"What an engaging story. Bunn continues both to elevate the quality of his writing and to astonish with his vision. In *Burden of Proof*, he explores fundamental issues of human relationships, regret, and the need we all share to gain wisdom. I was profoundly moved."

Joseph Raia, chairman, American Bar Association
International Division

"*Burden of Proof* hit me with the emotional equivalent of a Mack truck. Beautiful and complex characters and plot. The prodigal's dilemma brought me right inside the mystery, all the way to the surprising one-two punch on the final page. I loved this story and its profoundly personal message. Wonderful!"

Sarah Gunning Moser, president, Lighthouse for Literacy

"This is the first Davis Bunn book I have read, but it will not be the last. *Burden of Proof* beautifully demonstrates that a life spent in pursuit of selfish ends holds the makings of profound emptiness. Bunn's rich characters and compelling plot beautifully reveal how hope is still possible, even here."

Dr. Brian J. Grim, president,
Religious Freedom & Business Foundation

"Bunn has outdone himself this time. *Burden of Proof* kept me hooked from the very first page. This legal thriller invites us to consider the nature of the world itself. It challenges our worldview of the human experience and is both a powerful legal drama and a heartfelt love story. Bunn has opened my mind to a new vision of the human spirit."

Jeffrey Arresty, president, Internet Bar Association

"Novels with otherworldly themes normally are not my cup of tea, but Bunn's latest work is an amazing exception. In fact, the final line in its utter simplicity moved me to tears! The way he brings together all the story's various components is truly memorable."

Carol Johnson, founder, The Christy Awards

BURDEN OF PROOF

BURDEN
OF PROOF

DAVIS BUNN

Revell

a division of Baker Publishing Group
Grand Rapids, Michigan

© 2020 by T. Davis Bunn

Published by Revell
a division of Baker Publishing Group
PO Box 6287, Grand Rapids, MI 49516-6287
www.revellbooks.com

Printed in the United States of America

Library of Congress Cataloging-in-Publication Data
Names: Bunn, T. Davis, 1952– author.
Title: Burden of proof / Davis Bunn.
Description: Grand Rapids, Michigan : Revell, a division of Baker Publishing Group, 2020.
Identifiers: LCCN 2020017927 | ISBN 9780800727888 (paperback) | ISBN 9780800739041 (cloth)
Classification: LCC PS3552.U4718 B87 2020 | DDC 813/.54—dc23
LC record available at https://lccn.loc.gov/2020017927

20 21 22 23 24 25 26   7 6 5 4 3 2 1

For Joseph and Carmen Raia

With deepest affection

CHAPTER
ONE

Ethan paddled his kayak slowly across the inland waterway, heading into the dawn. The sun was a glorious red-rimmed blister rising straight ahead of him. The strengthening light made it impossible to actually see where he was headed. Not that it was a problem. Ethan had been coming and going from this particular dock since the ripe old age of nine and a half months.

The pain in his chest was worsened by the paddling motion. He needed to take his morning meds. But the pain medication left him somewhat removed from the world. That was not altogether a bad thing, since it was precisely what would be happening soon enough. Permanently. Even so, Ethan wanted to make his last journey out here with as clear a head as possible.

Skin cancer was a risk for every aging waterman. Over recent years Ethan had lost far too many friends to the aftermath, when the skin disease invaded the body. The week after he turned fifty-five, Ethan learned the melanoma had landed in the lining around his heart and lungs, what the doctors called thoracic sarcoma. Because he had waited so long to be checked out, treatment was simply not an option.

He minded, but not as much as he might have suspected. This dawn paddle was the first time in quite a while that he allowed his regrets to almost overwhelm him. Ethan did what he had been doing since the diagnosis. He pushed the bitter taste aside as best he could. By this point, the mental action was almost second nature.

His brother, Adrian, used to love telling and retelling the story of Ethan's first trip out here. How their father had basically ruined the best-ever father-and-son outing by insisting they bring the worm. That was what ten-year-old Adrian had named the family's unexpected newcomer. The human worm.

Needless to say, there had not been much love lost between the two brothers early on.

Their father and Adrian had been passionate about kayak fishing, which perfectly suited the marshes and shallow waters of Florida's inland waterway. As he grew into adulthood, Ethan had kept it up mostly because of his brother's love for the sport. He personally found it a little ridiculous, maintaining an impossible sense of balance while casting. Not to mention the nightmare of catching and landing a large fish. But Adrian treated it like his drug of choice. And because of how close the two brothers had become, especially after their parents were taken from them, Ethan continued to paddle out and fish and paddle home. Even now. Thirty-five years after Adrian was murdered on the Jacksonville courthouse steps.

In the past, Ethan had also made an annual trek up to the Saint Augustine cemetery where his brother and parents were buried, marking the trio of losses. Customarily this paddle-out took place the day he returned home to Cocoa Beach. But the graves were too far away now. And Ethan wouldn't be asking anyone to cart his remains up to the family plot. He'd already arranged for buddies to cast his ashes over his beloved Atlantic surf.

Ethan could make out the silhouettes of homes and carefully planted tropical gardens that now rimmed the Cocoa Beach waterfront. None of this had existed when he and his brother used to come out here, of course. The world had moved on. Soon it would continue without him.

The pier was pretty much derelict now, used mostly by locals who remembered how things once had been. Back in the eighties, when the Holiday Marina was the center of their young lives, Cocoa Beach had positively hummed with energy and people and new money. The space race had ended, and *I Dream of Jeannie* had shifted from the nation's number-one show to late-night reruns. But NASA was still going strong, and Cocoa Beach had become a choice winter destination for the nation's college students.

The Holiday Marina's owners had retired twenty-three years ago. Because they loved their hometown and the folks who had been their regular clients for decades, they willed the place and the land to the city. The marina had been razed, and the pier was badly maintained by volunteers. But the boat ramp and parking lot were still jammed almost every weekend.

As Ethan made the final approach, two silver-grey dolphins swam up alongside his kayak. They were the smaller brackish-water breed, and so tame that one let him reach down and scratch the slick pelt beside its dorsal fin. The other peeped a soft welcome, or perhaps a farewell.

Then Ethan saw who was waiting for him, and he wished the dolphins had managed a clearer warning.

There on the end of the pier stood Professor Sonya Barrett, widow of Ethan's late brother. The reason Ethan had not been with Adrian on the day he was murdered. The point of the worst—and the last—argument the two brothers ever had.

Sonya had not aged well. Ethan had not seen her since the day after the funeral, but he remembered her as a lithe figure with a ballerina's grace. Now her hair looked chopped off with garden shears, blown by the dawn breeze into a bird's nest of grey and silver. Her face was heavily lined. But at least the eyes were the same. Angry and tight. Ethan remembered that gaze.

Sonya started in on him even before Ethan docked. "I've been waiting here over an *hour*."

If he'd had any doubt about who the woman was, her attitude confirmed it. He'd had no reason to think she'd be showing up today. Even so, she treated Ethan like he had been born permanently in the wrong.

He swung the kayak around as though readying for a quick getaway. "Did I miss a message you were coming?" Ethan left unspoken the fact that if he'd known, he'd still be paddling in the opposite direction.

She gestured impatiently. "We don't have time for that. Get on up here before it's too late for *everything*."

It had always been this way between them. Ten seconds together and they were circling each other like curs, hair bristling, looking for the chance to draw first blood.

Only not today.

The weight of knowing this would be his final paddle-out, and all the wrong moves that had brought him to this point, left Ethan immune to Sonya's ire for the first time ever. On any other day, he might have found a bit of humor in the thought that struck as he gripped the lower railing. How being close to death proved to be the only way to put up with his brother's widow.

He reached out, offering her the line. "Want to make me fast?"

Sonya hesitated, as if needing a moment to search out the hidden barb. She took the rope. "I positively loathe to be kept waiting."

Sonya had always been impatient with a world that refused to spin at her frenetic pace. He remained silent as he clambered onto the dock. But he pushed himself erect too fast, and the pain in his chest went from bad to unbearable. He clamped his arm to his chest and managed, "Give me a minute."

"I don't *have* another minute." She lashed the kayak to a rusting stanchion. "And by the looks of things, neither do you."

He breathed around the pain, waiting. Gradually the discomfort fit itself back inside a manageable space. When he could breathe easy once more, he asked, "You heard?"

"Of course I heard. Why else do you think I'd be out here?"

A younger voice called from the shore, "Okay, Mom. That's enough."

"Well, really. Timing is *everything*." Sonya waved an irritated hand in Ethan's general direction. "And this man is making us late."

"Mom. You told me to say when you were being a pain.

This is me doing my job." The woman walked closer. She was tall and willowy and good-natured, the exact opposite of her mother. "Go start setting up, why don't you."

She so resembled Ethan's late brother that it took his breath away to look at her. "You're . . ."

"Delia. Nice to meet you, Uncle Ethan. Finally."

A blade of rage sliced through him. But he could no longer indulge in fury, even when it was justified. Anger magnified what he lived with constantly and turned his pain into a branding iron. Ethan tilted slightly to his left and breathed in and out, waiting for the world to resume its rightful course.

Even so, the look he gave Sonya was enough to send her scurrying down the pier as she said, "Tell him to *hurry.*"

Ethan said to Delia, "I can't believe I'm just meeting you."

"It's not what you think. Well, okay, maybe it is. At least partly." Delia had her father's hair, dark and long. She wore it woven into a rope as thick as her arm. And those eyes. Crystal grey and incredibly intense and constantly looking for a reason to smile. "See, a couple of weeks after I was born, Mom was taken to court by her Washington investors."

"Thieves and brigands, the lot of them," Sonya called back.

"Fighting them cost Mom everything," Delia went on. "Her job, her research, her reputation, the works."

Ethan allowed himself to be gently ushered back toward the shore. The pier was missing a number of planks, which meant he had to take his gaze off his niece.

His *niece.*

He said, "That was thirty-four years ago."

"Right. Thirty-five next week. After that, life just kept getting harder. Her investors claimed the right to buy her company. Mom being Mom, when they pressured her, she somehow misplaced crucial elements of her research."

"Correction. I destroyed anything they could possibly use and handed over a smoldering wreck."

"See?" Delia smiled. "What could possibly go wrong with a plan like that?"

"They gave me no choice at all," Sonya huffed from up ahead. "And if you insist on telling our entire past history to this man, you really should try to get it right."

Sonya's ire left her daughter untouched. "Okay, then the investors charged her with theft, larceny, breach of contract, the works. So Mom up and vanished and officially became a fugitive from justice."

Sonya reached the end of the pier and stomped across the parking lot. "Give my work to those idiots? I'd rather die."

Ethan asked, "Why didn't you contact me?"

Delia gave him the sort of patented look that had been Adrian's trademark in front of juries. A sideways glance that invited everyone to peer beneath the surface and see the truth. "Okay, point of order. You were nine thousand miles away at the time, am I right?"

"I came home. Occasionally."

"So my mother, who did not consider you her closest pal, should have tried to track you down whenever your global surf trek brought you back to this part of the world? Please."

"You sound so much like your father it hurts." And it did. Terribly.

Delia reached out and took a companionable hold on his arm, like she had been doing it for years. "The short version of what happened next is, I changed my name. Legally became a Smith. Cut all ties to Mom's past. It was the only way to keep working with her." She flashed her father's smile. "Plus, the way Mom described you, I had no reason to contact the ogre from the east."

Sonya called back, "How long do we have?"

Delia checked the timer on her phone. "Fourteen and a half minutes."

Sonya paused long enough to glare at Ethan. "Could you *possibly* walk any slower?"

When Sonya resumed stomping across the lot, Ethan asked softly, "Why did you bother staying with that woman? I mean, why not just cut and run?" He had to know.

Delia even had her father's shrug. A good-natured lifting of chin and shoulders both, a smile that never went further than those incredible eyes. "Mom's a genius. You need to accept that and move on. Because she's right. We don't have much time."

Four trucks with empty trailers were parked alongside the boat ramp. The only other two vehicles were Ethan's ride and a vintage refrigerated truck.

Ethan watched as Sonya headed for the truck and asked, "Time for what?"

"We're here to offer you a chance to save my father's life."

TWO

Delia's casual comment stopped him entirely. "Is this a joke?"

"Does Mom look like somebody who has ever, in her entire life, told a joke?" Delia took a firmer grip on his arm and urged him forward. "We know the process works. At least, it does on mice, hamsters, an egret, and three young pigs. You're our test goat. That's what Mom calls you."

Sonya's hearing was as sharp as her mind. She yelled back, "You're not helping!"

"Actually, I am." To Ethan, "We know you're dying. Mom's been checking. You've got, what, three months?"

"Maybe more."

"We understand your pain is getting worse. That much is true, yes?"

"By the hour."

"We're hoping you would be willing to try and do the impossible." She offered the day's best smile. "With a little help from your friends."

Ethan only half pretended that his discomfort forced him

to walk even slower. She certainly had a point. What was more, despite all the impossibilities he felt a faint spark of hope. It was ridiculous, of course. But there was something to these two women and their intelligence and urgency. Something that defied the fact that Ethan was just weeks from checking out.

How many nights had he awoken and lain there wishing for a chance to do that day over? Be there by his brother's side? Save Adrian's life, even if it meant giving up his own?

Ethan realized she was watching him. "Can I ask a question?"

"Manners. Nice. Go for it."

"Did Adrian know? About you, I mean. Because he never mentioned that little tidbit to me. I would have remembered."

"Mom didn't know until a couple of weeks after Dad's funeral."

"Wow."

"Yeah. Drinks all around, right?"

"Your father used to say that."

"I know. I used to beg Mom for stories about Dad. I guess some of them just slipped into my psyche."

Sonya reached the truck's rear doors and paused long enough to glare at her daughter before wrenching open the long metal handles. The doors groaned loudly as they opened.

The truck had been crudely whitewashed. A faint impression of the grocery chain's smiling-pig logo was still visible on the side. The paint was blistered by rust spots, but the engine rumbled smoothly, and the refrigeration unit hummed atop the rear hold.

Delia's speech became crisp, tight, faster. "Back to the matter at hand. Basically, we've created a warp in the quantum time field. This requires a focus of vibrational energies with a laser's pinpoint accuracy. The end result is, we can shoot your consciousness back to a specific point in time. You need to understand, time is not linear. Our physical perception of time is. At the quantum level, time is a map. We have calculated the map coordinates of you eighteen days before Dad's death."

Ethan tried to concentrate. He struggled to come up with a half-decent question or objection. But as they approached the truck's open rear doors, his mind and heart were swamped by how much he wanted this to be real.

Yet there was more at work here.

The most vital part of his existence had been surfing big waves. A crucial element to killer surf was that the risk of injury or death was always present. Always. The tiniest error in judgment, the slightest shift in wind or current, and the finest wave could instantly become the final ride. Surfers who hunted the globe's biggest waves did so for one simple reason.

They lived for this.

The risk was simply part of the ride.

For Ethan, nothing in his entire life had ever compared to the thrill of standing on the shoreline and looking out, seeing those liquid mountains march invitingly toward him, knowing the best was yet to come.

That was exactly how he felt now. For the first time in years.

As he studied Delia's excited, intelligent face, Ethan became filled with the single element of his past that he missed almost as much as his brother. The thrill of facing the impossible.

Delia broke into his thoughts. "We know at least some key components of the subject's current mental awareness and thought processes travel back. If we train the animals to do some highly complex task, they maintain this knowledge even when they have never seen the trial before."

Ethan stopped by the rear doors and forced himself to pay attention. "How is that even possible?"

"We know they're test subjects because they run the maze or perform the task the first time they see it. At first we couldn't believe it. Test animals with no training whatsoever suddenly just danced their way through the most complex maze we could design." Delia seemed delighted by the memory. "We had no idea what was happening. I mean, these were not actually registered as test subjects! So we would train them weeks or months later, then transit their consciousness back to the period before they ran the maze." She gestured to the collapsible metal steps. "Climb in."

Ethan remained planted on the asphalt. "Why don't you two go?"

Sonya cackled. "Who calibrates the machines then? You?"

"Mom, please." Delia said to Ethan, "The simple reason is, forcing your consciousness to transit kills your physical body. What's more, you'll most likely expire in the past as well."

"Wait, what?"

"All our test subjects perish twice. As far as the current physical body goes, the energy required to make the transit stops the subject's heart. Plus our subjects have had a very short life span once the transition takes place. At first we thought it was due to how the trained subject couldn't meet their untrained future self. But we separated them, and the pattern continued." Delia might as well have been discussing the current heat wave. "Think of it as a rejection of a transplanted organ. Only in our case, it's the individual's future consciousness that is rejected."

"How can a past subject die and a future one still be taught?"

"Good question. The answer is quantum logistics, which are totally wild. But they clearly govern the conscious mind and its temporal location. A longer answer would put you to sleep."

Her matter-of-fact tone helped Ethan mightily. "How long will I have?"

"My best calculations suggest about a month. Six weeks tops."

"Long enough to save Adrian and rechart all our courses," Sonya added.

Ethan stared out over the dusty parking lot. A flock of pelicans drifted by, painting the sky with their graceful script. He had loved parts of his life, sure. The travel, dawns on the water, great waves, good friends. But how did that song go? Regrets, he had a few. That was the understatement of the century. The time since learning of his upcoming departure had been filled with the bitter longing to correct wrong moves, starting with his brother's death. And a lot more besides.

Sonya tapped the electronic timer set in the truck's right-hand wall. "Will you *please* get in here so we can start? We have four minutes."

Delia remained unfazed. "Correction. We can't do anything for another four minutes. And Ethan needs to understand."

Sonya went back to working the machinery. "Understand—him? Humph."

Delia told him, "We would have come sooner. But we only learned about your condition the night before last."

Sonya bristled. "Three minutes!"

Her mother might as well have been in another room. "Plus the calculations require hours at a supercomputer, and we only accessed one last night. But the biggest reason is that you are here, we know you're here, and Mom remembers you were precisely in this same spot eighteen days before Dad died. She and Adrian talked about it in their last conversation . . ." Delia waved that aside. "Positioning at the corresponding quantum point is crucial for this to work."

"Positioning is not nearly as crucial as timing!" Sonya pointed at the gurney occupying the center of the truck. "Which is why you need to get in here and lie down!"

This time, when Delia offered her hand, Ethan started up the steps.

She went on, "Establishing a precise physical location between present and past is utterly crucial. We know you were working here before Dad was murdered. And we know you come here every anniversary. So . . ."

Ethan remained standing as Delia pulled the doors shut and locked them in place. The truck was wall-to-wall electronic equipment. A spiderweb of wiring was suspended from the roof directly above the gurney. It looked like something straight out of a B-grade horror flick.

Ethan figured he probably should be afraid. Running away, or at least limping, was the logical next step. But the simple fact was, these two women were offering the first chance he'd had to make a decision about his own destiny since receiving the fatal diagnosis. He knew he should be terrified. Instead, though, Ethan felt as awake and hyper as a clown on a unicycle. He knew all this probably led to a spectacular failure. But just then, his only response was to silently shout, *So what?*

"You really do need to step on it," Delia said. "Else we'll all miss the dance."

CHAPTER

THREE

Delia kept talking as she strapped him to the gurney. "There will be two separate processes. They happen almost simultaneously, but not quite. First, a precise vibrational jolt will be applied to your frontal cortex, harmonizing your mental processes at the quantum level and preparing you for the transition."

Ethan's attention gradually shifted away from her, the truck, Sonya, even the straps Delia fastened around his body. He had noticed this happening more often as the pain increased. As though part of him was already gone. As though there was some unseen door, and he had accepted that the only way to rid himself of the growing burden was to walk through.

Only now, for the first time in what felt like years, the sense of disconnect was not driven by pain. Ethan was filled with the electric buzz of anticipation. The thrill of danger, the high of attempting the impossible—he had lived for this. The incredible moment when he was drenched in adrenaline and his heart grew wings and every second became split and parsed . . .

He was *back*.

The transition, Delia called it. The logical side of his brain kept repeating the word. Like how doctors kept telling him to prepare himself for the inevitable, that his only choice was to get ready, because in a matter of days he was checking out. All options stripped away.

Not anymore.

"This will probably be painful," Delia went on, fitting the padded strap across his chest. "I've not been able to discuss pain with our animal subjects, but they don't appear all that happy. The good news is, it only lasts seven seconds." She shifted down to his ankles. "The second stage compresses your consciousness through the quantum keyhole." She looked up, her good humor gone now, her gaze somber. "Like I said, this jolt will stop your heart."

Ethan gave a mental shrug. For the first time since he'd received the news, his fear of death was balanced with the power of choice. Perhaps if he'd had more time to think things through, he would have gone with living out his few remaining days. But he doubted it. He could feel the cancer eating its way through his body, consuming in its path all the goodness he had known.

Delia fit a final strap to his forehead and wrenched it tight. "Sorry. But we need to make sure you're fully immobilized."

Ethan watched as Sonya took her daughter's place and fit a plastic mesh helmet over his hair. "We should have shaved his head."

Delia was already standing by a bank of instruments. "The trial subjects' fur made no difference."

Sonya buckled the strap under his jaw and told him, "Grit your teeth." When he did so, she tightened this final strap until he could no longer open his mouth. The buckle dug into his right cheek, but there was no way of telling the ladies that it hurt. Nor, Ethan suspected, would he mind for much longer.

Delia said, "Twenty seconds."

Sonya lowered her face to within inches of his own. For once, her constant irritation was gone. Instead, she looked at him with a yearning so deep the agony filled her eyes with tears. "Please, please, *remember*."

"Ten seconds," Delia said.

Sonya's face disappeared, and all Ethan could see were the dangling cables and the ceiling lights and the truck's rusty roof.

"Eight, seven, six . . ."

Ethan had no sensation of a life flashing in front of his eyes. Instead, he remembered just one event. The memory was so vivid he felt as though he was actually there once again. For three and a half years after Adrian's death, Ethan had traveled the globe, surfing many of the finest breaks on earth. One day, on the island of Mauritius in the Indian Ocean, he'd slipped inside a tube twice his height. The day was windless, the waters so clear he could watch the sunrise through the wall of water. He was back there now, inside the tube, so deep the opening seemed a mile or so ahead of him. He could hear the thunderous roar, smell the salty air, feel the ocean spray cover him in a liquid blanket. It was . . .

Bliss.

Then the circular opening far ahead flashed a brilliant white. The light became so intense it compressed his brain.

There was nothing anymore, no room even for thought. Just the light.

Then the second jolt struck, so fierce he actually felt his heart freeze solid.

And then he died.

CHAPTER
FOUR

Ethan was staring at the moon.

He sat up, gasping and choking. He rolled off the padding and clawed at the raw planks of the floor.

Then he heard the water.

A soft summer breeze blew up tiny waves. They splashed like cymbals against the pilings that rose to either side of where he lay. He gripped the nearest strut and forced himself to his feet. The night was utterly dark. He was dressed in a pair of raggedy cutoffs and a T-shirt. On his feet were leather sandals curled and cracked by salt and hard days. He was completely alone.

Ethan cried out, a choking sound wrenched from the terror and confusion that filled him.

He knew where he was.

What was more, he knew *when*.

The summer before his final year at the university, when he and his best friend had wrangled jobs at the Holiday Marina. The long pier ran back to the shore, every plank in place, the pilings straight as arrows. The marina's unmistakable form was silhouetted by yellow streetlights. Four A-frames housed the sailing classes, the repair shop, the store, and the stockrooms.

An old canvas inflatable raft lay on the pier, with a towel for a cover. The dockhands rotated the task of hanging around until sunset and bringing in the day's last rentals and hosing them down. The marina's sixteen daysailers formed a floating perimeter to him now. The boats ducked and weaved in the gentle breeze, lashed to safety pilings, dimly visible in the moonlight. Nights like this were one of the reasons he had loved the job so much. When the last craft was in place and the gear stowed, Ethan often blew up the inflatable and ate a solitary sandwich and watched the sun set. Then he stretched out here, alone, and fell asleep to the cry of gulls and the liquid cymbals.

Back in a summer filled with impossible potential.

Now, as Ethan walked the lonely road, he knew flashes of very real terror, fearing it all might vanish and he'd find himself trapped on the gurney with electrodes zapping his brain. One thing was certain. This was not a dream. The reality was too, well, *real*.

The eighties version of Cocoa Beach was undergoing a drastic shift. The cheap motels thrown up in the early NASA heyday were being replaced by high-rise condos, luxury housing, elegant restaurants, and refined hotels. Here and there, however, a few remnants of the simpler world remained.

The Holiday Marina lay at the end of a hard-packed clay road. To Ethan's right stood one of the last remaining orange groves within the Cocoa Beach city limits. The blossoms opened fully at night, and the fragrance was as powerful a confirmation as the body he occupied.

The year was 1985. Again.

He was twenty years old, with a youth's ability to shrug off the fact that he had worked a ten-hour shift in the hot August sun, had slept maybe six hours on the end of a pier, and had not consumed a cup of coffee in forever. Back in the day, Ethan's only caffeine kick came from the occasional Coke.

He arrived back at the rental cottage just as the first rose hues of dawn appeared in the east. He stood in the front yard, surrounded by everything he thought lost and gone forever. The unkempt yard was just as awful as he remembered. A line of surfboards flanked the cottage entrance. Leashes and board shorts and rash shirts littered the weeds and hung from the branches of two banana plants. Six plastic chairs stolen from some bar served as garden furniture. The house was squat and narrow and constructed of unpainted cinder blocks. There were no locks and nothing to steal inside.

A cold nose poked Ethan's ankle as he opened the front door. He bent over and lifted the whining pup. His best buddy, Sawyer, had rescued it from the pound because he had fallen for a girl who volunteered there. Ethan and his buddies had named the pup Banzai, after the North Shore surf break. He had not thought of the dog in years.

He carried Banzai into the bathroom and shut the door. The house had a lot of serious flaws, but there were four closet-sized bedrooms and a huge screened rear porch that served as an indoor-outdoor kitchen. Ethan pulled the light cord, and there he was, staring back at himself from the cracked mirror over the sink.

When he groaned, Banzai responded by licking his face. Ethan watched his hand stroke the pup. His skin was tanned almost black. White-blond hair contrasted with his pale blue eyes. Scared eyes. Still, the face was definitely his. Staring at himself, Ethan had no choice but to accept what his reflection truly meant.

The transition, or whatever Delia and Sonya called it, had worked. He was four months from his twenty-first birthday. Again.

Ethan let the dog out, then showered and dressed in fresh shorts and a T-shirt. He grabbed the all-too-familiar keys and surfer's wallet from his dresser. As he started for the front door, a voice called from the next room, "Did you sleep on the dock again?"

Sawyer had married his childhood sweetheart and moved to Oregon. Four years ago he had been diagnosed with adult-onset type 1 diabetes. Ethan had not spoken with him in months. Now his best friend sounded so young Ethan could have wept.

"I did. Yeah."

"Not sure that was a good idea. Ready for your big day?"

The question pushed Ethan faster out the door. He had no interest in staring any more mysteries in the face. "Absolutely not."

Ethan's car was a cast-off Jeep Wagoneer, with rusty springs and a wobbly ride and no gas mileage to speak of. The Jeep had been his brother's since college. Earlier that summer, Adrian's boss had ordered him to sell it, junk it, do whatever necessary so it never again stained the firm's parking lot. Adrian had sold it to Ethan for the whopping sum of twenty-five cents.

Ethan drove the lonely dawn-streaked road on automatic

pilot. He couldn't listen to music because the radio had not worked in years. His two favorite boards were jammed between the seats. The smells assaulted him, ratty beach towels and melted surf wax and exhaust. Everything formed ingredients of a life he had assumed was lost and gone forever.

His destination was the Cocoa Beach pier, whose restaurant served a fisherman's breakfast twenty-four hours a day. His stomach growled in anticipation. That was good for another empty grin. He had not eaten breakfast in six months. Longer.

Ethan pulled into the parking lot and braked hard. The lot was full for that time of day, and the reason shouted at him from three banners stretched above the pier's main entrance. The top one read "Bash at the Beach." Below that, the second banner read "Cocoa Beach O'Neill Pro-Am." A third canvas standard had been lashed into place below the others. It had one word stamped in glittering letters: "FINALS!!"

Ethan's stomach growled a second time. But he was no longer paying attention.

Bleachers rose on either side of the pier's breakwater. Beside them loomed two walls of loudspeakers, ready to blare music and comments at a crowd that would eventually number over ten thousand.

An East Coast surf contest didn't normally draw that sort of audience. This one was different. A hurricane had threatened to demolish the contest before it even got started, but at the last moment the storm had veered northeast, away from landfall.

The waves thrown up by the storm had arrived Saturday, just hours before the first heats. Legendary surf. Mountainous. The sort of waves that remained a marvel for decades.

Ethan saw the workers pausing now and then and staring out to sea. The surrounding structures blocked his own view. But he did not need to see the ocean to know what they were watching.

Pandemonium.

The sun rose over a crystal-blue sea and cloudless sky. There was not a breath of wind. The waves were *huge*. The biggest and most perfect conditions to hit the Florida coast in a generation. The local press was calling it fifteen feet, but at this size, such measurements were meaningless.

As Ethan rose slowly from his car, he heard the compressive *crump* of very big waves falling far out to sea. The ground beneath his feet shook slightly from the shorebreak's constant roar. As he stood there, the first television van careened around the corner and skidded to a halt, and the crew spilled out with their equipment.

Remember, Sonya had begged him.

Ethan remembered every moment.

The adrenaline pumping through his veins, the spicy smell of the salt spray blown up by the massive surf, the place . . .

Ethan breathed the words aloud. "I'm back."

FIVE

Ethan grabbed two breakfast burritos and settled on the stand's top tier, away from the growing crowds down below. The loudspeakers played some electropunk surf music that Ethan did not recognize.

The first time around, he and other local surfers had waited atop the judging platform for the quarterfinals to begin, using the elevated deck to watch the waves and find some hint of assurance in the company of buddies. This time, he took another bite and studied the group seated to his right. One of the pros dragged here by O'Neill was the South African Hennie Bacchus. Hennie had not announced it yet, but this was going to be his last year competing. He was twenty-nine, old for a pro, and had helped shape the current trends in surfing. His grace was as strong on the beach as in the water, and his smile and looks would eventually help him build a successful career in politics. Hennie was also a pastor and ran a surf ministry that within a decade would plant a counselor in every pro tournament around the world.

When the O'Neill guys drifted away, Ethan slipped over and introduced himself.

Hennie studied Ethan and asked, "You a local, mate?"

"Born and raised in Cocoa Beach," Ethan said.

"You did all right out there yesterday. Have you ever made it to a big-wave spot?"

Ethan hesitated, unsure how to respond. The answer was, he had surfed his way around the globe four times. But that all remained in a future that had yet to become reality.

Hennie seemed to take his silence as fear. "Listen up, mate. No matter how good you are or what you think you know about your local spot, you need to adjust your surfing to fit the size. Because straight up, those monsters can kill you stone dead."

Ethan studied the honeyed skin, the clear eyes, the genuine concern. "I've admired you ever since I read my first surfing magazine." He offered Hennie his hand. "See you in the water."

As the clock wound down to the start of the quarterfinals, Ethan filtered the day through two different lenses. He vividly recalled how the contest had gone down before. The previous day, he had eked by with four second places in a row. He was the surfer with the lowest overall point score who made it into the quarter round. That night, he retreated from his buddies and slept on the end of the Holiday Marina pier. The water and gentle breeze worked their magic, which was why he felt even semi-rested. Not that it had helped.

This particular morning, he had suffered a bad wipeout on his first wave and never recovered. It was to be his one brush with fame. In the years to come, when his buddies spoke of that day, it was mostly about watching him go over the falls on an eighteen-foot behemoth.

Had he returned on any other day, Ethan would have been consumed by the impossibility of this. But today was different, unique. There simply wasn't room to implode. He had dwelled on this day his entire life. The contest and the loss had defined so much of what was to come.

The desires, the fears, the inability to handle the ocean's force—Ethan had run from this and toward this for years. He had surfed seven of the biggest waves on earth. And repeatedly on the days when he had surfed his best, from Hawaii to Australia to Chile to Portugal, he'd ended with the same wish. If only he could have gone back and relived this contest, knowing what he did now.

This time around, Ethan gathered on the shore with the other quarterfinalists. When the horn sounded, he launched his board into the water, reveling in a twenty-year-old body honed by constant workouts and youth. Added to this was what he brought from the first go-round: years of surfing the world's big breaks.

The paddle-out was grueling. But Ethan had been through worse. Of course, that was in the months and years still to come.

Then he was in the lineup with four other guys. All of them staring out to sea, breathing hard from the paddle-out, hearts close to redline.

When the next set formed shadow lines on the horizon, Ethan moved into position.

Ready.

CHAPTER SIX

The next morning, Ethan woke up to discover Banzai snoring softly at his side. He rolled from his bed, knowing today he would face everything the contest had kept at bay.

He stood by the cracked window in his eight-by-ten room and recalled being strapped to the gurney. Sonya hissing for him to remember. Then the blinding mental flash, the crushing weight of a stopped heart, the clenching pain, the immobility, the end.

Banzai scratched at the door and whined, drawing him back to the new present. Ethan slipped on a pair of board shorts and opened the door.

Sawyer called, "Yo, champ."

"I didn't win," he replied and slipped into the bathroom. When he emerged, Sawyer was still standing there, grinning. Ethan added, "Not even close."

"That's not what Hennie said. He told the reporter that if Florida was growing a crop of surfers like Ethan Barrett, the pro tour had better watch out. On account of—"

"I heard it already." He walked out back and greeted his other roomies. They looked so young, so confident. The invulnerability of youth shone from their sleepy faces. Ethan made himself a bowl of cereal and endured their play-by-play, wishing he could lose himself in the simple pleasure of rewriting his own memories.

The contest final had been better than any midnight imaginings. He and Hennie had dominated the heat. The other finalists were basically left fighting for third place. The waves backed off a trifle, the closeouts had lessened in number, and the two of them had started taking incredible risks. Pushing each other's envelope, shouting encouragement, laughing and joking and owning the hour.

Ethan had intentionally let Hennie take the top three waves and build up an insurmountable lead. Hennie responded with a warrior's honor, twice telling Ethan that he should go pro and Hennie would back his play. The second time he said it, Ethan paddled up close. The waves were bunched and muscled, but it didn't matter. Nothing did. They owned the day.

Hennie's mother was Indian, and his father was a Zulu chief. He had been barred from competing in apartheid South Africa, so with O'Neill's support, he had taken his act abroad. The year he first won the world title, the pro surfing association gave the South African apartheid regime a choice: let Hennie compete, or they would never support another contest in their country. Surfing was the third most popular sport in South Africa after rugby and soccer. The Botha regime caved.

Ethan had actually visited the slum outside Port Elizabeth where Hennie was born. By the time Ethan arrived, Mandela was in power and Hennie was a rising star in the new South African parliament. Botha's regime had been relegated to the history books, along with his hated secret police. But as Ethan had walked the rutted road with the sewage spilling down the open trench, he could almost hear the snarling police dogs.

Ethan said to Hennie, "This is your heat. Your contest."

"What is this, some new form of a psych-out?"

"I'm not . . . I don't want to go pro."

Hennie checked to make sure there was no incoming set, then asked, "You sure about that?"

"This is your last season," Ethan said. "Win here in Florida. Rejoin the main circuit and take Hawaii. Go out as the world number one. When you return home, you lift up some other kid from the slums of Durban."

Hennie's jaw bunched up tight as a fist. "You really know how to blow a mate out of the water."

"Some other kid the world wants to dismiss as a no-account," Ethan went on. "Some kid who is almost ready to give in to the temptation of futile rage."

Hennie's tension grew to where he looked ready to fight. Or weep. He pointed out beyond Ethan and said, "Here comes your wave, mate."

He was right. The peak was taking aim straight at Ethan. He glanced around and saw one of the finalists flailing through a ragged closeout, the other struggling down in the impact zone. It was Ethan's wave.

Sometimes the wave communicated through the board, or so it seemed to Ethan. Sometimes the connection to the ocean was so strong that the concept of limits, of fear, even of thought, just vanished. For one fleeting instant, he did not just bond with the wave. He joined it.

This was one of those waves.

Ethan entered the tube, came out, spun off the lip, slipped down to the pit, saw the lip curling over, and got tubed a second time. When the ledge started to feather and close out, Ethan took a ridiculous risk because he *knew* he could make it. He lifted up so that his board actually danced along the feathering lip. It was a small-wave maneuver, when there was not the sort of power and risk of today's swell. When the wave crashed down, Ethan did not slide off and finish as logic dictated. Instead, he kept surfing the broken wave, riding on top of the foam ball. The move was called a floater, because that was exactly how it felt, just coasting over air and spume. There was no control, no way to even steer. But instead of eating him like it should, the wave did not completely fall. Rather, it sectioned, and up ahead the wall held up like a pristine invitation. Ethan's floater brought him into an inside section where he crouched down, so tight his knees met his chest, and was tubed a third time.

When he came out and the wave ended and reality gripped him once more, he was close enough to the shore to hear the crowd screaming.

The clock showed less than three minutes left, not enough time for him to paddle out. Ethan rode the next break to shore, then watched Hennie take the wave of the day. The tube was so large that Hennie stood up straight, all six feet two of him, and extended his arms out wide to either side without touching water. He emerged and threw two sweeping trough-to-lip maneuvers that sent rooster tails up high as the sky. He rode and he flipped and he rode, and when it was all done and the Klaxon had sounded, Hennie had stepped off the board onto dry sand.

Now Ethan ate his cereal and studied the photograph that dominated the *Florida Today*'s front page. He and Hennie were on the winners' stand, cups and checks in one hand, arms around each other's shoulders, still laughing from the thrill of owning the day.

Sawyer rose from the table and tapped his watch. "We've got to clock in."

There were good-natured groans from the others, until Ethan said, "I'm not coming. I quit."

The guys who had formed his team through college stared at him. Sawyer said, "There's the matter of your paycheck."

One of the others said, "Second place paid twenty-five thou. I'd already be gone."

Sawyer whined, "But you love that job."

"I did," Ethan agreed. He felt a flutter of nerves over changing the course of history already written. Again.

Sawyer demanded, "What are you going to do?"

Because he was his best friend, Ethan replied, "I need to give my brother a hand with something important."

———

Ethan did not bother to call Adrian and say he was coming. His brother had made Ethan a key to every place he had ever lived. They were never much for personal discussions, especially when it came to family. Adrian was a closed book. He lived for work. Where so many of the firm's young associates burned out after a few years of eighty-hour weeks, Adrian thrived. When he finally married, fourteen months before getting murdered, his widow-to-be was a neurobiologist running her own research company. Sonya was as driven as Adrian.

There was a bland comfort to the drive up I-95. Ethan had the highway and the late August day pretty much to himself. He drove with all the windows open because the AC had not worked in years. As the humid air washed over him, he pulled out the central question and let it hang there in the heat.

Ethan's task was to change the course of time.

He knew at a gut level that simply alerting his brother to a coming threat would not work. Besides, he did not want to *warn* Adrian. He wanted to *rescue* him. Keep him alive to enjoy a full life, raise his daughter, become the rising star in the Jacksonville legal world, fulfill the potential Ethan knew his brother possessed.

The question that accompanied him was *how*.

In his previous existence, Ethan had made this very same drive, only fifteen days from now. That time, he had not quit his job. There was no second-place check to justify such a move. Instead, he worked the final two weeks, received the bonus payment the marina paid every dockhand who stayed through the entire summer, then traveled to Jacksonville to tell Adrian he was quitting school.

Of course, Ethan didn't put it that way. What he said was he wanted to take a year off, surf some of his dream locations, and come back revived and ready for the real world.

But Adrian, being Adrian, saw straight through to the truth. The reality was, Ethan had no interest in ever returning to his brother's idea of a life.

Their parents—a community college lecturer and a county librarian—had been far from wealthy. But their pensions and life insurance had been enough to ensure both sons could complete college without debt. What remained of Ethan's share was in a trust run by his brother. Ethan had made the journey north hoping Adrian would release funds and cover his traveling expenses, at least for a while.

Instead, Adrian blasted him with a barely controlled rage. He accused Ethan of running away.

Ethan was utterly shocked by his brother's wrath. He had expected to spend hours dickering, laughing, pressing, begging if necessary. Instead, Adrian accused him of being lazy, gutless, and living his life without a shred of direction. And then turned Ethan down flat.

Hurt, still wounded by the contest loss, desperate to escape, Ethan lashed out with a fury of his own, saying that Adrian was blind to everything but his own ambition. That he had no life to speak of. That he had married a woman equally ignorant of life outside their comfort zones.

It was the last time the brothers ever spoke.

Two days later, Adrian was murdered on the courthouse steps.

———

When a heavy afternoon thunderstorm struck, Ethan took the next exit and stopped for a late lunch. Rain blurred the truck stop's windows and washed away the outside world. Ethan stared at his reflection in the glass and saw the impossible task ahead of him.

Adrian was a trial attorney. He lived to grapple with facts. He thrived on courtroom combat. He loved nothing more than to hunt below the surface, find the opposition's hidden weakness, and tear it apart.

Ethan ran through various scenarios of trying to tell his brother what had happened, what *would* happen, and . . .

His brother would laugh in his face. Accuse him of doing a nosedive into drug culture. And walk away.

Approaching Sonya was a nonstarter. The woman would not give him the time of day.

Which meant . . .

The waitress stopped by his table. "Everything all right, hon?"

"Sure. Thanks."

She picked up his plate. "You need anything else?"

Ethan started to ask for coffee, his standard reply for years. "Maybe some more water."

"You got it."

The longer he sat there, the clearer his only course of action became. The only way for him to save his brother's life was to do it himself.

Yet this raised any number of dilemmas. Ethan had not been anywhere near Jacksonville when the events happened. He had no idea precisely how they had gone down.

What if the threat was not just an isolated gunman? The authorities had never identified the shooter or given any definite reason for the attack. The police's public statements alluded to a criminal who was sent to jail and vowed revenge. But why that day? Why in such a public place, in broad daylight?

The questions and doubts hammered at his brain and heart while the storm continued to lash the window. Ethan grew increasingly frightened by everything he did not know.

The waitress returned, set down another glass of water, and laid a copy of *Time* magazine beside it. "Here you go, hon. A customer just left this. Thought you might like some company."

"That's really nice. Thank you."

The waitress's scuffed shoes squeaked across the linoleum floor. Ethan picked up the magazine and started leafing through the pages. Anything to escape the thoughts that chased him round and round . . .

Then he realized what he was staring at.

The page coalesced with the same blistering intensity he had known back on the beach.

The waitress passed by his booth and asked, "How about some dessert, hon? We make the best pecan pie in five states."

"No thank you. Could I have the check? It looks like the weather might be clearing."

"No problem."

"Thanks." Ethan looked back down at the page. Staring up at him were photographs of America's current tennis greats: Chris Evert Lloyd, Jimmy Connors, and John McEnroe. The article was about the US Open, scheduled to begin the next day.

Ethan rose from his seat, filled with an electric sensation of things coming together. He knew what he was going to do.

SEVEN

Adrian's firm was located in the Allstate building. The high-rise had been sold after Allstate stopped insuring homes in hurricane-struck Florida. But of course that wouldn't happen for another twenty years.

Ethan parked in one of the law firm's guest slots, took the elevator to the fifteenth floor, and exchanged hellos with a receptionist who was clearly disappointed when he did not remember her name. He wore the best clothes he had found in the packing crate he used as a clothes cupboard—unironed chinos, scuffed boat shoes, and an Izod knit shirt so ancient the lizard was frayed around the edges. Ethan ignored the stares shot his way by the Armani brigade clustered to one side. He soon lost himself in the *Time* magazine article.

His brother stepped into the reception area and announced, "Okay, everybody, can I have your attention? This young stud here is Ethan Barrett, who just won the Florida Pro-Am in killer surf." Adrian did his version of a television game-show hostess presenting the car of the day. "Beat last year's runner-up for the world title in the quarters, no less. All hail the conquering hero."

The shock was worse than he had imagined. There alongside Adrian's grin was the misery of loss, the pain of seeing his brother's coffin lowered into the ground.

Ethan barely managed, "I came in second."

"Don't pay my modest brother any mind. He was robbed. NBC says so."

Adrian hauled him back through the arena of researchers and legal aides and secretaries, one arm locked around Ethan's neck, introducing him to everybody, taking great pleasure in Ethan's embarrassment. When they arrived in his office, Adrian said, "There's half a dozen young lovelies out there who've semi-volunteered to have your children."

"Lay off, man."

"What, lay off? You're the closest to a famous face these people are likely to see." Adrian dropped into his leather executive chair. "Take a load off, bro."

Ethan gripped the arms of his chair and struggled desperately to maintain control. "It's good to see you."

"Did you call to say you were coming? Because I don't recall seeing that memo."

"I didn't know where I was going until an hour before I left." His voice sounded strangled to his own ears. "I needed to get away."

"Sure, I get that. Only, I'm leaving in . . ." Adrian checked his watch, a gold Rolex. Naturally. "Eight hours."

"New York. I know."

Adrian's sideways glance took Ethan straight back. It was his brother's tell, a hard inspection that was partly masked by how fast and indirect it came. Adrian became overly casual. "Must be important, whatever brought you north."

In that instant, Ethan realized that his brother already knew.

The first time around, he had been too preoccupied with all he had bottled up inside to notice. But as he sat there and studied the man he thought lost and gone forever, he realized his brother was waiting to hear that Ethan was checking out.

That could only mean one thing. Ethan had been laying down hints for some time. Planting seeds. Why? Had he suspected all along that he would lose the contest? Had he planned this departure in advance of the contest, regardless of what happened? His head spun with the sudden flush of fear that everything this time around was actually different. What he remembered no longer applied. Events were not the same, his memories didn't mesh . . .

Adrian began shifting his chair in tight quarter circles, an unconscious motion that mirrored the billing clock he was always tracking. "Sorry, bro, but I'm due to meet opposing counsel in a big case."

The words were exactly what Ethan needed to clarify his direction. He did not have time to doubt. If the threat was real, he needed to act. He needed to act *now*.

Ethan said, "The situation involving Sonya's company."

"You've been paying attention. Yeah, the attorneys for the opposition are coming in today. Basically their goal is to tell us our case isn't all that great. But Sonya insists we take them on in court." Adrian glared at the blank yellow pad on his desk as if angry the page did not hold answers. "I can't say I blame Sonya. Her life's work is on the line."

Ethan did not remember his brother being so stressed over

his wife's court case. He knew Sonya had been working on an alternative method for treating chronic pain and her investors had suddenly decided to buy her out. But Adrian's raw blend of fear and pressure and anger was something new.

Ethan pushed away the uncertainty and said, "About New York."

Adrian slowly refocused on the room and his brother. "I'm flying up with the partners today. Sonya follows tonight. We really need this break. We'll have two days together, then it's back to the trenches for us both."

"Can I come?" Ethan said what he had decided on the drive. "I won't attend the matches. And I guarantee to stay out of your way. I have an investment opportunity. Something that's just happened."

Adrian studied him a long moment. He had been trying for years to get Ethan to join him for the US Open, Adrian's all-time favorite sporting event. He lifted the phone, punched a button, and said, "Gloria, call the hotel and see if they can add one more room to our booking. I know . . . Still, try to sweet-talk them. That's my girl." He hung up the phone. "So what's your business plan, a new line of bikinis?"

"This is real, Adrian."

"Is that so."

"Real enough that I'm investing all my winnings." Ethan showed his brother the second-place check.

"What? *All* of it?"

"Every cent. And I need your help. I don't have time for this to clear, and I need the money tomorrow."

"You're asking me to give you"—he took the check and inspected it carefully—"twenty-five thousand dollars."

"In cash. Please."

Adrian gave Ethan another dose of that tight courtroom gaze. "Is it drugs?"

"What? No, Adrian, this is totally legit."

"Is it."

"I have never lied to you."

"No, that's true enough." When his phone rang, Adrian answered while still staring at the check. "Yes, Gloria. Did they. A last-minute cancellation. What do you know. Okay, book it in my brother's name, please. And try to get him a seat on our flight up. Thanks. No, wait, Gloria, I need you to do something else. Come in here, please."

When he hung up the phone, Ethan said, "Thanks for trusting me. It means a lot."

"Sign the back and make it out to the firm." Adrian watched his brother. "Are you sure you know what you're doing?"

Ethan struggled through several responses, then settled on, "This could be a major breakthrough."

"Seeing as how you're investing the first real money you've ever had, I sure hope so." Adrian looked up at a knock on his door. "Come in, Gloria. I need a draw from petty cash, please."

"Okay. Congratulations, Ethan." She accepted the check. "How do you want this?"

"Whatever. Hundreds would be fine. Thanks."

Adrian continued to show Ethan that hard courtroom stare. "Add another five thou and put it down to my account, Gloria."

"Right away. Oh, and downstairs reception just phoned. You asked to be informed when Jimmy Carstairs and his team arrived."

"Put them in conference room B, please. And call Hank and say my brother's coming over. Tell him I want Ethan made ready to meet clients, and Hank is to put everything on my tab." When the door shut, Adrian said, "Three things. First, I insist on sharing some of the risk. You can't just go and dump it all. I want you to hold a little back as a buffer. And don't argue with me."

Ethan fought down yet another surge of emotion. Adrian had always been there for him. Up until their final confrontation. "I don't know what to say."

"I'm not done. There's a men's shop across the street. I want you to go over there and buy a jacket, a suit, dress slacks, a sweater, some dress shirts, shoes, a couple of ties . . . No arguments, Ethan. Ask for Hank."

Ethan had to swallow twice before he could say, "And number three?"

"Get a haircut. You'll be traveling with the big dogs. You need to look the part." Adrian was already rising from behind his cluttered desk, shifting through the piles of papers and coming up with a couple of thick files. "We meet downstairs at four. Cars will take us to the airport. Be on time."

"Thanks, bro," Ethan said. But he was already talking to an empty room.

EIGHT

Ethan flew to New York in an outfit unlike any he'd owned before. The trip itself was part of a growing divide between his memories and the new reality.

His brother had captained the University of Florida tennis team through two winning seasons. Adrian's passion for professional tennis was real and enduring. Every year since joining the firm, Adrian traveled to the US Open in New York. Big firms like his had at least a couple of events they used for client stroking. Adrian happily served as the firm's official host whenever his caseload permitted.

The clients kept Adrian occupied throughout the trip. When their plane landed at LaGuardia, a pair of black town cars swept them into Manhattan, where they had a block of rooms at the Waldorf Astoria. Ethan had been there once, on a holiday with his ex-wife. It had been a last attempt at patching things up, an expense they could not really afford. But they had gone anyway, and it had been a miserable failure. Now he stood in the art deco lobby, filled with remorse over things that had not yet happened.

Adrian guided him into the bar, where the firm and their clients took over a trio of tables and regaled each other with tales from other moments on the tennis world circuit. Ethan listened to them take excited pleasure in what everyone assumed would be America's year.

World tennis had become increasingly dominated by foreign players. But this year would be different. Everyone said so. John McEnroe and Chris Evert Lloyd were expected to bring the trophies back where they belonged.

Only Ethan knew it would not turn out that way.

The first go-round, Adrian had phoned Ethan most evenings, offering a quick recap of the day's events. But really what his brother intended with the calls was to be there in the midst of Ethan's own contest loss. Adrian had done what he always did in the bad times. He made sure Ethan knew he wasn't alone.

Those phone calls had formed the last significant bond the brothers ever shared.

The next morning, Ethan met with Adrian's group before they headed out for the first round at Flushing Meadows. As he walked with Adrian to the door, his brother offered, "I could probably get you tickets for the early-round matches."

"I told you," Ethan said, "I'm here on business."

"What happened to taking time off to celebrate?"

"I am, in a way." Ethan followed his brother out the Waldorf's front door. "Have a great day."

"Watching Jimmy Connors clean the decks, you kidding?

What could be better?" Adrian gave him five seconds of the laser stare. "You sure you're doing the right thing?"

"Yes. I am."

Adrian nodded and kept whatever concerns he had inside. "You'll tell me what's going on when we can kick back alone?"

"Everything you want to know," Ethan replied. "Everything you can handle."

"Well, you clean up good, I'll give you that much." Adrian strode to the limo's open door, then turned back and said, "Be careful. Do that for me. You're the only brother I've got."

Ethan waved him off, then went back upstairs for the Samsonite briefcase he had bought the previous evening. He spent another long moment at the bathroom mirror, inspecting a man he had never seen before. He had not owned a decent outfit until he returned from his global trek. Now he stood in a Hugo Boss jacket and gabardine trousers, polished Bally loafers, and a haircut that was a vast improvement on his previous unkempt style.

He retrieved the manila envelopes holding his cash from the hotel safe, took a taxi to Penn Central, then hopped on the next train heading south by east to his new place of business.

CHAPTER

NINE

Atlantic City was a town made for the blues.

That was the strongest impression Ethan had, strolling from the train station to the boardwalk. Behind the rising hulks of the glitzy new shorefront casinos stretched block after block of sheer misery. Even the brightest shop looked tawdry, as if the signs were meant to mock everyone who passed.

The sea breeze was welcoming, but little else gave Ethan any sense that he was where he belonged. The people were pasty white and brash as only New Jersey locals could be. They showed a lifetime's experience of ignoring everyone else and focusing on whatever it was they wanted next.

Ethan walked through the summertime crowds, utterly alone.

He chose the Trump Casino first. It was still new and glistening and full of promise. The hotel's bankruptcies and the boardwalk's decline were all in the future. Atlantic City was busy reinventing itself as a New England alternative to Las

Vegas. The day was filled with the sound of jackhammers, and the sky was etched with skeletal cranes.

A smiling hostess greeted him as he entered the vast lobby. He passed through the main casino, the tables already crowded at eleven in the morning. Beside the bar were the betting windows. The only one with no line was for hundred-dollar-plus bets. Ethan approached that window.

"May I help you?"

"I'd like to place a bet on the US Open."

"What round?"

"The finals. Men's and women's singles." He was fairly certain he also remembered who had won the men's doubles, but he couldn't be sure. He had decided to limit himself to the two events where his memories were clearest. If his memories applied at all.

The woman was attractive in a hard-edged fashion, with heavily caked makeup and eyes of brown glass. "You want to place one bet on both, or two separate?"

"What's the difference in the odds?"

In reply, she lifted the phone and dialed. Ethan could not hear what she said until she leaned toward her mike and asked, "Who are you backing?"

Ethan glanced at the line of bettors to his left and hesitated.

The woman had clearly seen it all. Wordlessly she slid a piece of paper and pen through the money slot. Ethan wrote on it and slipped it back.

She spoke into the phone, then leaned forward and asked, "What's the size of your bet?"

Ethan motioned for the paper again. This time she sighed her exasperation, at least until he returned the page and she read what he had written. She glanced at him, read it again. Then she cupped her hand around the receiver, hiding her conversation. She watched Ethan as she waited for a response. They waited for what seemed like hours.

Finally she said, "Twelve to one on the women's, fourteen on the men's. If you go for both, thirty to one."

"I'll take them both together."

She spoke into the phone another time. "One moment."

Ethan started to object to another round of waiting, but he saw the blockade in her gaze and knew he had to do what she said. He realized he was sweating. His legs were trembling slightly. Eighteen-foot waves were apparently easier to handle than placing a bet.

A door beside the bettors' windows clicked open. "US Open, right?" The man wore a suit of sharkskin grey and a Countess Mara tie, his silver hair razored to precision, his face mechanically tanned.

"Uh, yes."

"This way, sir."

Ethan saw another man lurking farther back, a brute in navy serge, and said, "Thanks, I'd rather stay where I am."

The guy was as polite as he was firm. "Sir, we're just trying to protect your interests here."

Ethan knew every eye at the counter watched as he reluctantly entered a windowless chamber. It was clearly used for counting the spoils, because a pair of long steel tables and several adding machines were the only furniture.

The guy pulled the door shut, then said, "Five thousand to win, right?"

"Yes."

"Mind if I see the cash?"

Ethan had no choice but to open the briefcase. The guy saw the additional bands of money, accepted one bundle, counted it swiftly, then handed it to the brute. "He'll make your tickets."

"Okay."

"You planning on laying all that out on the match?"

"I . . ."

"Look, I understand you're a little spooked." The guy might have spoken the same words a thousand times already that day, he was so calm. "I'm only asking because we can offer better odds if you lay it all off here."

The brute returned and handed Ethan a bunch of tickets. He studied them a moment, long enough for his tension to ease a fraction. "Thanks, but I prefer to spread it around."

The guy cast an experienced eye at the closed briefcase. "Tell you what, you lay out another five with us, I'll loan you Jeff here. He'll escort you down the boardwalk, make sure none of the bettors who spotted you here get itchy fingers."

Ethan had been worried about that very issue. "Agreed. But only if Jeff takes me around, then I come back here."

"And you lay out our second five at the end. Sure, I can live with that."

Jeff was a silent mountain who fitted himself a step and a half behind Ethan. He had a killer's flat gaze, completely uninterested in anything except doing his job. But entering a casino with a bodyguard guaranteed a level of service that few people even knew existed.

Ethan worked his way down the boardwalk, placing five-thousand-dollar bets in the next three casinos. When he returned to the Trump, he counted out everything he had left, then held back seven hundred for expenses.

The same man in the grey suit counted Ethan's money with fluid swiftness. "I make that as nine thousand three hundred."

Ethan used both hands to clear the perspiration from his face. He had decided on the train ride up that he was going to add Adrian's five to the pile. If his memories still worked, Adrian needed to benefit. If everything was wrong or off or whatever the word was . . .

Ethan realized the man was waiting for him to respond. "Correct."

Jeff left and swiftly returned with another batch of tickets. The guy showed no interest in Ethan's nerves. As far as he was concerned, Ethan was simply another mark, here to lose. There was nothing different about him except the size of his bet.

The man in the grey suit watched Ethan slip the tickets into his briefcase and asked, "Where are you headed now, sir?"

"Back to the train station."

"I believe we can arrange a ride. Jeff?" As the brute departed the back way, the man ushered Ethan through the casino proper with a meaningless smile. He did not offer his hand as he said, "Good luck, sir."

The stretch limo's rear doors were emblazoned with the Trump logo. After it took him to the station, Ethan thanked Jeff and watched the limo disappear. He knew a sinking feeling as the limo swam down the asphalt stream, a mindless carnivore already hunting its next meal.

Ethan waited less than five minutes for the train, collapsed into his seat, and gave in to the tremors. He'd had no idea how hard it was to gamble.

TEN

The next morning, Ethan returned with Adrian to Jacksonville. He was already tired of walking the New York streets and being alone in a crowd. Plus he wanted to try to start preparing to save his brother's life. How, he had no idea. But he had to begin.

Fifteen days.

Adrian had left earlier than planned because of another meeting with the opposing counsel. He spent the flight studying legal papers and staring grimly out the side window. Sonya had just arrived in New York that morning, and Adrian intended to return as soon as he could.

When he and Ethan settled into a taxi outside the Jacksonville airport, Adrian asked, "You okay, little bro?"

"Fine. Why?"

"You seem really worried."

"I'm okay."

"Is it the deal?"

"My investment," he corrected. "Partly. Sure."

"Anything else you want to tell me?"

A huge amount was his response. Ethan felt locked in a straitjacket of tension he couldn't share or unload. "Thanks for asking. It means a lot."

"That's a no, right?"

"For now."

Adrian reopened his files and asked, "Okay if the driver drops me first by the office?"

"My car's still in the office lot, remember?"

"Sure." He scrawled an illegible notation in the margin. "When does school start?"

Ethan had no idea, nor did he know what he was going to do, especially if the outcome was not as he remembered. "Not long now."

Adrian looked up from his pages. "Any word on the investment?"

"Nothing yet."

"When should you hear?"

That, Ethan could answer. "Eleven days."

"Pretty specific for an investment."

"I know."

"You holding up okay?"

Ethan shrugged. "Depends on the hour. Nights are tough."

Adrian nodded slowly. "It's all gone?"

"Not gone. But invested. I kept a little back."

"How much?"

After the expense of New York . . . "A few hundred."

"Yeah, I figured you were going to blow my five on this too." Adrian leaned forward and extracted his wallet.

"Bro, look, I can't . . ."

"Quiet." Adrian pulled out everything he had, kept a few

bills, then offered the rest. When Ethan did not accept it, Adrian stuffed the money into his hands. "Add it to the balance. You win, you pay."

Ethan stared at the money. Then he looked at his brother, who was already lost once more in his work. "Adrian . . ."

"Don't get all gooey on me. The Barrett boys don't do mush."

———

Ethan waited until Adrian disappeared inside the building, then shifted his car from the firm's visitor space to a relatively unused floor. He swiftly changed from his New York duds into clothes he had brought up with him from Cocoa Beach, locked the suitcase in the Jeep, and carried his backpack into the humid afternoon.

He found what he was looking for a block off the waterfront, an aging city hotel now standing in the shadow of the city's new Skyway. The hotel mostly catered to the monorail's construction workers. Its rusting sign outside the wire-glass doors offered air conditioning and clean rooms. And very little else.

He could have stayed at Adrian's. But that would have required him to explain why he was hanging around. Plus there was the risk of Sonya coming home early from New York. Ethan was definitely not ready for that little confrontation.

His room was on the sixth floor and faced north, away from the Skyway's platform under construction. The noise and dust were manageable. His bed sagged like a tired old man, but Ethan had spent time in far worse places. Not in a long while, but still. After a decent enough meal at a local diner, he made a pallet on the floor and slept fine.

Ethan spent the next two and a half days reacquainting himself with the city. He had visited Adrian there any number of times, but not for years. His annual visits to the Saint Augustine cemetery had never included a visit to the city itself.

Jacksonville was pretty much as he remembered. The place was busy shrugging off its roots as a sleepy southern sister to the much larger Augusta. The Jacksonville of 1985 was a city on the rise.

The downtown districts contained Jacksonville's historic core, courthouses, and central business districts. The first major high-rises were taking shape, soon to house regional or national headquarters of CSX, Fidelity National, Bank of America, Wells Fargo, AT&T, and Aetna. Already the sidewalks were fronted by shiny new restaurants and upscale shops. The former derelict port area was being refashioned into Riverwalk, a trendy pedestrian zone with some of the south's hottest nightlife. Most of the faces Ethan saw were young, vibrant, excited to call Jacksonville home.

Ethan sectioned the downtown region with the Duval County Courthouse at its center. For two solid days he scoured the area surrounding East Bay Street, walked the courthouse corridors, studied the stairs and front plaza soon to be stained with his brother's blood.

But not this time.

All the while, he argued with himself over tactics. By his third morning walking the city streets, Ethan had decided his original plan was the right one. If or when he scored on the Open bet, he would bring in his version of heavy artillery.

The nights were awful and endless. When the pallet grew too hard, he walked the room's threadbare confines, trying to formulate a plan that did not depend upon money. He would have to tell Adrian everything. He repeatedly imagined his brother's scorn, the accusations of drug use, the questions for which he had no answers.

Adrian would change his tactics, of course he would. Ethan would give him no choice. But say his brother didn't appear on the courthouse steps. Say he survived that morning. What then? The police had never identified the shooter.

The dread prospect of Adrian living through that attempt, only to die a few days later, finally drove Ethan from the city. As he took I-95 south in the decrepit Wagoneer, the wind rushing hot and fragrant through his open window, Ethan's mind kept pounding through a desperate refrain.

He had to win that bet.

ELEVEN

While the early rounds of the US Open continued, Ethan did his best to remain detached. He surfed, cruised the beaches, ate with his friends, and watched a tennis tournament that seemed to last for months.

The United States Open Tennis Championship was a hard-court tournament held annually over a two-week period. It was the fourth and final tourney that made up the Grand Slam events—Australian Open, French Open, Wimbledon, then New York. The main tournament consisted of five championships—men's and women's singles, men's and women's doubles, and mixed doubles. Since 1978, the tournament was played on acrylic hard courts at the USTA Center in Flushing, Queens. All this Ethan learned in the local library, where he spent at least an hour each morning, checking the newspapers and researching a world he only half remembered.

Boris Becker and top-seeded John McEnroe continued on their collision course, winning their third-round matches with surprising ease. Becker was only seventeen years old and was already being referred to as the new wunderkind.

Ethan spent far too many hours in the confines of his summer rental. He watched parts of matches on their awful television. The sound was scratchy and the image worse. He could have gone to one of the new sports bars and watched on a wide screen. But if he had wanted to spend the tense hours being lonely in the company of strangers, he could have stayed up north.

Mostly he fretted.

His lack of forward momentum grew more frustrating by the hour. Twice he started to head back to Jacksonville, only to be halted by the utter futility of the act.

Added to his internal cauldron were any number of questions he could not answer. Time and again he returned to how Sonya and her as-yet unborn daughter had confronted him. In the aftermath of Adrian's death, Sonya had lost her lab and her life's work. What if more was at stake here than a crazed gunman acting on his own? Ethan was no professional sleuth, but the more he pondered the upcoming events, the more he feared his dilemma did not end with bullets fired on the courthouse steps.

His growing suspicions only magnified his mounting anxiety over the Open. If his suspicions about Sonya's work were correct, then his task required not just stopping a gunman but uncovering a conspiracy.

And for that to happen, he needed cash. Lots of it. Security, a team of investigators, and something more besides. He had to convince both Adrian and Sonya the entire issue was real.

Adrian liked to describe his professional life as high-stakes gambling in the harshest casino of all. He lived and breathed facts and evidence and tactics and the arguments required to win over a jury.

Sonya was certainly no easier a sell. Ethan had no idea if telling her about the pregnancy would be enough. And if not, what could he possibly say? The woman could hardly bear to be in the same room with him. Would it be enough for him to declare what had happened at her own hand and beg her for help? Or would she toss him and his threats to their security out the door?

It all came down to having hard evidence.

Ethan needed to win.

His buddies started their final chaotic weeks of summer, drinking themselves insensible each night. They closed down the bars and slumped into work in pain-wracked stupors, then did it all again the next night. Ethan played designated driver, even though the term had not yet entered current culture. He went to the bars, sat in the corners, nursed his ginger ale, and smiled at girls who were impossibly fresh-faced and innocent and young. They were often magnetic in their appeal, until they opened their mouths. And then they only made Ethan feel ancient. But at least it gave him something to do while he endured the endless wait.

On the other side of the chart, Ivan Lendl and Yannick Noah both advanced into the third round. In the women's competition, Chris Evert Lloyd crushed a south Korean in her third-round match, and Martina Navratilova trounced Lisa Bonder.

By the time the next stage began, Ethan was hardly sleeping.

Jimmy Connors and Chris Evert Lloyd, the two winningest players in US Open history, both advanced. The battles were fierce. Lloyd, the number-one seed and hunting her seventh Open title, reached the semis for the eighteenth consecutive year by defeating Claudia Kohde-Kilsch. Her next foe would be Hana Mandlíková, an unseeded Czech who had stunned the world by defeating Helena Suková.

Ethan's heart stopped several times watching Ivan Lendl's match against the seventeen-year-old Jaime Yzaga of Peru, a qualifier. Lendl self-destructed in the first set with seventeen unforced errors. But the Czech right-hander finally found his accuracy on his crucial ground game. The quarters would match Lendl against Yannick Noah of France, ranked seventh in the world.

The next day, defending Open champion John McEnroe overcame a ridiculously bad call and a wild temper tantrum to beat Sweden's Joakim Nyström in straight sets. The crowd was then stunned by the young Steffi Graf of West Germany, who beat fourth-seeded Pam Shriver. The previous year Graf had been crushed by Shriver in the first round.

Then former ball girl Hana Mandlíková shocked the world by beating Chris Evert Lloyd in a three-set nail-biter. The victory sent her into the title match against Martina Navratilova, who crushed Steffi Graf in straight sets.

Ivan Lendl ignored the 112-degree courtside heat and powered through the semis, crushing Yannick Noah in straight sets. Later that evening, Jimmy Connors defeated Heinz Günthardt in a match that even the announcers said was lackluster.

Then on Saturday it started to come together.

When Adrian called from New York that night, he was

hoarse from cheering. He greeted Ethan with the exact same words as the last time. "The bridesmaid stole the show, shot the priest, hijacked the limo, and is currently headed out on somebody else's honeymoon."

This time Ethan knew what he was talking about. "I saw. Parts, anyway."

"It was some of the best tennis of any time, any race, any match—male, female, Chihuahua. I tell you, bro, that lady deserved her win." Adrian went on to give Ethan a blow-by-blow of Mandlíková's stunning defeat of world champion Martina Navratilova. Ethan did not interrupt, mostly because his tension had grown to where the power of speech belonged to a different guy.

Adrian asked, "You watch any of the men's semis?"

"Some." Ethan had paved a new track around the house, popping in occasionally, catching the scores, then doing another round.

Adrian said, "Lendl pounded Jimmy Connors into the dust. It was embarrassing."

Ethan let Adrian talk, trying to take some comfort in getting it right so far. But when he hung up the phone, there was nothing to do but pace.

CHAPTER
TWELVE

That evening, Ethan used some of his remaining cash and took a room at the beachside Holiday Inn. The summer season was over. September and October formed the slowest tourist season unless there was a launch, but NASA's next rocket was scheduled for Thanksgiving week. Ethan got an oceanfront room for the cost of a highway single.

He walked down to a strip mall serving the local business community and bought a portable calculator. But he left it in the bag on the shelf in the closet. He didn't want to think about it just then. He simply wanted to be ready. In case.

Ethan spent most of the finals match out on the balcony. The ocean had returned to standard Florida calm, so the play was clearly audible. He was tempted several times to shut the doors and just wait. His hands shook and his eyes felt scratchy. He had not eaten a decent meal in six days. He had slept a maximum of a few hours each night.

The announcers kept up their standard patter through the

first two sets. In their eyes, John McEnroe had already won. It was just a matter of time.

Ivan Lendl had been defeated by McEnroe every time they had met but one. Earlier that year, McEnroe had defeated Lendl in straight sets at two different major tournaments. Lendl's expected defeat would mean he had lost in the finals four years in a row, a record matched only once before, by William Johnston in 1925.

When the third set started, the announcers finally changed their tune. And Ethan found the courage to reenter his room. He watched the entire third set standing in front of the television. He did not breathe. He could not move.

Lendl forged ahead with a magnificent series of blasting serves. Then he set himself up for the title by breaking McEnroe's own service twice. Lendl did not just win. He obliterated the world number one in straight sets.

When Lendl lifted the cup over his head, Ethan crashed to the floor.

He lay there through the interviews as Lendl described how he had changed tactics and sought to lead a normal life throughout the tournament. Ethan lay on the carpet and let Lendl's accented words wash over him. "I tried to do everything like I would every other day and just went to my matches. I went to aerobic classes. I played golf. I played with my dogs. I tried to keep myself relaxed."

Ethan rolled onto his back and laughed at the popcorn ceiling. He and Lendl should have had this conversation a week ago.

Finally Ethan managed to crawl over and turn off the set. He sat there awhile, gathering strength, staring at the ocean. Then he rose, went to the closet, opened the bag, and got out his calculator. He did not need to check the tickets. He remembered the odds. All of them.

Each of the casinos had offered slightly different odds, ranging from 29–1 to 34–1. Ethan's fingers trembled so badly he botched the first three attempts. On the fourth go he grabbed the pad and pen off the bedside table and wrote down each set of numbers in turn. Then he had to stop and go out on the balcony before he could work up the nerve to add them together.

He had invested $29,200. He had won $905,200.

Adrian's money and his share of the winnings came to $155,000.

Which meant Ethan was going to walk away with $750,000 and change.

He staggered back out on the balcony and blindly stared out over the crystal-blue sea.

He was rich, and he knew what was going to happen next. He had a month to try to make things right.

It would all begin with saving his brother's life.

THIRTEEN

Ethan did not sleep well. Becoming an almost millionaire changed nothing in that regard.

On Monday morning he was the hotel diner's first customer. The banked-up stress and fatigue felt like tight electric sparks shooting through his brain. His hands trembled slightly, and his eyes felt grainy. Even so, nothing seemed to affect his appetite. He worked his way through a Spanish omelet, home fries, sausages, toast, and two glasses of milk.

When the waitress cleared away his plates, Ethan brought out the notepad and pen from his room. On the first page, just below the Holiday Inn logo, he wrote his future ex-wife's full name. Angelina Grace Devoe. She would return from Europe tomorrow. It was a date etched in his memory, almost as vivid as the gunshot he had never actually heard.

The previous time, Gina had phoned him from her parents' home. There was a new note to her voice, an eagerness without reservation or any hint of doubt. Ethan promised to meet her in three days, once he finished his last week of work at the Holiday Marina.

Gina drove up with him for Adrian's funeral and heard his decision to drop out of school and take a world tour of his own. She responded by promising to wait for him.

And she did. For three and a half years.

They met occasionally. Every four or five months, she flew out to wherever he was surfing and working at some menial job. Four times in four years, he flew home. He claimed it was because he missed her. And he did, in some vague fashion. But mostly it had been to test the waters. See if he was ready to reenter the world he was running from. Things like responsibility. Family. A regular job. A paycheck.

An hour later, Ethan was still sitting there, staring at Gina's name written on the otherwise empty page. He sighed defeat, rose to his feet, paid the cashier, and departed. He checked out of the hotel, returned to the rental house, packed his meager belongings, and drove straight to the Jacksonville airport.

The travel websites that had driven down the cost of airfares were a thing of the future. Ethan paid an eye-watering sum for a last-minute return flight to Newark.

When he landed in New Jersey, he debated taking a limo. But an ad in the arrivals terminal claimed a bus left for Atlantic City every twenty minutes. He joined the line of other dedicated gamblers heading for the end of the road.

Ethan's first stop was a First Union branch between the terminal and the boardwalk. The duty manager offered empty congratulations at the news of his win and helped him open an account.

Any concerns Ethan had over being treated as a gullible youngster were erased the moment he presented his tickets to the Trump Casino cashier. Ten minutes later he left with a cashier's check, which he took straight to the bank. Ninety minutes later, he had completed his rounds and was back on the bus. He did not even stop to eat until he had checked in for his flight.

He grabbed a burger at the terminal diner, then bought an AT&T long-distance card from the news agent and claimed a pay phone by the terminal's side window. There were very few things he missed from the new millennium. But owning a cell phone would definitely have made his next steps a lot easier.

One positive outcome of Ethan's enforced delay was having time to plan. At the top of that list was gaining the help of a local security specialist. The only investigator he knew personally worked for Adrian's firm. Gary Holt was a former cop, a highly decorated gold-shield detective who had spent twenty years in white-collar crime. After taking his retirement, Gary had earned his private investigator's license and went to work for Adrian's firm.

Gary's father was a full-blood Seminole and considered by many to be the finest fishing guide in Florida. Adrian had befriended Gary soon after joining the firm, and together with Ethan they had spent countless weekends trolling the slow-moving Saint Johns River for sturgeon, rainbow trout, and large-mouth bass.

Gary was tied up with pretrial testimony and tried to put Ethan off until the following week. The PI's tone of voice said it all. He was a busy professional who did not want to make time for Adrian's kid brother. But Ethan pushed hard, and the investigator reluctantly agreed to meet him in two days for an early lunch.

Ethan hung up and dialed information. When the operator came on the line, he said, "This is going to sound crazy."

The New Jersey operator had the metallic voice of someone long dead. "Hon, crazy is the only way to define my day. Do you want a number or not?"

"Yes, I want a number. But I can't remember the name."

"Then you've got yourself a problem."

"It's a hotel in Jacksonville Beach. It's old and really nice."

"Not a lot to go on."

"The name is old-fashioned too. I remember that much."

"Do you remember the name of the lady you took there? That's the important question."

"It was my brother. His firm put him up there while he looked for a place to live—"

"Could it be Casa Marina?"

"Wow. You're good."

"Tell that to my boss. Hold for the number."

By the time Ethan finished booking a room, his flight was being called. He spent the two-hour journey working on his timeline. He knew it was mostly just a hypothetical exercise. Even so, it helped frame the coming days in manageable segments.

The drive to Jacksonville Beach was awful. The airport was north of the city, and to reach the beach meant passing through downtown at four in the afternoon. The heat was stifling, made worse by near one hundred percent humidity. Ethan kept all his windows down, but by the time he reached the Saint Johns bridge he had sweated through his shirt.

When he spotted the sign on Atlantic Boulevard, Ethan felt as if the Jeep turned of its own accord.

Tom Bush BMW had fueled the dreams of Jacksonville youths for years. Adrian drove a Lincoln and considered Ethan's fascination with Beemers to be a serious character flaw.

There was a brand-new BMW 633i in the showroom window. That particular machine had been Ethan's dream ride since he caught the car bug at the ripe old age of seven.

A couple of the salesmen drifted out of the rear shadows, but Ethan suspected it was to give his Jeep a closer look. They watched him enter the showroom, and all but one drifted away. The salesman whose turn it was walked over with the sort of smile he would offer every wistful youth. "Help you?"

"Yes." Ethan walked over to a vacant sales desk and opened the canvas satchel he had taken to New Jersey. "I need you to look at something."

"Kid, I'm really sorry, but this is a cash-only business . . ." The salesman's sneer vanished when he realized what Ethan held out for his inspection. "What are those?"

"First Union deposit slips," Ethan said. He pointed to the clock, which read ten minutes to five. "I need you to get on the horn and do whatever it takes so I can drive out of here today."

———

Three hours and fourteen minutes later, Ethan drove his first-ever BMW from the lot.

First Union had acquired First Atlantic Bank of Jacksonville, which gave them a branch just four blocks from the dealership. The branch manager agreed to stay open long enough for the salesman to rush Ethan over and obtain the necessary cashier's check. By this point, Ethan had decided a flashy new 633i would only confirm his brother's fear that he was dealing drugs. He and the salesman reviewed options. Ethan settled on a sensible ride, but one with a serious kick.

The three-year-old 535i had only 6,500 miles, a grey metallic exterior, saddle-leather interior with Recaro sports seats and, as the salesman put it, all the necessary bells and whistles.

Driving from the car lot, seeing the Jeep rust bucket in his rearview mirror, hearing the engine growl as he accelerated into traffic—all of it was good for a shout of pure, unbridled joy.

The Casa Marina was one of the oldest hotels in Florida, founded in 1925 and renovated every decade or so—compliments of the two-fisted beating all oceanfront hotels received from tourists and the weather. Ethan had no trouble with the check-in process because the bank manager had phoned ahead to confirm that his checks and credit were both good.

The floors of his corner suite were peg-and-groove Florida mahogany, the furniture heavy Spanish oak. He had a four-poster bed and a lovely two-way view over the beachfront in the last light of a very long day. Ethan ordered a room-service dinner, spent half an hour in the deep bath, and almost fell asleep over his meal.

He woke at six the next morning, after the first real rest he had obtained since the transition. He ate another room-service meal, dressed in his last clean shirt and trousers, and beat the rush-hour traffic into Jacksonville. His first stop was the same men's store where Adrian had sent him. The gun-to-his-head prices only slowed him down a little. From there he walked to First Union's main office and asked to speak to one of their brokers. A quick glance at his current balance was enough to bring out the division chief.

"Ethan Barrett? Reginald Firth. Are you related to Adrian?" The broker was in his mid- to late thirties and was already balding. His three-piece herringbone suit and pale complexion suggested he had recently arrived from somewhere farther north.

"He's my brother, and I need to know you won't speak to him about anything that happens here."

Reginald halted in the process of shutting his office door. "Can I ask why?"

Ethan knew the broker saw a know-it-all college student and did his best to stifle his impatience. "I want to tell Adrian in my own time, in my own way."

They remained standing in the middle of Reginald's office. "Tell him what?"

"That I'm doing this for both of us. I want both Adrian and Sonya to be co-owners of this account. And they don't know anything about it. Yet." When Reginald started in on another question, Ethan cut him off with, "Sorry, I don't have the time to go into further details." He handed over a sheet of notepaper. "I want you to buy shares in these companies."

Reginald slowly rounded the desk and waved Ethan into a chair opposite. "IBM is a sound buy. But these other two . . . Nintendo, did I say that right?"

It was the only clear recollection Ethan carried from that last fateful year, how he and Adrian had become hooked on the brand-new concept. "It's a maker of electronic games.

This year they're coming out with their own hardware system. It's going to remake the gaming industry."

"You're sure about that, are you?"

"I am. Yes. They're a Japanese company. But they're listed on the AMEX. I checked."

"And this last buy?"

"Motorola has brought out the first general-release cell phone. Another game changer."

"Those things weigh a ton and cost a fortune." Reginald flipped the paper onto his desk. "Nobody outside a few Wall Street jokers would dream of shelling out for one."

"Adrian has one. And I'm not here to ask your advice. I want you to buy shares. A hundred and fifty thousand dollars on each company." He waited as Reginald wrote down the figure. "One question. If I short a stock, how long can I hold it?"

Reginald took his time answering. "If your account holds the full market value of your short, then as long as you want. But normally—"

Ethan waved that aside. Nothing about this conversation had even a nodding acquaintance with normal. "I want you to short $150,000 worth of Apple."

The broker laughed out loud. "But they just fired Steve Jobs!"

Ethan nodded. He had read about that on the flight south. "Exactly."

"With that hippie gone, they'll take off like a California bottle rocket."

"I disagree." When Reginald looked ready to argue, Ethan rose to his feet. "I expect those deals to be executed by close of business today. Now I'm due at my next appointment. Where do I sign?"

FOURTEEN

The Jacksonville of 1985 was gradually emerging from its sleepy, slow-moving past. Adrian had moved here because he was as ambitious as he was impatient. He left law school already looking to become partner, which meant finding a good firm in a city that was on the move.

Ethan's destination was a new business-technology park rising from what had previously been a river port. The rusting warehouses and cranes were gradually being torn down and replaced by gleaming new waterfront buildings. Only three were completed, and they were surrounded by raw earth and construction noise. Ethan parked in the visitors' lot, entered the central building, and asked the receptionist to page Sonya. He took a couple of steps toward the exit, ready for a quick retreat, and steeled himself for what would happen next.

The first time he and Sonya met had pretty much defined their relationship from that point on. Ethan had shown up for dinner dressed in his standard college-casual garb—faded surfer T-shirt and cutoffs and sandals. As usual, Adrian made some caustic joke about Ethan's inability to dress for the occasion, then ignored it as inconsequential. Their relationship was not defined by clothes. Sonya's response was completely the opposite. She thought Ethan's attire showed her and their upcoming marriage a severe lack of respect.

But even in that first meeting, Sonya's hostility went far deeper. She saw in Ethan a young man who was completely uninterested in making the most of his life. She listened to him talk about college and loathed how he took that opportunity for granted. She thought he showed contempt for the investment his late parents had made in his future. In short, she despised his attitude and everything it represented.

Adrian watched in dismay as his brother and future wife fought their way through dinner. Their tight little snips grew into a full-fledged verbal battle. Ethan had finally stormed out and not spoken with Sonya again until the rehearsal dinner.

This time around, the shock of seeing Sonya again was worse in some ways than Ethan's first meeting with Adrian. Sonya Barrett, rising star in the world of microbiology and brain chemistry, was almost beautiful. She carried herself with a model's erectness. Her ice-blue eyes held a Nordic chill. Her hair was dark, her face unlined.

As he watched her cross the building lobby, Ethan knew he had been right to come.

Sonya wore a crisp white lab coat with her name sewn into the pocket, and an expression that showed him angry distaste. "What are you doing here?"

"Five minutes," Ethan replied. "Please."

"Adrian said he bought you new clothes." She crossed her arms. "You clean up okay, I'll give you that much."

"This is very important, Sonya."

The young receptionist pretended not to listen to them between answering calls.

Ethan asked, "Can we step away?"

Reluctantly she followed him over to the corner, where a trio of potted palms offered a hint of privacy. "I need to get back to the lab, Ethan."

He said, "You were right about me."

"Excuse me?"

"I was getting ready to walk out. Leave school, leave Florida, take off and surf the world." Ethan had spent the drive over debating how he might break through to her. Now that he was here, now that she was actually listening, he still had no idea. Except to give her the unvarnished truth.

"You've spent your entire university career floating."

He nodded. *Remember*, she had told him. Looking at her now, seeing everything that might still happen if he didn't get it right, if he didn't save his brother, if he didn't . . .

"What has gotten into you?" Sonya leaned closer. "Are you ill?"

"No. Well, yes. But it's not . . ." He unfolded his bank statement and passed it over. He realized his hands were shaking. "I need to show you something."

"What is this?"

"I've started investing. I'll explain everything later. But for now—"

"Is this drug money?"

"Adrian asked me the same thing."

"It's the natural response, given what we know of you." She studied him. "Is it?"

"No, Sonya. This is legit. And it's only the beginning."

"Why are you showing me this?"

"Because I want to invest in your group."

Sonya opened her mouth. Closed it. Opened it again. "I don't . . ."

For the very first time, Ethan glimpsed beneath her frigid exterior and saw the woman his brother loved. The burning intensity, the incredible intelligence . . . the heart.

"If I'm right, I'm going to make a lot more. It's yours—all of it. In a month. Maybe six weeks."

She said weakly, "What is going on?"

Ethan glanced around the empty lobby. The receptionist continued fielding calls. They were isolated by the Muzak and the shrubbery. The afternoon glare through the side windows bathed them in a heat that defied the AC's wash.

"Ethan!"

So he began. But he did not tell her everything. Not even close.

He did not tell her about Delia. Or about Adrian's death.

Midway through his description, Sonya sank into a corner chair. Ethan lowered himself to the edge of the coffee table. The setting sun beat on the back of his head and shoulders. But that was not why he was sweating.

He talked about his life. It was the clearest way he knew to make the transition real for her. How he had returned after four years from surfing the globe. How for a while the hunt through various island jungles was enough. How he loved the island hopping. How the job he held the longest was as dockhand on a luxury yacht owned by the Lichtenstein royal family. How he walked off the boat in Tahiti and spent six and a half months playing a modern-day Gauguin. How in the end, he woke up one morning, just another beachcomber sleeping in a thatched hut at the shore, and . . .

Nothing. The joy of surfing, the fire of discovery, the sense of adventure . . . gone.

He left his boards and his clothes, took only his passport and his last seven hundred dollars, and flew back to Florida. Married his college sweetheart. Divorced seven years later. He spent the next twenty years doing precisely what Sonya had accused him of. He floated.

He got a job managing the Sebastian boatyard. He bought part ownership in a couple of small local companies—surf shops and board manufacturers. He surfed the local breaks. He made friends who wandered through their days with the same scattered emptiness as he did. Until the cancer came. And when the doctor told Ethan he was on final approach, what he felt most of all was . . .

This is it?

That was why, when Sonya had shown up, he found himself so incredibly eager to transit. More than that, he had been hungry to try to right some of the things he had gotten so wrong. So he had let himself be shot back through time . . .

"Stop," Sonya said. "Please."

Ethan took that as his sign. "I need to ask a couple of questions." He gave her a chance to object. When she remained as she was, gazing blindly at the sunlit vista beyond the side window, he went on, "What are you currently working on?"

"The same investigation since we met." Her words came out in a monotone. Like she was not fully aware that she spoke at all. "Treatment of chronic pain through brain-wave frequency modulations. You've heard Adrian and me talk about this any number of times."

He replied as gently as he knew how. "That was thirty-five years ago."

She breathed in and out through pursed lips, taking the news in deep.

Ethan felt a need to add, "To tell the truth, I probably wasn't listening all that well back then either."

She managed to focus on him. "You've changed."

He nodded. No question about that. "So you don't have anything to do with, you know . . ."

"Transfer of consciousness? No. Although there are several different avenues . . ." Her voice drifted off as her vision went back out of focus.

"You said when the initial test subjects showed they'd transitioned, it caught you totally by surprise."

She nodded slowly, but Ethan wasn't entirely sure she had heard him at all.

He'd started to ask about the Washington-based group that had invested in her company, when the door leading back to her lab opened. A young Asian woman emerged far enough to call over, "Sonya, we're late running the test. If we don't move, the results will be skewed."

Sonya rose slowly to her feet. "I have to go."

He stood with her. "I'm staying at the Casa Marina if you need to reach me."

As he headed back to the car, Ethan hoped he had been right not to warn her about the attack on Adrian. But there was no telling how she would take the news or what she would do. And the last thing he wanted was for her to try to take control and him to wind up with two deaths on his conscience.

As he started to reverse from the space, Sonya came running through the front doors.

He put the car in park, opened his door, and stood up. He wanted to meet this incoming assault on his feet. This being Sonya, he expected bitter argument, the sort of cold fury he had always elicited before.

Instead she halted in front of him and said, "I have questions."

"I'll do my best to answer them." Ethan hesitated, then decided he needed to repeat what he had told her inside. "I need you to not discuss this with Adrian. Not the money, not my return, anything. Let me do it in my own way, in my own time. Please."

She seemed to work through several thoughts so potent they pinched her entire frame. "This is the last thing I expected. To have my research extended in such a profound direction."

"Totally out of the blue. I know it must be—"

"And to have it come through you of all people." Sonya's desperate appeal raked his heart. "You haven't told me everything, have you?"

"Not even close."

"What you haven't said, it's bad, isn't it."

Ethan slipped back behind the wheel. "Not if I can help it."

FIFTEEN

The Beach Road Diner was a throwback to Jacksonville's roots, a Deep South restaurant that had been clogging arteries for over fifty years. Ethan's BMW was far from the only fancy car in the lot, however. Many of Jacksonville's movers and shakers considered the diner a weekly rite of passage.

As Ethan rose from his car, Gary stepped out of the porch shadows and tapped his watch. Ethan followed him into the diner. As they waited for a table, the former cop demanded, "What's so all-fired urgent it can't wait until next week?"

"Soon as we're seated I'll explain."

Other than a fresh coat of paint, the diner's interior had changed very little since the second World War. The tables were still draped in clear plastic sheaths, the silverware came wrapped in paper napkins, the drinks arrived in twenty-ounce plastic cups, the meals were piled on giant oval plates. Faces and fingers shone with grease. The smell was heavenly.

Gary waved away the menu and said, "Butterfly shrimp with everything. Extra creamed peas. Sweet tea."

"Same," Ethan said. When the waitress departed, Ethan said, "Thanks for seeing me."

"I've got to be back at the courthouse in"—he checked his watch—"thirty-seven minutes."

Ethan launched straight in. "I have information that Adrian is going to be murdered. Shot in cold blood."

"Is this some kind of sick joke?"

"Do I look like I'm joking to you? Here, take a look at this." Ethan passed over his deposit slips. "I'm showing you this because I need you to understand I'm not here as Adrian's brother. I'm a client, and the threat is real."

Gary was a handsome man in his early forties, but he was not aging well. Ethan watched the flat brown eyes inspect the documents, cop eyes that gave nothing away. He could see Gary in another ten years, bulked up with a hundred excess pounds. Maybe more.

Finally Gary handed the pages back. "Tell me about this source of yours."

"Not now, not ever."

"Look, kid—"

"See, that's where we need to reach clarity. I'm not a kid."

Gary gave him the cop's version of a graveyard stare. Dark, bottomless eyes that promised a world of hurt if Ethan dared get out of line. "You think money in the bank and a new set of flashy clothes make you a man?"

Ethan breathed in and out, waiting for the rage to dim. "I don't have time for this, and neither do you. I came to you first because my brother thinks you're the best there is. I want to hire you. In return, I expect you to treat me as a bona fide client."

The waitress delivered their meals. They ate in silence.

Ethan spent the time reviewing alternative next steps. Not having Gary agree to take him on meant building a relationship with people he had never met. He had researched the city's three other security firms. Sinclair would be his first call. But going in cold probably meant no better reception than now.

Gary broke into his thoughts. "Say I agree. Which I haven't. Not yet. What are you after?"

Ethan pushed his half-finished plate aside. "Protect my brother. The attack is supposed to take place tomorrow at four in the afternoon, as Adrian exits the courthouse."

"They're going to shoot your brother in broad daylight?"

"Exactly."

Gary spooned up the last of his peas. "What else can you tell me?"

"The gunman is Anglo, mid-forties. That's all I know. I don't have a name. His escape vehicle is a stolen minivan. I'll cover all costs."

"You sure this is legit?"

"I am."

Gary balled up his napkin tighter and tighter. "That it? We stop an attack and we're done?"

One look into that hard, suspicious gaze was enough. Ethan wanted to discuss his concerns and his suspicions with someone. But Gary Holt still viewed the world from a cop's point of view. He was as addicted to hard evidence as Adrian. Before Ethan went any further, he would have to prove the threat was real.

So all he said was, "The message I received was incomplete. This might be a lone gunman, it might be more. Once this first attack has been foiled, I'm going to try to convince

Adrian to accept a security detail on him and Sonya both. Round the clock."

"Kid, you have no idea . . ." Gary smiled, and in doing so he rearranged the grim lines. Ethan remembered him then as their fishing buddy, the man who knew the Saint Johns River like the back of his hand. "Sorry, that just slipped out."

"It happens."

"What I was going to say was, this could get extremely expensive."

"Would a fifty-thousand-dollar retainer do for a start?"

It was Gary's turn to take it in. "All right. I'm your man. At least for the next two days."

"You need to get this in place today. That includes hiring people we can rely on to secure the street in front of the courthouse."

"Soon as I'm done with this deposition, I'll get started."

"And you treat this as you would any other confidential assignment. Nobody in the firm hears a thing until I decide and I act."

"Understood." Gary waited while Ethan paid, then followed him outside. He offered Ethan a second grin. "Guess I won't be calling you kid ever again."

SIXTEEN

Ethan used the phone on the restaurant's outside wall and called Gina's home. Her mother's voice came on the answering machine, which was good for a shock. In his first go-round, his future ex-mother-in-law had passed away twelve years before. Ethan fumbled over the words, managed to say he was driving down, and hung up sweating from far more than the heat.

Once he hit I-95 south, the miles flowed smoothly, which only granted his memories more space to roam. Gina had spent that entire summer backpacking through Europe with her sister and two friends from UF. Three days before she departed, Gina had asked him not to write or call or make contact in any way. For the entire summer. She felt conflicted, she explained. And scared. She needed time to sort things out and see if indeed they were meant to build a future together.

Of course Ethan agreed. He felt all of those things himself.

They had met at the beginning of their junior year at UF.

They were drawn together with a fierceness that frightened them both, and almost instantly they found themselves fighting. Their relationship remained as it had begun, with their growing love regularly shattered by explosive breakups.

Right up to the day of their divorce.

———

An hour or so later, the vegetation began shifting from temperate to tropical. Pine trees and kudzu vines gave way to palms and blooming oleander. As Ethan passed the Daytona exit, he was struck by a memory from his childhood.

Like all beach kids, he'd considered himself completely invulnerable. His parents knew he would never be kept out of the ocean, so they had paid good money to have a professional lifeguard teach him about safety and the sea. That particular day, the investment saved Ethan's life.

That autumn, the king tide had arrived while a hurricane churned through the Caribbean. The proper name for the phenomenon was a perigean tide, and on its own the rising waters often flooded low-lying coastal towns. Combined with a distant storm, the event carried deadly force. What made it especially dangerous were the day's conditions: warm temperatures, crystal-clear sky, placid seas that sparkled and beckoned and drew eight-year-old Ethan out farther than he should have gone. And suddenly he was caught in a king-tide rip. Literally one dive under water was all it took. When he went down, he was playing on the edge of deep water. When he came up . . .

The shore was gone.

The lifeguard had stressed time and again how, if Ethan got caught by a rip, the only hope of safety would come from moving *with* the flow, not against. That sounded fine when he was sitting on the beach. But as the currents pulled him fast as a river and fear rose in his throat, all Ethan wanted to do was scream.

Then the lifeguard's stern voice sounded in his head. *"Do not fight. Do not panic. Swim steady and easy in the flow's direction. And above all else, keep careful watch."*

Unlike the sappy films they showed in every Florida school, rips caused by major events like the king tide did not reverse flow in a clear pattern and simply head landward. They were too strong, too big. Rather, they fragmented.

Ripples tracked the moment when streams broke away and headed inland. You had to watch, stay calm, and be ready when the moment came.

Now, as Ethan drove the almost-empty highway, he remembered that incredible moment—actually, three of them. The first had come when the tiny feather waves broke free from the current and turned toward the setting sun. And he was ready.

The second came when the beachfront condos came into view. Nothing in his entire short existence had looked as beautiful as those buildings, gleaming soft and golden in the late afternoon light.

And the third, that incredibly sweet moment, was when his feet had touched the sandy bottom.

As Ethan passed the Canaveral exit, he felt that same immense flow of events, accelerating as it pulled him further and further from his own past. The rip was too powerful to fight against, even now, as he was pulled so far out he could no longer even define his own comfort zone.

He had no choice but to move with the flow. He could only

hope that somewhere out there, beyond the empty horizon, was confirmation that he was taking the right course.

———

That final hour of the drive probably should have been worse than it was. Ethan turned on the radio and found himself listening to a soundtrack from his own life. Huey Lewis's "The Power of Love" was followed by Whitney Houston singing "Saving All My Love for You." Then came Phil Collins and "One More Night."

Kissimmee's main artery was the 192, which drilled a straight line from the Atlantic beaches to Disney's southern entrances. Already by 1985 the highway was lined with tawdry castoffs—cheap motels, trailer parks, strip malls, and apartment complexes with walls so flimsy the occupants could hear other families breathe.

Old-town Kissimmee, where Gina's family had lived for three generations, was another world. Spanish moss dangled from the branches of live oaks that had taken root before America became a nation. Stately homes were framed by blooming perennials. Kids played kickball on emerald lawns. A passing motorist welcomed him with a languid wave.

Gina's father was an orthodontist, her mother a nurse who since their marriage had run her husband's office and served as his surgical aide. The Devoe clan had migrated southeast from the Louisiana bayou country. They were Southern to their roots but with a distinctly Cajun spice. Their bloodline was mixed, their skin the color of sourwood honey, their eyes dark as a cloudy midnight, their women beautiful. Gina's parents were both quiet, stern, reserved, aloof. Her own nature hearkened back to a more distant lineage. The only way to describe Gina's personality was *effervescent*.

Ethan parked across the street from Gina's home and sat there, remembering their fights. He had naturally blamed her mercurial nature for their frequent breakups. He had often accused her of knowing which button to press and taking pleasure in setting him off. And that was true enough, but it was far from the entire story.

A magnolia tree wafted its heavy fragrance through his open windows, and he breathed it as he would a truth serum. Because from this new temporal distance, Ethan realized he had been as much to blame for their quarrels, perhaps even more so. He had set Gina off so he had an excuse to leave. And he had been very good at leaving.

Ethan rose from his car. Nervous as he was, he found himself grateful for a chance to try to get it right. This time.

Gina's mother opened the door, and for a moment she did not seem to recognize him. "Ethan?"

"Good afternoon, Mrs. Devoe."

"You look . . . Is Gina expecting you?"

"Not exactly. I phoned from Jacksonville. May I come in?"

She held herself impossibly erect, this small woman. Ethan had forgotten how tiny Gina's mother actually was. Of course, the last several years before he and Gina divorced, a stroke had confined Marie to a wheelchair. Several months after the stroke, Gina's father had been felled by a massive coronary. Gina had returned home so that her mother was not forced to move into hospice care. It was as good an excuse as any to end a marriage that was already over in all but name.

Gina's mother surveyed him from polished loafers to

freshly trimmed hair, then took a reluctant step back. "Do you have a new job?"

"Something like that."

Marie shut the door behind him and said what she always did when Ethan arrived. "You can wait in the parlor. I will see if Gina is available."

Marie Devoe had a Southern woman's ability to dismiss with a single motion, wagging one finger to both point him into the living room and reject him at the same time.

Ethan crossed the foyer and walked in the direction she indicated. But when he reached the open doorway, he was halted by unwelcome memories.

He remembered the whiteness. The bone carpet held an ivory sofa set and coral table and a pale sideboard covered with starched damask. The fireplace's mantel was varnished white. Even the picture frames. How he had despised this place! No doubt Marie had been aware of his repulsion, which was probably why she always insisted he wait here.

He surveyed the room and recalled the last time he had entered. It had been to sign his divorce papers.

"Ethan, did you not hear—"

He turned, and something in his expression seemed to stifle her demand.

Ethan said quietly, "I'll wait by the pool."

Marie's crisp footsteps followed him back across the foyer and through the kitchen. "I don't recall you ever being back here—"

Again she was halted by Ethan unlocking the French doors and stepping onto the covered veranda. A trio of paddle fans marginally reduced the afternoon heat. Ethan pulled two cast-iron chairs close to the pool's border and seated himself. "I've always loved this place."

Frangipani and booming oleander formed a living boundary to the pool. Several dozen palms rose like green sentries around the rear garden. Ethan sensed Marie standing there, probably debating whether she should order him back inside. But finally she moved away, and moments later he heard her calling for Gina to come down *now*.

"Ethan?"

His heart felt ready to grow wings and burst free. Unlocking his limbs and rising to greet her was quite possibly the hardest thing he had ever done.

"Wow. Mom said you'd changed. But this . . ." She rounded the chair and hugged him hard. "Look at you!"

As soon as she released him, Ethan's legs gave way. He was glad the chair was there to catch him. "You are so very, very beautiful."

She did a quick little pirouette. "You like?"

His voice sounded strangled. "Very much."

He remembered now. Gina's last stop had been four weeks of intensive language school in Paris. She'd returned with her hair bobbed in the latest French fashion. She wore a striped, off-the-shoulder top and navy shorts that were fashioned like a small skirt.

Gina slipped into the chair next to his and took hold of his hand. "I almost didn't recognize you."

He remembered her beauty, of course. She had inherited her mother's lithe form and her father's stature. What he did not remember was . . .

Everything that their years together had stolen.

Her dark eyes sparkled, her face shone, her smile for him was unbound by cares or hurt or disappointment. She was so free, so full of joy and promise. Her incredible eyes, the dark depths that had always invited him to dive straight in and lose himself, were filled now with unshed tears of happiness over seeing him again.

And yet . . . overlaid upon this Gina was the way he had last seen her.

Eight years after their divorce, Gina had sent him the formal notice of Marie's death. He had come out of respect and spent the entire service regretting the deed.

He remembered how pale Gina had looked then. Almost ghostlike, as if grief and exhaustion had combined to form an affliction that would finally claim her as well. He remembered how she had looked at him. Like he was a stranger drawn from some long-forgotten era. Like a shadow of former times. Just another mourner to greet in her mother's long procession.

"Ethan? What's wrong?"

He bowed over his knees, cupped his face in both hands, and wept.

SEVENTEEN

Half an hour later, Gina was the one weeping. "But you *can't* be dying!"

There was nothing Ethan could do about it except press on. "I'm sorry you have to learn this so soon after your return—"

"You're twenty years old! And I love you!"

Hearing her say the words, after so many years of loveless acrimony, lanced him with a pain so fierce he cradled his heart with the hand not holding hers. Even then, he did not shift his gaze from her face. Because there in her tragic beauty was the truth. She did. She really did love him.

Gina was so young and eager to be with him. And so certain that he was the one for her. Yet he knew the utter ruin he had made of her world. So many of those lost years came down to Ethan's selfish determination to live his life exactly as he had intended.

Ethan kept a loose grip on her tear-dampened fingers and remembered his dawn paddle. He recalled how crimped his motions were. He had been determined to make that final journey without his morning meds, even when each stroke was a trial by fire. Out there on the water, there was nothing ahead for him except, well, dust. Having his ashes sprinkled over the Sebastian Inlet break. And after that, a world of dawns he would never see.

Ethan had spent much of that pre-dawn paddle looking back, seeing the stubborn pride and iron-hard determination not to change, not to give in. To be his own man.

Now, seated here, he saw what those years had cost him. He had turned Gina's love to ashes. He might as well have made that final paddle-out for their relationship.

And for what? Because he wanted to stay a waterman? Was there no way he might have compromised? Been flexible enough to fulfill her dreams as well as his own? Helped her through the crises of losing her beloved parents? Been there in her hours of need? Accepted that a love as beautiful and fierce as this deserved to be nurtured and fed?

Apparently not.

Ethan realized he was crying again when Gina's mother went out of focus. She hovered just inside the kitchen doors, arms clasped tightly across her middle, her porcelain features crimped so tightly she looked ready to shatter with shared grief.

He spoke the only words that came to mind. "I'm so sorry, Gina."

"But I want to *marry* you!"

Gina's mother jerked forward, ready to halt that before it took hold. Ethan lifted his free hand, stopping her approach. "I'm not marrying anyone. But you will. Just not me."

He allowed her to weep a bit longer. Then he pried his hand loose, gestured to Marie, and rose so that she could take his place. "I have to get back to Jacksonville."

Gina cried, "You can't just *leave*."

"Sonya, my brother's wife, needs to run some more tests." That much was true. "I'm staying at the Casa Marina."

Marie's voice dropped a full octave. "I know it."

"Call me whenever you—"

"How long do you have?"

She had already asked him that. Three times. But some truths required more than one telling. "Sonya thinks about a month." He watched Gina melt into her mother's arms. "Goodbye, Gina."

Ethan drove north feeling distinctly removed from the trip. His mental and emotional fog only cleared when he arrived back at the hotel and accepted two message slips from the receptionist. Gary Holt had phoned to confirm he was putting things in place, and he would call again at seven the next morning. The second message was from Sonya, saying it was urgent that he call.

Ethan waited until he was upstairs and had ordered room service to phone Sonya back. As soon as she answered, he asked, "Is Adrian there?"

"He's still in the office, preparing for tomorrow's hearing. Why?"

Sooner rather than later, Ethan needed to tell her all the missing fragments, including why she had sent him back. Only not now. "Just asking."

"You sound exhausted."

"I am." And more besides. Ethan rubbed the hollow place over where his heart formerly resided.

"Does Adrian have something to do with what you haven't told me?"

"No." Another half-truth. Adrian had everything to do with it. "Sonya, I need to ask about these investors and the case against your company."

The harsh judgmental tone he remembered so well came back in a rush. "You need? *You* need? I'm handed confirmation that my research is actually founded in reality, and you want—"

"I'm hanging up now."

"No, don't!" A hard breath, then, "Ethan, you have to answer my questions."

"I will. Just not now, okay? Give me two days. Forty-eight hours. There are issues I have to work through. As soon as they're done, I will tell you everything."

"Your word?"

"Yes, Sonya. You have my word. Day after tomorrow, you and I will talk. No holds barred." He gave her a moment to protest, then asked, "Will you please tell me what's happening with your case?"

"I don't understand why you need . . ." Another hard breath. "Cemitrex is a Washington-based financing group that funded my early research. Adrian and I met when he replaced my original attorney."

"I remember that." Actually, what he remembered was how Adrian had gone on and on about this scientist. *Stunning* was the word he had used to describe Sonya.

"Cemitrex has announced they want to buy me out. They already own fifty-one percent—that was the price I had to accept to obtain their investment funds. Adrian thinks my original attorney made some serious mistakes. He's gone to court to try to save me from losing everything."

"And tomorrow?"

"It's just more of the same." Talking about her court case clearly aged her. "Adrian says it's just a question of time."

Ethan rubbed his forehead, wishing he was not so tired. "I don't understand."

"Neither do we. I answered your question. Can I ask you one in return?"

"Go ahead."

"Why did I send you back?"

He nodded. Leave it to the scientist to see to the heart of the matter. "Two days. I promise."

CHAPTER

EIGHTEEN

Amazingly, Ethan slept.

He had expected to spend the night pacing. Instead, he lay down after setting his dinner tray in the hallway outside his door, and was gone. The next thing he knew, a hand holding a gun emerged from some indistinct dream and fired off a single shot.

Ethan jerked awake to discover dawn painting pale watercolors over the ocean. The clock read a quarter past five. The hotel restaurant would not open for another forty-five minutes. He dressed in shorts and sandals and a T-shirt and went for a walk along the shore.

He felt enormously guilty taking such pleasure from having the beach and the sunrise to himself. His heart tripped an electric beat every time he thought of what this day would hold. But for the moment, he felt strangely comfortable with himself. It was an odd sensation, one he had not felt in, well, years. A mile or so down the shore he turned around and wondered if perhaps, just perhaps, this was his reward for having done right by Gina. This time.

The previous day's sorrow was gone now. As he returned through the strengthening light, he felt a distinct separation between himself and all that had gone before. Not just in this latest encounter but in his entire relationship with Gina. The ashes of a failed marriage and the deeply embedded pain were so much a part of who he was, he had simply learned to live with the inevitable. But as he started back up toward the hotel, Ethan wondered if this was what it meant to heal.

He ate breakfast, then returned upstairs and showered and dressed. As he knotted his tie, the phone rang. Gary greeted him with, "Everything's in place."

"You're sure?"

The detective's tone was languid and tough. "This is me doing my job. I've hired a team from Sinclair Security. You know them?"

"The name, sure."

"They're costing you a bundle."

"Money's not the issue here."

"Yeah, well, I've run through the situation half a dozen times with their team. We're prepped and good to go."

Ethan turned to the window. The beach was still there. The sunlight sparkled on the open waters. The only thing missing was his former calm. "I guess that's it."

"Unless you decide to tell your brother what's going down."

"That's not happening."

"You've got a rumor of a hit. You come to me, I do what you say, which means spending a ton of your money. I say alert Adrian to the threat, according to this source you won't identify."

The previous day's irritation returned. "Just for one moment, let's assume I'm not some punk who's wasting everybody's time. On my dime, let's not forget. Say my source is real and the attack is happening today. We tell Adrian and he actually listens. And he doesn't show. Then what? We have a gunman we can't identify who may or may not have accomplices. And Adrian of course refuses to take any further precautions, since the initial attack never happens. Then the next time—"

"Okay, okay, I got it." Gary chuckled. "You sound, I don't know . . ."

"Older. I'm getting that a lot."

"I was going to say 'like a pro.' So what now?"

Ethan had been thinking about that as well. "Check with your pals in the firm. See if there's any unexpected development in Adrian's case."

"Something to do with his wife's company, right?"

"Correct. I'll meet you at the courthouse at nine."

After Ethan hung up, the phone rang again so quickly he assumed Gary had forgotten something. He answered with, "What now?"

"Ethan?"

It took him a moment to recognize the voice. "Gina, now isn't—"

"I don't care! We have to talk!"

In truth, he didn't need to be anywhere for another hour and a half. "What is it?"

"What is it? For starters, the way you left yesterday! First you drop your bombshell, then you walk out on me. That was terrible, Ethan! You should be ashamed of yourself!"

Ethan lowered himself onto the edge of his bed. He took a mental tumble through half-forgotten memories. How many times he had heard Gina's tone rise like that. He used to call it her Cajun launchpad. She fired up her emotional engines long before he came into view. Then he came within range, and she took aim.

He said softly, "Not today, Gina."

"How *dare* you take that tone with me—"

"Either you quiet down or I'm hanging up. And I'm telling the front desk to refuse all calls from this number."

Gina went quiet.

"I'm leaving now for an extremely high-stress day. You can't add to it. You just can't."

A trio of seagulls floated past his top-floor window. One backed up slightly so as to glance inside. Ethan liked the sense of floating with the bird. Sharing an impossible moment, caught in forces neither of them could fathom.

Gina asked with little-girl weakness, "Don't you love me anymore?"

It was Ethan's turn to go quiet.

"We said we'd take the summer to decide. Well, I've decided. And then you say . . ."

Ethan finished the sentence for her. "That the decision has been made for me."

He knew she was crying, but he could find no words that might comfort her. Truth be told, his own emotions were such a tumble, it was hard to say what he felt. There was certainly an affection, strong as the sorrow and the ashes. But it was all a very long time ago. And she was so young and so fresh.

Ethan breathed in and out. The gull swept out of sight,

but Ethan remained hanging there, trying to find his way through the invisible lines of force.

Gina sniffed, took a shaky breath, and said, "I want to see you."

He nodded to the empty sky beyond his window.

"Ethan?"

"I'm here."

"Can I come?"

"Of course you can. I'd love to see you. But there are conditions, Gina. You'll stay in your own room. We'll see each other as friends."

"But I *love* you."

"And I love you."

Her voice took on a new timbre. "You've never said that before."

"Really?"

"You think I would forget such a thing?"

"Of course not. It's just . . ."

"It was one of the reasons why I left for Europe. Because you wouldn't commit. I had to decide whether I could stay with you as you are. Because I thought . . ."

"I'm sorry, Gina. So sorry. You deserve better."

"I don't *want* better. I want *you*."

Ethan rubbed his chest. "It has to be this way. You know it does. And you have to agree to my boundaries before I will see you."

He let the silence linger for a time, then said, "Call me when you decide." Another empty space, then, "Goodbye, Gina."

He tightened his tie, checked his collar in the mirror, and found himself inspecting the sadness in his gaze. He wondered if every conversation with her would hurt him so terribly. Even so, as he grabbed his jacket and left the room, he was filled with the comforting sensation of having gotten a very important moment very right.

This time.

NINETEEN

The Jacksonville courthouse was a dramatic mix of the city's Southern roots and its rising ambitions. The original section dated from the early twentieth century and would have looked at home on Mount Olympus. Corinthian columns and broad central stairs led to a shaded portico and huge bronze doors. A high-rise office building was connected to the back, as bland and bold as all the other towers that dominated the city's changing skyline.

Gary Holt was waiting for Ethan just inside the main entrance. He sat on one end of the foyer's long bench with his back on the stone side wall. His legs were stretched out, his heels resting on the marble floor. One of the security guards leaned on the wall beside him and laughed at something Gary said. When Ethan entered, he waved a languid hand and motioned to the bench beside him. The guard took that as his cue and sauntered off.

Ethan asked, "Should we go somewhere private?"

"What for?" Gary waved at the domed portico. The stone

floor and walls formed a massive baffle. "No one beyond arm's length can understand a word we say."

Ethan seated himself. It took a moment for him to realize what was missing. No security. No metal detectors. No tension, no lines, no ID's. The two uniformed officers were basically playing at guard duty.

Gary brought him around with, "I just checked on our preparations."

"And?"

"Everything is good."

"Are you sure?"

Gary smirked. "Do I look stressed to you?"

"If you were any more relaxed, you'd be snoring. And *that* worries me."

"I'm telling you, everything is in place."

Ethan's perspiration defied the building's cool wash. "It better be. My brother's life hangs in the balance."

"If your source is giving you the straight dope."

"You're being paid to treat this as credible. You and your team, who better be out there and ready."

Gary inspected him carefully, his eyes searching deep. But all he said was, "Your brother's in courtroom seven."

Adrian's courtroom was in the modern sector and as cold as a meat locker. Gary led Ethan into the next-to-last row. When they were seated, he murmured, "Judge Durnin insists it stay one degree off freezing in here. His regulars think he does it to make things move faster. He's not one to let attorneys waste the court's time."

Ethan had no interest in discussing the judge's preferences. "Did you find out anything about this case?"

"Not a lot to tell, according to people around the firm. When Dr. Barrett incorporated, her primary investor was Cemitrex, a DC-based fund manager. They went in for fifty-one percent. Now they want to buy the rest. She doesn't want to sell." Gary's low drone carried the same air of boredom he'd showed in the front hall. "No fireworks, no drama. Your brother is fighting the good fight. But the odds are stacked against him."

"Then you're missing something."

"Look, I've been around this basically all my life. On the force my beat was white-collar crime. Twenty years for the good guys, another eight with your brother's firm. I know the signs. And I'm telling you, the only reason Adrian is fighting so hard is because it's his wife's company."

Ethan did not bother arguing. There was only one way he was going to convince Gary. He checked his watch and felt his heart rate surge to double time.

Ninety-eight minutes and counting.

The courtroom was as sterile as it was frigid. There were no other observers and nothing really to see. Adrian and another attorney stood in front of the judge's dais, talking too softly for Ethan to hear. The judge was a stern-faced man whose unblinking glare tracked the attorneys with molten intensity.

Gary followed Ethan's gaze and murmured, "Judge John Jacob Durnin. Been on the bench since Eisenhower, seems like. Adrian claims Durnin is on their side, which would be a first. The man's got a hide of pig iron."

The courtroom's silence only fed Ethan's rising tension. Despite the chill, he felt perspiration trickle down his spine.

Even the lawyers up front seemed subdued. Then the opposing counsel turned and walked back to his table. He was a heavyset gentleman with a receding hairline and a neck that spilled over his collar when he leaned. He flicked through several files.

The judge had a deep voice with a sandpaper edge. "We're waiting, counsel."

"One moment, Your Honor."

A blonde-haired woman sat directly behind the opposition attorney's empty chair. She leaned forward and whispered something. When the lawyer responded, she opened her briefcase and extracted a sheet of paper. The attorney examined it briefly, nodded once, and returned to the judge's dais.

Ethan asked, "Who's that?"

"Jimmy Carstairs. He's top dog in a firm his granddaddy founded."

"Not him. The woman."

Gary shrugged. "Ask your brother. He's the one with the inside track."

"I'm asking you," Ethan replied. "See what you can find out about her and who she represents. And remember what I said about confidentiality."

Ethan watched as Adrian continually shook his head at whatever the other lawyer said, then responded softly, one hand curled over the front of the judge's dais. Finally Ethan could remain still no longer. He rose and slipped from the row. He thought he heard Gary snort softly as he left the courtroom.

CHAPTER

TWENTY

During his early investigation, Ethan had spent hours wandering around the courthouse. At least once each day he had stood where he was now, at the top of the courthouse stairs. The newspapers and television stations had repeatedly shown this very spot, with his brother's blood staining the concrete. He shifted over to the shadows formed by the columns and the high front portico. The stifling midday heat and humidity cast a languid blanket over the city. The sidewalk fronting the courthouse was empty. Even the traffic along the boulevard seemed mired in the sullen heat. Or perhaps it was just Ethan's racing heart that made the day appear to move in slow motion.

Gary stepped up beside him and asked, "You okay?"

"Tell me the Sinclair team is in place."

"Three seasoned officers. I'd trust them if my own life was on the line." Gary squinted into the empty distance. "I'm not going to point them out because I don't want you staring their way."

Ethan checked his watch. The news articles had been very precise about the timing, witnessed as it was by the two guards inside the front entrance. Nine minutes to go. He told Gary, "Let's say it's not a lone gunman with a grudge. Say it's the case. Say it's the case *now*. Today. What has changed?"

Gary showed him the same stare as in the courtroom. "You're getting yourself all worked up, and over what?" When Ethan remained silent, he pressed on. "If this source of yours is so solid, why won't you reveal it? Give me something I can take to the cops."

Ethan checked his watch again. Seven minutes. He knew Gary wasn't listening. But talking helped. "Say something just happened. Adrian struck a nerve."

Gary kept on watching. "Same question, same comment. I'm still waiting."

Fear and adrenaline squeezed his thoughts like a vise. "Say Adrian is approaching a secret they will do anything to protect. Even kill him."

"Kid, you're so far out of reach I doubt you can even hear me. *Nothing has happened.*"

Another check of his watch. Four minutes. The more he tracked down this mental path, the more it resonated. "So they go for him. They figure killing Sonya's husband would be a sure way to strong-arm her. Make her give up the company. Especially if somebody else was assigned this case. Like you said, they wouldn't fight nearly so hard."

Gary shook his head. "This beats all I've ever heard of."

Ethan went back to scouting the street and the empty courthouse steps. Gary continued to complain, about Ethan's silence and the day's heat and the lack of anything concrete to go on. Ethan found it increasingly difficult to pay him any attention. He felt his awareness reaching out, probing unseen distances.

Abruptly he had the distinct impression of a hurricane on the approach. Every Florida waterman knew the signals— the gathering humidity, the oppressive stillness, the clear and breathless air. Somewhere in the distance, clouds massed and swirled and sucked in nature's force, growing into the most powerful maelstrom on earth.

Just like now.

But the attack did not happen.

Four o'clock on the nose, the moment stated by both guards, came and went. Ethan did not move. He had nowhere else to go. His shirt was plastered to his skin now. His face was covered with sweat. Nothing mattered. He would stay there all day if need be.

Ninety seconds later, Adrian appeared through the courthouse doors. He was deep in conversation with a younger man Ethan had never seen before. The younger attorney nodded and wrote hastily as Adrian spoke. Ethan could see his brother was angry. Furious, in fact.

Gary leaned against the neighboring pillar, looking bored and hot and increasingly angry. Which was why he missed the attack when it came.

The shooter did not climb the stairs. He emerged from inside the courthouse. He wore a tan jacket over dark slacks and carried a white paper bag with the blue RX symbol from some drug chain. He was middle-aged, not short or tall, almost bald but with long, greasy strands of grey-black hair combed over a deep indent in the middle of his skull. Ethan only noticed him because of two distinct traits. The man's eyes darted about, a rapid-fire search that touched nowhere for very long. The only place he *didn't* look was directly in Adrian's direction.

What focused Ethan's attention was the man's speed. He was the only part of the day that moved fast. He was not running, but he was not far off. And he headed straight for Adrian.

Ethan did not risk alerting Gary, who watched the empty stairs and sidewalk with cop-like patience. Gary's view of this ordinary-looking guy was blocked by the pillar.

Ethan rounded in front of Gary, which meant the attacker went out of sight for two seconds, perhaps three. Long enough for him to reach inside the white pharmacy bag.

Ethan saw a metallic glint catch the sunlight as the bag dropped to the stone. And he knew that this was his move. It had been all along.

The gunman's pistol looked big as a cannon. Big as the hole it had blown in so many lives.

Ethan leapt down, covering three steps and thirty feet in half a heartbeat. He clawed at the gunman's back and neck and arm. And he snarled.

The gun went off, impossibly loud.

The air became filled with shouts and screams.

Ethan was on top of the gunman, climbing over his head and shoulders in an attempt to wrest the weapon free. The attacker shouted obscenities and flipped Ethan. When Ethan refused to let go, they tumbled down the steps together.

Ethan caught quick glimpses of fractured action as he fell. Two security people shouted and raced up the stairs. Gary shoved Adrian down and yelled something and raced after Ethan. The gun kept firing, so loud it sounded like the shots were inside his head.

Then he bounced wrong, and his head struck a corner of the stone step. As Ethan's vision flashed brilliant, the gun went off again, only this time a bright flame seared its way across his left shoulder.

And the world went away.

TWENTY-ONE

When Ethan opened his eyes, he viewed a scene utterly removed from everything that had come before. Adrian and Gary and Sonya stood outside a glass-walled hospital room. Gina was there as well. The room was semi-dark, and night was draped over the exterior window. They listened as a doctor spoke. The middle-aged man was dressed in surgical blues and gestured with long pianist's fingers as he talked. His mannerisms were easy, and he smiled as he listened to something Adrian said. As the doctor responded, Gina glanced over and saw that Ethan's eyes were open.

She rushed into the room, clearly wanting to throw her arms around him. But she stopped a pace away and offered a tremulous smile. "How are you?"

"You're here."

"I'm here. Please don't send me away. Please."

"I'm glad you're here, Gina."

"Really?"

"It's good to see you. Wonderful, in fact."

His words only made her appear sad. "Nothing's changed, though, has it."

"Not how you mean."

"The doctor says he can't find anything wrong that might lead to you dying—"

"Tell Sonya I need to speak with her."

"Don't you want to know what . . ." Gina stopped talking as the others entered.

Up close the doctor had the dark shadow of a heavy beard and long hours. His eyes were red-rimmed, but his manner was friendly enough. "How do you feel?"

"All right. Sore. My head hurts worse than my shoulder. And my shoulder hurts a lot."

"We'll get you something for the pain. But first I wanted to check your reflexes." He had Ethan track his light, then inspected the throbbing point behind his right ear and finally his left shoulder. He straightened and slipped his flashlight back in his jacket pocket. "You've probably had a minor concussion. You needed a few stitches to close the skin. Our initial X-rays showed no sign of serious damage."

Adrian asked, "And his shoulder?"

"As I was saying, it appears your brother was struck by a ricochet. The bullet penetrated less than a centimeter. We cleaned the wound and repaired the musculature." To Ethan he said, "I want the physical therapist to give you some exercises, but I don't think you'll suffer any lasting damage."

"That's great to hear."

"I want you to remain with us over the weekend, just to be certain there's no lasting impact from either injury." The doctor hesitated, then went on, "Your friend tells me you have recently received some serious news."

Ethan nodded, then wished he hadn't. "I don't want to talk about it."

"That seems a rather odd attitude to take. And dangerous."

"You don't know, you can't imagine, how many doctors and tests I've been through."

He stared down at Ethan for a time, then said, "Will you at least tell me what your diagnosis was?"

"Cancer."

"Do you remember the name?"

"Sorry, no."

"Can I request your records?"

"I won't be here that long."

The doctor looked ready to argue, then changed his mind. "I'll stop by tomorrow."

As soon as he left, Ethan told the others, "I need to speak with Sonya. Alone."

Adrian put up a fuss, of course. He was a lawyer, it had been his life that was threatened, his brother had been wounded, and so forth.

But Sonya revealed a new side to her personality, as different from the face she had always shown Ethan as everything else about the night. Ethan watched his brother's resistance melt away under Sonya's firm insistence. She was wise and she knew things, her attitude said, and Adrian needed to trust her. So he left and took Gina with him. They stood outside the doorway and spoke in somber tones, observing the two of them through the interior window.

Sonya asked, "Should I close the drapes?"

"No. Let them watch."

She seated herself next to his bed. Took her time. When

she was ready, she released the words carefully, one by one. "Was this why I sent you back?"

"Yes."

"And you couldn't tell me."

"No."

"Whatever else you need to say, I will accept. I have to. Because you saved my husband's life." She stared at her hands. "Before, he died?"

"Yesterday."

She pursed her lips and breathed softly. In and out. "I owe you . . . everything."

He gave her a moment. She wiped her face twice. Otherwise there was no sign that she was weeping. Ethan saw Adrian watching his wife and knew they did not have much time. "I need you to handle the doctor. And Adrian. And Gina."

"Handle . . ." She straightened and gathered herself. Another quick swipe of her eyes, and Sonya was back in control. "What should I tell Adrian?"

"He needs to know what's going on."

"I agree." A pause, then she asked what Ethan knew she would. "And Gina?"

"For the moment, only that I don't have very long to live."

He half expected her to argue. But Sonya's combative nature had been erased, at least temporarily. "You are certain you only have a few weeks?"

"No, Sonya. You were."

"Yes. All right . . . Anything else?"

There was. A lot else. But just then his head hurt so badly he had to stop. "Go ask the nurse for my pills."

TWENTY-TWO

Ethan next woke to bright sunlight and the duty nurse offering him a cheerful good morning. There was a dual pounding in his head and shoulder, but the pain was far more manageable. The nurse ignored his declaration that he was feeling better and stood over him as he downed his meds. Only when she canted his bed up and left to get his breakfast did Ethan notice the figure in the far corner. Light streaming through the exterior window draped the man in shadows, but Ethan knew from the way he held himself that it was Adrian.

His brother continued to read the file open in his lap until the nurse returned with Ethan's tray. When the door closed once more, Adrian slipped the file back into his briefcase, rose, and pulled his chair closer. "How do you feel?"

"Better."

"You should. You've slept around the clock."

"So today is . . ."

"Friday." Without being asked, Adrian filled a plastic cup from the pitcher by his bed and handed it over. Since childhood, every morning both brothers woke parched. When Ethan drained the cup, Adrian asked, "More?"

"I'm good, thanks."

Adrian refilled it and set it on the bedside cupboard. He seated himself and watched his brother eat. "Someday I'm sure the words will come to me."

"You don't need to say a thing. Not now, not ever."

"We both know that's not true."

"Adrian, you have made a profession of being there for me." When Adrian did not respond, Ethan asked, "What time is it?"

"Just gone nine."

"Don't you have to be somewhere, off fighting the good fight?"

"The battles are put on hold this morning."

Ethan watched his brother cross his legs and adjust the knot of his tie, and he felt a flood of relief and affection for the guy. Adrian was preparing himself for the formal deposition, the verbal struggle that he had been born for. Ethan's heart swelled from the simple pleasure of being there in Adrian's company. Today.

He said, "It's good to see you."

Adrian nodded. "Sonya told me . . . everything."

"Sonya doesn't know everything."

Adrian smoothed an invisible crease in his trousers. "That's why I'm sitting here instead of putting out fires. So you can tell me everything."

Twice during the telling, Adrian rose to refill Ethan's glass. Ethan could have done it himself, but it would have meant reaching his good arm across his wounded shoulder. So he let Adrian serve him. Then he resumed describing to his brother how he had volunteered to end a lonely life in order to return and save Adrian's.

As he finished, lightning flashed a long illumination. Rain spackled the window. The flickering light turned the drops into liquid prisms. Both men turned to watch the storm's arrival. The move granted Ethan a chance to study his brother and remember other storms from long ago. Back when they were two orphans, dealing with a world that had stripped away the comfort of parents and redefined the word *family*. Ethan saw that Adrian's cheeks were wet and wondered if he was remembering the same thing.

Adrian cleared his face and turned back around in one smooth motion. "Might be a hurricane brewing."

Ethan nodded, then winced from the pain the motion caused.

"You need something?"

"Not yet."

"I can call the nurse."

"Later." First Ethan needed to deal with the issues his brother was bound to raise. Two of them. And for that, he needed a clear head.

Adrian's gaze was lit by another flash of lightning. Grey eyes that burned with an electric force as potent as the storm. "You told Sonya you don't have long to live."

That was one issue. "Back before the transition, she was pretty definite on that point. She said the present me would reject the old consciousness. Like a transplant gone bad."

"You sound pretty calm for a guy on death row."

"You have no idea what I left behind. The cancer. The pain. At least this way I get to live a few more good days."

"Not to mention saving my life."

Ethan nodded. There was certainly that as well.

"How long do you have?"

"Four, maybe five weeks tops." Not to mention what getting shot and suffering a concussion might do to the timing.

Adrian rose to his feet. Lifted his jacket from the back of the chair. Slipped it on. Adjusted his lapels. Ethan understood his brother's slow-motion acts, the attempt to retreat from imminent loss.

When he spoke, Adrian had resumed his dry courtroom voice. "Your saving my life, that was primo circumstantial evidence. You understand where I'm headed?"

"Yes." Here it came.

"But there are so many impossible issues I'm being asked to take in." Adrian waved at the world beyond the door. "This means I need to redefine my entire existence. And our relationship. And Sonya . . ." His arm dropped, the attorney rendered speechless. "Ethan, don't take this the wrong way. I need . . ."

"Something more," Ethan said. "Something concrete."

Adrian's gaze tightened. "You were expecting this."

"Of course. I know you."

"So tell."

"The business deal that took me to New York," Ethan replied. "It was a bet."

Adrian's shoulders slumped. "The Open?"

"My first time around, I lost the surfing contest in the quarterfinals. You knew I was in trouble. You called every day. Tried to keep me connected to the world beyond my defeat by telling me what was happening at the Open. Those were our last conversations. I remember every word, seems like."

Adrian opened his mouth, but no sound came out.

"I won just under a million. Your share comes to just over a hundred and fifty thou. I've invested most. The account is in all our names."

A pause, then, "Sonya knows?"

"It's why she believed me."

"That and how you've changed. It's all she talked about."

"I asked her to let me tell you."

"So . . . this is real."

"As real as it gets."

Adrian did a slow-motion turn to the door. The way he fumbled for the knob, it was unlikely he saw much of anything. "I need to think. We'll talk—"

"There's something else, and it can't wait."

Adrian did not turn back. "I don't know if I can take—"

"You need to hear this. For Sonya's sake as well as yours. She's pregnant, Adrian. She doesn't know yet. You're going to have a daughter . . ."

Ethan stopped talking because Adrian was no longer there.

TWENTY-THREE

Ethan slept through much of the day. Around five the duty nurse woke him, checked his vitals, fed him more pills, then brought him dinner. The surgeon arrived while he was eating, changed the two bandages, and probed the wounds, leaving Ethan very glad he had not refused the meds.

The physical therapist entered as the doctor was leaving. An hour of having his arm twisted and extended left Ethan utterly washed out.

He dozed off, then opened his eyes only a moment later. Or so he thought. But the world beyond his window was awash in strong morning light. Gina was curled up in the chair that had been moved back to the far corner. A blanket was tucked up tight below her chin, and she was breathing in a deep-throated pattern that was one notch off a snore. Ethan remembered her making that sound, back when they shared a home. It was strange, the things that made his eyes burn. He might have become a great deal more caught up in memories from a different era, except that Gary passed by in the hallway, saw he was awake, and entered the room.

The PI smiled at Gina's slumbering form and said, "Found her a couple of hours ago trying to sleep in the waiting room. Kids squalling and families fretting. Gina looked about done in. So I brought her up. Hope it's okay."

Having the former cop ask for his approval about anything was definitely a step in the right direction. "It's fine. Thanks."

Gary kept his voice down to a soft rumble. "How's the shoulder?"

"It hurts almost as bad as my head."

He grinned. "A better man than me would say something about how I should have been the one to catch that bullet. But I ain't that guy."

Ethan asked, "Any line on the shooter?"

"Name's Rickie Schofeld. Two-time loser. Drugs, assault and battery, B&E. Adrian represented him pro bono. The guy went away for ten to twenty, got early release for good behavior and time served."

"Will you check on him, see if there's any connection?"

"To what?"

The question was simple enough. Gary's easy tone suggested he was finally all in.

Ethan glanced over at Gina, made sure she was still asleep, and said, "I need to walk you through some things."

"About time."

"None of this is definite. It's basically what I've come up with since . . ."

"Hearing from that unnamed source of yours," Gary offered.

That worked as well as anything. "I'm worried that this guy might not have been acting alone."

"You mean, a second gunman?"

"No. Well, yes . . ."

"Just take it slow and easy," Gary said. "Working on the what-ifs is how cops make their best busts."

"What if . . ." Ethan breathed easier now with the pro on his side. "What if the gunman is fronting for some hidden threat? One that doesn't just vanish after this shooter goes back inside?"

Gary rocked slowly, his bulk causing the chair to creak. "Which is what you were saying on the courthouse steps. Only I was too busy disbelieving you to listen."

"You listened," Ethan corrected. "You just didn't have any reason to believe."

"Schofeld hasn't said a word since he was arrested. Not even to give his name." Gary kept rocking, as if his nods required the motion of his entire body. "I could go through his priors, see if there's any connection to a bigger organization. It's doubtful the group buying Sonya's company would stand that close to a smoking gun. But there might be a link." He nodded slowly. "I can do that."

"Adrian is being protected?"

"Twenty-four seven." Gary started to say something more but stopped when Gina's breathing changed. The men glanced over. She settled and her eyes remained closed. Gary's voice lowered another notch. "Pretty lady. I'd call her a keeper."

"Do me a favor. Book her a room in the Casa Marina. Tell them to put it on my bill."

"Sure thing." Gary smiled at Gina. "I imagine she won't complain about a bed with a sea view."

131

"Any idea when I can get out of here?"

"The doc is still saying tomorrow afternoon. He wants them to change the bandages again, make sure your head is behaving, take you through another PT session."

Truth be told, another day of bed rest sounded just fine. "My car's still at the courthouse."

"Nah, I took it back to the hotel." Gary stood, walked over to the curtains, and swept them closed so the interior hallway was blocked from view. Then he turned back to Ethan, started to say something, and stopped.

"What is it?"

"The doc and Sonya got into a spat out there. He wanted to run tests. Sonya chopped him off at the knees."

Ethan heard the unspoken question. "There's something you need to know. I've gotten bad news from some other doctors. I'm checking out. Four more weeks is the best guess."

Gary's response was cut off by a nurse knocking on his door. The sound startled Gina from sleep. While the nurse took his vitals, Ethan explained about Gary booking her a room. Ethan liked how she tried to protest, much as she clearly wanted nothing more than a shower and a non-hospital meal and real rest in a real bed. She hugged him gently, kissed his cheek, and promised to come and pick him up first thing the next morning. The nurse instructed Gina in best medical fashion to sleep late, as the doctor would not show up until the early afternoon.

As soon as Gary and Gina left, the nurse fed him more pills, then brought him dinner. When he finished eating he tried to watch the news, but the words were a jumble. Half an hour later, he was sound asleep. He dreamed of Gina's smile.

———

The physical therapist arrived late Sunday morning and worked on Ethan until his morning meds felt like a distant memory. After lunch Ethan slipped into the bathroom to change and found a surfing shirt, drawstring trousers, and sandals that he assumed were all Adrian's. His clothes from the attack were hung on the back of the door. A jacket sleeve and both knees of his trousers were torn. All the buttons from his shirt were missing. As he dumped them into the trash, he caught a whiff of potent odors, his own sweat and something more, perhaps burned cordite. The scent took him straight back to the steps and the shooter and the closeness of failing his brother again.

He waited until the shakes subsided to slip on the trousers. When he opened the door, he found Gina and the nurse waiting with a wheelchair. "Can you help me with the shirt?"

"Of course." Gina eased his arm from the sling, threaded it through the sleeve, did the other arm, then buttoned up the front. The act drew them close enough for Ethan to see the stains of stress on her own face as well. She did her best to smile and said, "There. All better."

Once he was seated, Gina took hold of his hand while the nurse pushed him down the hall. Gina looked as tousled and weary as he felt. And achingly beautiful. When the elevator doors shut, she said, "Adrian and Sonya are off handling something to do with her family. I wasn't supposed to tell you, but they feel really guilty leaving you."

"They shouldn't. Life doesn't just stop."

"It's something about her mom needing care. They set up the appointments before . . ."

"The attack. I understand."

"Gary was here when I arrived. He's going to drive us back to the hotel." She reached out her free hand and traced his hairline with one finger. "Thank you for arranging a room."

"I'm glad you're here, Gina."

"And I'm beginning to think you mean it."

Gina pushed him through the foyer and out the front doors. The heat and humidity were September intense. Even so, the air smelled heavenly. Florida locals called this the sweet season, when the orange trees and wild jasmine bloomed and filled the air with a comforting flavor. This was the other side to the height of hurricane season, as if nature offered such perfumed days as a promise of better things to come.

When Gary pulled up in his Buick, Ethan rose from the chair, thanked the nurse, and offered Gina the front passenger seat.

Gary waited until they were passing over the Saint Johns bridge to ask, "You mind if we talk work?"

"We have to," Ethan replied. "I'm going to fade as soon as we reach the hotel. Maybe sooner."

"The detective in charge of this case is a former partner. He's given you this time to get back on your feet because I asked nice. But you need to give him your statement."

"Set it up." He settled his head onto the seat back. "You also need to extend that security to include Sonya, her lab, and their home."

"I imagine the lady will kick up a fuss."

Gina said, "I like her."

Gary glanced over. "I don't often hear newcomers say that about Sonya."

"The lady does have her ways," Ethan agreed.

"She tells me the truth," Gina said. "She answers my questions. She treats me as an equal."

"Well now," Gary said.

Ethan asked Gina, "Do you want to help out?"

"More than anything." She paused. "Almost."

"Handling Sonya would take a huge load off my mind," Ethan said.

"That's your first mistake." Gina turned in the seat so she could address both men. "Thinking you can *handle* her."

Ethan pressed on. "There are a lot of questions we need Sonya's help with. Starting with exactly what makes the Washington group so eager to buy her out."

"You need to give me more than that," Gina said.

"And I will," Ethan replied. "Tomorrow."

Gary said, "That it on my end?"

"One thing more. I need you to set up an appointment for us to meet with Adrian. You and me and him. Nobody else." His head was throbbing now. Each bump in the road caused his shoulder to complain. He closed his eyes. "Might be best not to let him know it's me. Just say it's a new client."

Gina asked, "Can I come?"

Ethan nodded his head and regretted it. "I wouldn't have it any other way."

When they arrived at the hotel, Ethan excused himself, saying he needed to rest. He knew Gina was tempted to insert herself into his evening, his world. To her credit, she merely kissed his cheek and wished him a good rest.

Ethan ordered room service, took the most exquisite shower of two lifetimes, ate by the open balcony doors, watched another late afternoon storm sweep in from the Atlantic, then eased himself into bed and let the rain sing him to sleep.

That night he dreamed of a world that never was.

After two difficult miscarriages, he and Gina had stopped trying to have children. By then, the fractures had already begun to appear in their relationship. They never seriously considered adoption. Which made his dream a complete and utter impossibility.

In it, he and Gina were seated and holding hands on an almost empty beach. In the strange awareness of dreams, Ethan knew they were in Tahiti. The wave breaking far outside, beyond the coral shelf protecting the bay, was called Teahupo'o.

It was also the place where Ethan had finally grown disgusted with his rambling, empty, self-absorbed days.

He had never taken Gina there, though she had asked. Many times. For Ethan, Teahupo'o represented all the wrong turns and dead-end days. Remembering those final months in Tahiti always filled Ethan with a sense of defeat. He had gotten everything he ever wanted, and on his terms. And look where it had brought him.

In the dream, though, he and Gina chatted happily while their two children played in the shallows.

Their children.

As soon as he glanced their way, Ethan knew them intimately. Pablo was Colombian, orphaned by the cocaine trade. Christine's Jamaican mother had abandoned her at a Miami orphanage when the child was four months old. Nothing was known about her father.

Pablo was seven now, and a scamp. Christine was six and incredibly mature and so intensely intelligent it astonished and awed her parents. Pablo often treated her as an older sister, except when they fought, which was often. They formed the greatest joy Ethan had ever known.

The scene shifted in the easy abruptness of a good dream. Ethan found himself seated in Tahiti's international airport. They were checked in for their flight and were making a picnic of fruits and nuts that Gina and the kids had bought at the local market. They chattered and laughed as they ate. Ethan could not make out precisely what they were saying. He only heard them clearly say one word. Each of them said it over and over.

Home.

He watched the three of them and was filled with a joy so intense it threatened to shatter him.

The dream shifted again.

He was still seated in the Faa'a international airport of Papeete, the Tahitian capital and main island. Exactly the same place as before. Only now he was alone.

Now the scene was as Ethan had actually lived it. A violent late-spring storm had struck the island chain and shut down all flights. Anyone who spent time in the tropics learned to take such delays in stride. Ethan watched wealthy tourists berate the man behind the check-in desk, as if they expected the manager to rewire the day and banish the storm to Tonga. The attendant smiled in that special way the Tahitians used to deal with impolite tourists, pouring scorn on them in silent ease. Each time the tourists paused for breath, he repeated the same word. *Bientot.* The official French definition was "soon." Tahitians more often used it for "sometime" or "next week."

Ethan watched the argument with a sense of bitter emptiness. He was neither of one world nor the other. He belonged nowhere. He had chased some elusive dream of perfect days and wound up here. Utterly alone, saying farewell to an empty life, and going back to . . . what? He was twenty years old and felt consumed by an ancient's sorrow.

When he woke, he found his pillow wet from tears.

TWENTY-FOUR

Monday morning Ethan took his time showering and dressing. His head and shoulder were both much improved. When the clock struck nine, he walked down to Gina's room.

As he had requested, Gary had booked Gina into an ocean-front room located in the hotel's opposite corner. As he raised his hand to knock, he heard two women's voices.

They were trying to be quiet, given the hour. But it was clear they were locked in a fierce argument. One or the other hit a strident note, sounding as sharp to Ethan's ear as a slap.

As soon as he knocked, the voices cut off. "Gina?"

She opened her door a fraction. "Did somebody complain?"

"I don't . . . Is everything all right?"

"No." Her tousled look was a throwback to their own lengthy quarrels. Gina's hair was delicate as woven silk. When she became angry, she generated a current that turned it into a rat's nest. Just like now. "Mother is here."

"I just wondered if you'd like to join me for breakfast."
He raised his voice. "Hi, Mrs. Devoe. You're both welcome."

Gina shot a tight look beyond his field of vision. "Mom?"

"That . . . sounds nice."

"Come up to suite 404."

As he turned away, Gina asked, "You have a suite?"

By the time they finally arrived, the room-service waiter
had brought chafing dishes of eggs and breakfast potatoes
and bacon and biscuits and two thermoses of coffee. Gina
tapped on the open door, then stepped back to let the waiter
depart. "Ethan?"

"I'm on the phone, come on in." To Gary he said, "I'll
see you at noon." Adrian's calendar was fully booked, but
because it was Gary who asked, the secretary had scheduled
them for sandwiches in the conference room.

"Come at 11:30," Gary replied. "There's a lady from
Sinclair Security you need to meet. One thing more. The
detective I told you about wants you to come in and give
that statement. And Ethan, you need me with you on this."

"Whatever you say." Ethan hung up the phone. "Ladies.
Welcome."

"Gina was correct. You have a suite." Marie took in the
broad plank flooring, the brass chandelier, the dark Spanish-
style furniture. "It's not to my taste, but very nice just the
same."

"Sorry we're late," Gina said. "Mom took forever."

Marie was immaculately dressed as always, in coral-
colored linen pants with matching cork-heeled sandals and
an off-the-shoulder silk sweater. "Well, a lady doesn't simply

march upstairs to a gentleman's room in garments wrinkled from travel and a quarrel." She ignored how Gina rolled her eyes. "Am I allowed to ask how you come to be staying in such nice accommodations?"

"I've been investing," Ethan replied.

"And doing quite handsomely, by all accounts. How long will you be staying?"

"Hard to say," Ethan replied. "I'm booked in here for two months."

She tried to hide her shock and failed. "I must say that seems a bit extravagant. Forgive me for asking, but are you sure you can afford it?"

Ethan did not mind her polite probing in the slightest. "I've done so well I won't even feel it."

"How remarkable. You really must share your secret with Gina's father."

"Absolutely. Happy to."

"That's very kind. Wouldn't you agree, dear?"

Gina slumped into the central sofa. She was dressed in cutoffs and a man's shirt knotted below her ribs. She pulled her feet free of the sandals and tucked them under her thighs. Her hair was the same mess. "Swell."

"Can I pour you a coffee, Mrs. Devoe?"

"Please. Just milk."

"Gina?"

"Same as always."

"It's been a while, Gina. Remind me."

"Milk, one sugar."

He served the ladies, then said, "Maybe we should eat while the food is still fresh."

Ethan could see Gina wanted to refuse, to stay planted

on the sofa and sulk. He followed her mother's example and pretended all was just fine. "Room service insisted I take something called Jacksonville potatoes. I have no idea what they are."

"My family has always referred to them as Orleans potatoes. They're exactly the same as what you'd find anywhere from Alabama to Savannah. Only with a Florida attitude." Marie glanced at her daughter, then offered Ethan a little smile. "Slice and boil small potatoes, then refry them with peppers and shallots and a tiny hint of garlic."

Ethan did a one-handed job of loading his plate. "That sounds fabulous."

"If you took away grits and Orleans potatoes from his diet, the average Southern male would positively shrivel up." Marie waited as Ethan walked over and pulled back her chair. "I don't recall ever seeing you demonstrate such manners, young man."

"I'm a fast learner." He walked over to where Gina sat scowling at the side wall. She was so angry, and so beautiful, he leaned over and kissed the top of her head. "Hungry?"

Gina rose from the sofa and huffed as she crossed the room to the side table. "You think I don't see what you're doing? Sticking me as far as you can get from your room? I might as well have stayed in Orlando, I'm so far away."

Ethan stayed a pace or so back, watching her use the spoon with the same vigor as an angry drummer. "You didn't complain last night."

"I saw how tired you were." She marched over and stood by her chair. "What, I don't get the same service as Mom?"

The tone of her voice as much as her words carried him back to all the arguments that had started just like this. Only now he remained utterly removed. Perhaps it had been the dream. "Of course." He pulled back her chair and remained standing there until she was settled. "More coffee?"

"I'll give you more coffee."

"Gina, dear," her mother said.

"Don't you dare start. Who said you should come to Jacksonville anyway? That's what I want to know."

Ethan seated himself. "I was going to ask you to invite her."

That halted both women.

Marie said, "Excuse me?"

Gina said, "You're making this up as you go along."

That was so close to the truth he had to laugh.

"Now you're laughing at me?"

"Gina, you are without a doubt the loveliest woman on earth."

"Well," Marie said.

"No I'm not. I'm a mess."

"An angry mess. And still so very beautiful."

That calmed things down to where they ate in a more or less civil silence. When the two ladies were finished, Ethan gathered their plates and asked, "More coffee, anyone?"

Marie replied, "I wouldn't say no to another cup."

He plied the thermos, then asked, "Now, will somebody tell me what you two were fighting about?"

"You, of course," Gina replied.

"Only indirectly," Marie said. "You're much too charming a host to be the object of so much ire."

Ethan reseated himself. "Why, Mrs. Devoe. Did you just pay me a compliment?"

She offered Ethan what might have been her first full-fledged smile ever. "Perhaps. It's such a novel move, I'm not entirely certain."

"I'll take it just the same." He smiled back. "In a heartbeat."

Gina crossed her arms. "You two are so happy-sappy I'll just go back to my room and throw a fit."

"Why bother, dear? There's more than enough space right here."

"That is so completely not funny." Gina huffed. "Mother drove up to demand that I come home."

"School begins next week, dear."

"For the tenth and final time—"

"Your mother does make a very good point," Ethan said in hopes of stopping the quarrel before it could resume.

This time, the silence lasted until Marie said, "Please excuse me while I pick myself up off the floor."

Ethan could see Gina was still working on a full head of steam. He kept his voice calm, steady. "I need to explain what's happening at my end."

"We know all that. You're dying. And if that's not enough, you're trying to make it happen faster by getting yourself shot." To her mother she said, "And I am *staying* here because Ethan needs me."

"I do," Ethan said. "Need you."

Marie said, "Clearly I am missing something here. You just said you wanted her to leave."

"I need help. Desperately. The question is, does Gina want to offer what I need? And is it in her best interest to do so?"

"Who precisely am I addressing?" Marie's head angled slightly. "Every time you open your mouth, I am flummoxed as to who it is in the room with me."

"Getting shot at will do that to a fellow, Mrs. Devoe."

"I think it's time you called me Marie."

He smiled his thanks, then said to Gina, "I need to tell you what's happened to Adrian. And Sonya."

Marie said, "I'm sorry, that name . . ."

"Ethan's sister-in-law," Gina said. "Don't interrupt."

Ethan went on, "More importantly, I need to explain what I'm afraid might be happening next."

By the time the waiter returned to clear the table, Ethan's head and shoulder throbbed. It felt as if the telling had pummeled his body. Marie noticed and asked, "Should we take a break?"

Ethan shook his head. "I'm due downtown in a couple of hours, and there's more you need to hear."

Gina asked, "Didn't they give you something for the pain?"

"Two different pills. And both of the bottles have written in bold, 'Don't take these and drive.'"

"I can drive you," Gina said. "And Mother can get back to Daddy before it gets dark."

"I have no idea how long these appointments will take," Ethan warned.

"I want to help," Gina said, giving her mother the eye.

Marie, however, did not seem willing to resume their earlier dispute. "Why don't we take this outside and enjoy the air?"

Ethan downed his morning meds and met them in the lobby. Marie had changed into a designer cover-up over a bathing suit. Gina wore a surf-shop tee over a bikini and looked stunning.

They walked the shore for a time in silence. The heat and the movement and the meds worked on his wounds until he was breathing easy enough to say, "I'm the luckiest guy on the beach, sharing the day with two beautiful ladies."

"Give Mom time," Gina said. "The charm wears off."

Marie responded by giving her daughter a one-arm embrace. "Why don't you tell us what else we need to know."

As they walked, Ethan described his concerns about the future. That the gunman might in fact not have been acting alone. That some nefarious concern might be hiding behind a supposed revenge shooting. That the Washington investment group seeking to acquire Sonya's company might in fact have a hand in it all. Which would mean the danger was far from over.

As the hotel came back into view, Ethan said, "We've moved a long way from what I know. None of what I've just described is definite."

Marie said, "We needed to understand your concerns."

Gina's former ire was gone now, replaced by a calm that mirrored her mother's. "Mom, I want to stay and help him."

Marie responded by asking Ethan, "Will my daughter be safe?"

"Gary's arranged for security details on Adrian and Sonya. I think—I hope—that should be enough to protect them." Ethan gestured to the hotel. "You see where we are. There's no reason for us to become targets."

Marie reached for her daughter's hand. "I suppose we could ask the university to give you a semester off."

Ethan heard Gina release a tightly held breath. He said, "I could really use her help."

"Doing what, exactly?"

"I have no idea."

She managed the trace of a smile. "Honesty is a most refreshing trait in a young man."

He told Gina, "I'd like to pay you for helping out."

"I don't want your money, Ethan."

"My investments have brought me a lot of income," Ethan persisted. "You might as well take some of it, use it for school or whatever."

Marie said, "It may help put things on an official footing with the university, dear."

Gina did not respond as they crossed the veranda and entered the hotel. As Ethan returned upstairs to shower and change, he realized the meds had created a somewhat muffled distance between him and the day.

When he appeared downstairs, the ladies were waiting in the lobby. Marie gave him a long look—polished loafers, jacket and tie, well-trimmed hair. "Who are you and what have you done with my daughter's former beau?"

They walked Marie out to her Buick, where she embraced him almost as tightly as she did her daughter. "I scarcely know what to tell my husband."

"It would be nice if you two could come up next weekend," Ethan said. "My treat."

"Say yes, Mom," Gina agreed. "Please."

"I had best depart before you two say something more and my eyes pop out of my poor head." She hugged her daughter again, then slipped behind the wheel and was gone.

Gina's ride was a bright yellow Volkswagen bug, so Ethan insisted they take his BMW. Gina snapped the keys from his grasp and danced her way around to the driver's side. It was only when she gunned the motor and blasted from the lot that Ethan recalled how awful a driver she had always been. Too late. When she burned rubber at the first traffic light, he could not completely stifle his groan.

She said, "Don't fuss, else I'll put you in the back seat."

"Gina, you don't need to kiss that truck's rear end. It won't make him go any faster."

"Now you sound like Daddy."

"Orange light, orange light!"

"Are you feverish?" She shot him a look of mock concern. "Maybe you should tilt your seat back and have a rest."

"You don't know where you're going."

"I'll just drive around breaking laws until a cop pulls me over. Then I'll ask directions." She smiled brightly. "Does that make your feverish little head feel all better?"

As they entered downtown, the slow-moving traffic gradually brought a semblance of order to Gina's driving. Ethan leaned against the door so as to study her.

She glanced over. "What is it now?"

He shook his head. "I'm glad you're here, Gina."

Her face crimped up tight, an instantaneous change from bright and sassy to tragic. It was one of her defining traits, how her emotions could shift with the speed of a hummingbird's wings. "Don't, Ethan. I'm driving."

He did not turn away. Her driving slowed somewhat. Twice she cleared her face with one hand, quick swipes to either cheek. As if doing it fast would keep him from noticing.

Ethan said, "We haven't talked about your salary."

"I told you I don't want money."

"I understand. Really. But I want to pay you just the same. It will be something you can show your parents if things get rough."

"Will it?" His words had the desired effect, bringing her down from the emotional tumult. "Get rough?"

In truth, he had been thinking about his own departure. But this was definitely not the time to bring that up. "Maybe. I hope not."

Her grip tightened on the wheel. "I want to help you."

"You already are."

"No, Ethan. I'm not talking about being your driver." She stopped for an orange light, ignored the horn from the truck behind them, and swiveled in her seat to face him straight on. "I want to *help* you."

Ethan closed his eyes and was instantly swamped by memories of the women he had left behind. The sorrow that had become permanently stained on his ex-wife's face. Marie's final days trapped in the wheelchair. And Sonya, leaning over his gurney, old before her time, seamed by loss and despair. He could not blame himself for everything. Some of it, most definitely yes. But what clenched his throat up tight was how he wished he could go back, redo his life and those relationships, and be there for them.

"Ethan?"

He cleared his eyes. "I'm thinking five thousand dollars a week."

TWENTY-FIVE

Ethan and Gina left the car in the visitors' parking at Adrian's office building. He led her across the street and into the clothing store. She protested, "I thought you said we were in a hurry."

"This can't wait."

The owner, Hank, was a dapper gentleman in his late fifties or early sixties, as immaculately groomed as a china doll. "Hail the conquering hero. How is your damaged wing?"

"Healing."

"I'm glad to hear it. We can't afford to be losing clients to deranged gunmen." Hank swept his gaze over Ethan's clothes. "My, don't you look dashing. Whoever does your clothes, I wonder."

"You wouldn't know him," Ethan said. "He runs with a bad crowd."

"I take that as a compliment." Hank smiled at Gina. "And aren't you a lovely young lady."

"This is my assistant, Gina Devoe. I need you to work your magic."

Gina said, "I can't afford a place like this."

"You're not. I am." To Hank: "Gina needs to look like the top-class young executive she is."

"It will be my pleasure. Right this way, Ms. Gina."

The women's area was reached through a wide archway that formed a mock divide between the two shops. The decor was pastel and muted, whereas the men's side was leather and oiled wood.

Hank stopped in the middle of the pale blue carpet and swept his hand in an invitation. "See anything you like?"

"My mother would love it here."

"That is the wrong answer." He tilted his head at Ethan. "Don't you need to be somewhere urgent?"

"Absolutely." He turned to Gina. "Three outfits at a minimum."

"It will cost you a fortune."

"That is precisely what I want you to spend," Ethan replied. "A fortune."

"And here I thought it was going to be just another of those boring old days." Hank clasped his hands in front of his chest. "All of my tawdry dreams have just come true."

Ethan told Gina, "I'll meet you in Adrian's office just before noon."

━━━━━

Gary's office was a narrow afterthought at the tail end of the partners' corridor. A single window, less than a foot wide but four feet tall, offered light but no view whatsoever. Gary indicated the empty chair. "Detective in charge of our case just called. The meeting has been put off until tomorrow morning. They're caught up in something urgent."

"Fine by me."

"Meet Beth Helms, one of the senior people at Sinclair Security. If you can't reach me, you talk to her. We clear?"

Now that he was seated, Ethan's knees were only a few inches from theirs. Gary's desk was so narrow Ethan suspected it had been made especially for the place. If Gary minded, he gave no sign.

Ethan said, "What I say to you goes to her, and vice versa."

Gary nodded. "You okay with that?"

"We need outside help," Ethan said. "You tell me Sinclair is supposed to be the best."

"No 'supposed to be' about it," Beth replied. Her brown hair was neatly trimmed and tucked behind her ears, revealing simple gold studs. Her skin was tanned dark as old leather. Her hazel eyes were sharp and arresting in their intensity. "Gary tells me you like fishing the Saint Johns."

"It's his brother who can't get enough of the river," Gary said. "Ethan here is a surfer."

"That's right. Didn't I read something about a major tournament win?"

"Cocoa Beach Pro-Am," Gary said. "Ethan wiped the floor with last year's world champ."

"Me, I've always wondered how somebody can stand on one of those things, much less do those fancy maneuvers in the waves." She gave him a pro's smile, all teeth and no emotion. "Mr. Barrett—Ethan—I need to know about your source."

"He's gone," Ethan replied. "Smoke in the wind. Forget him."

"Told you," Gary said.

Ethan asked, "Were you a cop too?"

"Naw, the lady here was Treasury. Major league."

Beth had lost her smile. "Just the same, Ethan, we need to know what you know."

"I only heard about the attack by promising to protect his identity. Can we please move on?"

When she responded with more of that hard-eyed stare, Gary said, "Like I told you, the shooter's name is Rickie Schofeld. Multiple arrests as a teen, two stints in juvie. Then he graduated from simple B&Es to major armed burglary. Two years back, he got sent away for ten to twenty."

"His third conviction as an adult," Beth said. "The guy went to Raiford. You know Raiford, Mr. Barrett?"

"The name, sure."

"Hard place to do time. Very hard."

Gary said, "Adrian was assigned the case pro bono. Rickie is apparently holding to his story that Adrian messed up at trial."

"Which is truly absurd," Beth said. "Given his previous convictions, he could have gotten life."

"That may be part of his lawyer's strategy. His court-appointed attorney is going for a temporary insanity defense. They've insisted on a psychiatric evaluation."

Ethan asked, "Who's the lawyer?"

Gary smiled as if he approved of the question. "Jimmy Carstairs. Recognize the name?"

The office and the two people all took on a crystal clarity. Ethan's shoulder and head drummed in time to his accelerated heartbeat. For once he did not mind. "Carstairs represents the Washington group that wants to buy Sonya's company."

"I had a word with their PI," Gary said. "She's a pal from the force. Claims it was their turn on the pro bono circuit."

Beth asked, "Do you buy that, Ethan?"

"Not for an instant."

"Now you see why identifying your source is so vital."

"Asking me a dozen more times won't change a thing," Ethan replied.

Beth frowned at Gary, who shrugged in reply. She turned back to Ethan. "Can you at least tell us if there was any connection between your source and a motive that conflicts with the shooter's claim?"

"I know what you know," Ethan replied. "And nothing else."

"I doubt that very much. So your source made no suggestion about future attacks?"

"Asked and answered."

"Best move on," Gary said. "The man riles easy."

The three of them spent half an hour going through security arrangements for Adrian, Sonya, their home, and their respective businesses. Nothing they discussed required so much time, but Ethan did not complain. Beth was essentially outlining what he would be charged for. She was treating him as a client. He did his best to pay attention and respond in kind.

They emerged to find Gina waiting in the front lobby. Gone was the university girl's pants and top. In their place stood a lovely young executive in a pale grey pantsuit, navy silk blouse, and alligator pumps. The outfit went perfectly with Gina's Parisian hairstyle. Her dark eyes glittered, and all the males within range watched her every move.

Ethan introduced Beth, informing her and Gary that Gina

served as his PA, and they were to treat anything she said as coming directly from him. When Beth departed and Gary left to check on arrangements for their next meeting, Ethan said, "You look stunning."

"I'm afraid to tell you how much all this cost," Gina said.

"It was worth it."

She fingered the lapel of her jacket. "My mother is going to take one look and keel over in a dead faint."

"I'd probably join her on the floor," Ethan replied. "Except for how everybody is watching."

The firm's main conference room was fitted with a long oval table and leather chairs and two walls of shelves filled with law books. A side table was laid with a coffee service, deli sandwiches, soft drinks, and plates of fine china. The room's only ornament was a bronze Remington statue of a Wild West rider, which held pride of place on the center shelf. Ethan made his way around the table and stood looking at the rider. He had found the statue at a Cocoa Beach garage sale, rusted out and broken in four places. He had spent two months scouring off the grunge, then a surfing buddy who ran a welding shop did an artist's job refitting the broken segments. Ethan had given the statue to Adrian and Sonya as a wedding present. He ran a finger around where the cowboy's head was reattached and wondered if there would come a time when such memories did not stab worse than his wounds.

Adrian entered the conference room and did a comic double take at the sight of his kid brother, the firm's PI, and a beautiful young woman there waiting for him. "What on earth?"

"I'm here as a client," Ethan said. "This is Gina Devoe, my PA. Now please shut the door, sit down, and let's get started."

Adrian ate in the impatient manner of someone who refused to let good food get in the way of work. Soon after they started, Gina rose from her place and left the room.

Adrian watched her exit, then asked, "She's your girlfriend, do I remember that right?"

"She was."

"Something happened while she was in Europe?"

Ethan nodded. "I got news of my coming departure."

Adrian pushed his plate aside. "Oh. That."

Gina returned with a yellow legal pad and two different-colored pens. She slid her half-eaten sandwich toward the center of the table and made a note at the top of the first page.

Ethan took that as his cue. "We need to set some parameters."

"You should be on my team," Adrian said. "I keep telling them, parameters are the only thing from the whole deal getting dumped in the circular file."

"I keep worrying that the shooter was not just a lone guy with a grudge," Ethan went on.

"Gary told me about your concerns. I'm waiting to hear the reasons."

Swiftly Ethan ran through his thoughts and finished with what he had just learned from Gary and the security specialist about Rickie Schofeld. Though she had heard much of it while they walked the beach, Gina took notes throughout. Adrian spent the time leaning back in his chair, staring at the sunlit glass.

When Ethan went quiet, Adrian glanced at his PI and

asked, "You ever heard of a multiple offender getting off for good behavior?"

"Not from Raiford," Gary replied. "That place likes to swallow inmates whole. Of course, that doesn't mean it couldn't happen."

"Coincidences." Adrian said the word like an oath. "I hate them worse than cold oatmeal."

Ethan confessed, "I feel like I'm dealing out too many fragments and not enough wholes."

"Just the same, you might be on the right track." Adrian balled up his napkin and dropped it on his half-eaten sandwich. "I want you and Gary to take this potential issue and run with it. I'm already overstretched."

"That's why I wanted to ask you about your case. Assuming my fears are real and there is actually a 'they' hiding behind the shooter."

"Let me worry about the doubts. You go with your gut." He looked at Gary. "You okay with that?"

"I didn't want to believe him," Gary replied. "And if he hadn't been watching where I wasn't, we'd be gathered for a completely different reason." He looked at Ethan. "You point, I'm on the hunt. No more questioning."

Adrian turned to Gina. "What about you, Ms. Devoe?"

"Call me Gina, and I'm better than okay," Gina replied. She offered Ethan solemn eyes. "I want to help. That starts with trusting the guy in charge and following his lead."

Adrian said, "Someday my wife is going to tell me that."

"In your wildest dreams," Gary said. "Sorry, that just slipped out."

"Back to my question," Ethan said. "What's changed with the case? What has upped the stakes?"

"That's just it," Adrian replied. "The case is falling apart, at least for us. We're just counting down the days to a total loss."

Ethan felt as though the words beat him back in his seat, away from the table and all his partially formed plans. "So maybe I've got it wrong."

"No," Gina said. "I mean, I don't know anything about anything. But I've heard how you talk about all this. And I think . . ."

"What?" It was Adrian who spoke. "Tell us."

"I think there has to be something more than what we're seeing. Ethan is spending his last . . ." Her face crimped so tight she bowed slightly in her seat.

Adrian looked from Gina to Ethan and back again. His expression held a hint of the same grim sorrow.

"My cop brain says everything points at a lone gunman," Gary said. "But I'm definitely open to being convinced otherwise."

Ethan waited until Gina had regained composure, then said to his brother, "Break down the case for us."

"We're fighting a losing battle. The situation is terrible and getting worse." Adrian rose and went to the coffee service on the side table. He spoke with his back to the room. "Sonya's first attorney was a flake of the first order."

"Brad Crawley." Gary spelled the last name for Gina. "Right family, right credentials. Handsome, charming, and dumb as day-old bait."

"Sonya spent a year living a dual life. She worked on her project in the UF labs and taught her classes. Weekends and late at night, she began developing a totally new idea." Adrian held up his hand while still standing with his back to the room. "I know you want to hear about her work. But it's extremely complex and I don't have time to go into it now."

Ethan wanted to argue but knew it was futile. "I understand."

"Five years ago, Sonya's lifelong research reached the point where she thought she was really onto something. And in order not to show a conflict of interest with the university, she tendered her resignation and moved up here. Her family's from Jacksonville. Sonya managed to snag lab space at the new science park."

"At least old Brad got that much done right," Gary said.

"Yeah, old Brad is fine so long as there's no heavy lifting involved." Adrian carried his coffee back over to the table. "Six months later Brad negotiated the sale of fifty-one percent of Sonya's company to Cemitrex, a DC-based hedge fund specializing in cutting-edge research with high-profit potential. To their credit, it's only because of their investment that Sonya's made it to where she is now."

Gina asked, "Cemitrex was the only interested investor?"

Adrian stopped playing with his cup. "Now that is a very interesting question."

"Is it?"

"Cemitrex is the only group Brad didn't have to work hard to find." Adrian continued his tight inspection of Gina. "You're a student?"

"UF. We had a case study in last term's business class. I remember what the professor said. It always comes down to how many suitors want to take the lady to the dance."

Adrian smiled. "That's how he put it—suitors looking for a dance partner?"

Gina returned his smile. "The professor is from Alabama."

"Man's got to be from somewhere."

Ethan saw no need to join the exchange. Gina looked fresh and young and happy, rather than a lady facing the sudden loss of the man who would never become her fiancé.

Adrian continued to address her. "The problem is what Brad let Cemitrex include in the contract. Namely, the right to buy the remaining shares whenever they wanted. Brad convinced Sonya he had added a poisoned chalice. His words, not mine. His contract stipulates the sale price is twenty-two million dollars. Three times their initial investment."

"That is stupid."

"Is it."

"What if she comes up with a product that's worth a billion dollars?"

Adrian's smile returned. "You just took the words out of my first meeting with Sonya."

Gina's eyes flashed. "That man should be locked up for being an idiot with a license."

"No argument here." Adrian checked his watch. "Sorry. Time's up. I need to bolt."

As Adrian rose from the table, Ethan said, "One thing more."

"It will have to wait. I'm due at court—"

"The police want me to make a statement."

Adrian's progress toward the door slowed. "When?"

"Tomorrow morning," Gary replied. "Ten thirty."

Ethan said, "They'll want to know about my source."

"No," Adrian said. "That can't happen."

"Exactly."

"I'll handle it." As Adrian opened the door, he said, "I

almost forgot. Sonya wants you over for dinner tonight. Bring Gina."

"It'll be a pleasure. Right, Gina?"

"Absolutely."

"Gary?" Adrian asked.

"Can't. Kid stuff."

"Rain check, then."

Ethan called after his brother, "I won't let you down."

Adrian stopped by the door long enough to offer them all a genuine smile. "Bro, that is the last thing I'm worried about."

CHAPTER
TWENTY-SIX

In the months leading up to their wedding, Adrian and Sonya had bought a fifties-era teardown on Fort Caroline Road in the Saint Johns Bluff residential district. They spent a year and every cent they had in building their dream home, a haven from all the pressures the world was already bringing to bear.

Ethan had been there before, of course. But previous occasions had been marred by the bitter friction that had defined his relationship with Sonya. So in many respects it felt as though he saw it for the first time.

Adrian walked down the brick front walk as Gina pulled into the drive. As they rose from the car, he said, "Hope you're hungry."

"Very."

"Good." He smiled a greeting to Gina. "You look lovely tonight, Miss Devoe."

"Why, thank you ever so." She made a pirouette. "Ethan bought it for me."

"All I did was tell her to go spend," Ethan corrected. "Gina did the buying."

She wore sky-blue silk gabardine trousers, a navy blouse with pearl buttons, navy open-toed sandals, and a simple gold chain holding a small golden sand dollar. "It was a tough job. But somebody had to do it."

Adrian smiled as his wife slipped in beside him. "Sonya doesn't cook all that often. When she does, I become her lab assistant. I pity the jokers who have to deal with that lady every day."

"They worship the ground I walk on." Sonya stepped forward and kissed Ethan's cheek. "How are your injuries?"

Ethan touched the spot on his cheek and tried to remember if she had ever before shown him affection. Perhaps at the wedding. But if so, it would have been the sort of generic motion offered to any cheek within reach. "Much better, now."

The home's simple brick exterior was spiced by grey clapboard siding along the roofline and around the door and windows. A steeply pitched roof hid Adrian's second-story office. The house stood on a deep lot that extended back through a wooded marsh to a long deepwater pier and boat dock on the Saint Johns River. The house's rear was a brick-and-timber U, with three bedrooms running along one side and Sonya's home office occupying the other. The screened central veranda held a small pool, an outdoor living area, and exercise equipment. It was a functional and happy place that suited them perfectly.

Sonya asked Gina if she was willing to help in the kitchen, then issued a series of precise instructions to her and Adrian. Sonya's manner suggested she was used to being obeyed instantly.

She told Ethan, "You and I need a moment in private." She led him to a pair of cushioned chairs planted by the pool. A trio of candles burned on a cast-iron coffee table. "I'm having a raspberry tea. Would you like something to drink?"

"Maybe later."

Sonya seated herself and said, "We need to set up a protocol."

"I learned to hate that word, back when the doctors pretended they could do something to make me all better," Ethan said. "Protocol. It ranks right up there with treatment. They both sounded so glib, rolling off the doctors' tongues."

"Just the same." Sonya did not budge. "You are a treasure trove of information and data. And I intend to mine you to the fullest extent possible."

"Do I have any say in the matter?"

"Absolutely," she replied. "You can set the appointment times."

Ethan was not certain she was joking. "I'll think about it."

"You'll do more than that." She set her untouched glass on the table. "Even the smallest items, things you might consider inconsequential, may in fact hold the compass headings we require to understand what precisely has happened and how we should proceed."

"What do you want from me?"

"Blood, fluids, scans—"

"No, Sonya. I'm sorry. But no."

She went silent. "You can't refuse me."

"I just did. I have a few weeks to go and a lot of work to do. What free time I have left, I am not spending in your lab."

"Please, Ethan." She leaned forward. "I'm begging you. And I hate to beg."

"You're not good at it either."

"Once a week. An hour. No more."

He nodded. "All right."

"Really?"

"One hour."

She settled back in her seat, lifted her glass, and sipped. "Isn't this a lovely night? Adrian insists there's a major storm brewing out there somewhere. Do you agree?"

"You were never after more than an hour, were you?"

She smiled. "One can always hope. But no. An hour should be enough. Maybe a smidgen—"

"No." He studied her. "I would hate to play poker with you."

"Adrian loves the occasional game. He keeps saying that sooner or later he's bound to win one hand." She sipped again. "We'll see."

"I don't know a thing about you," he said. "All I remember from before is how we fought."

Sonya turned to the night and went quiet. Ethan waited with her, content to watch distant lightning illuminate the sky. It truly was a lovely evening.

"My father was a pipe fitter and a mean drunk." Sonya spoke to the darkness beyond their enclosure. "My mother was a dessert chef in an Orlando restaurant. She had the ability to become a shadow when my father was bingeing. My brother ran away when he was fourteen. I learned later he joined the merchant marine. When Adrian and I were getting married, I tracked him down. He's a captain now of one of the world's largest container ships. The people serving under him had nothing but good things to say. The word I heard most often was kind. My brother, the kind and soft-spoken skipper. His crew worships him."

Ethan could hear Adrian and Gina talking inside the kitchen. Gina's voice was too soft for him to make out the words, but it didn't matter. Adrian said something, and she responded with a quick burst of musical laughter, easy and fine. The two of them walked a course that had not existed in his previous world. Just like this conversation. He and Sonya, seated together as if they were friends.

Sonya went on, "I ran too, in my own way. When I was nine, I went to the police. I'm told that almost never happens, a child breaking with the family pattern and seeking help."

"You were special even then," Ethan said.

She acknowledged his compliment with a nod. "Social services became involved, and things became better. Not great. Not even good. But better. I hid in my books. Study became my refuge. Two of my teachers took an interest in me and helped prepare me for early release. That's what I secretly called my home life—a cage I was desperate to escape from."

The night wind rippled across the pool's surface, scattering the underwater lights. Their reflection shone against the boundary of oleanders. Their blossoms weaved a soft dance in tones of lavender and rose.

"I started at Princeton three weeks after my fifteenth birthday. It was absolute bliss. I was still an outcast, of course. The youngest in my class and small for my age. I didn't care. None of their looks or comments could touch me. I did what I always did. I lived for my work."

Ethan looked up as a soft rumble of thunder echoed across the starlit sky. Despite the calm and the beauty of this one night, the storm was out there. And it was headed his way.

"I earned my doctorate at twenty and went straight into research. Princeton made me a lecturer—teaching just one class a week, my own lab, two assistants. In a tight market for science grads, it was a dream position." She went quiet.

"What happened?"

Sonya rose from her chair and walked to the pool's edge. She stared into the water with her own brand of singular intensity, as if she could parse the weaving blue waters and discern the future. Finally she said, "I grew so restless. When the University of Florida offered me the post, I leapt at it. Two years later I realized I had changed nothing. It was this same restless urgency that drove me to start my own lab. For years I feared I was never made for happiness. Getting what I wanted in life would only make me want to move on." She looked at him, revealing a stricken gaze. "When I fell in love with your brother, I was so happy, and so terrified. Some nights I wake up and feel so helplessly in love, so afraid this bad part of me will rise up and tear us apart."

He breathed in and out, trapped by the sense of walking farther and farther down a path that only existed because of who he had never been before. What was it, he wondered, that had made him so willfully blind? If he had been different, if he had tried harder, could he have captured just a tiny fraction of this goodness?

Finally Sonya's sorrow drew him back from the dark edge, and he said, "If I know anything at all, it's this. You and Adrian will have bad times, just like everybody. But you love him."

"So much," she whispered.

"And he loves you. And you'll find a way through. To-gether."

Adrian chose that moment to pop his head out the back doors and demand, "What are you two up to out here?"

Sonya walked over and placed her hand on Ethan's cheek. "Becoming friends."

TWENTY-SEVEN

They dined on the rear veranda beneath slow-moving Bermuda fans. They talked in the easy manner of longtime friends, mostly about Gina's plans for the future. Twice the lovely young woman dabbed unshed tears from the corners of her eyes as she discussed life after Ethan. No one saw any need to comment. Gina was majoring in business and had already been accepted by UF's law school. Adrian had studied there and regaled them with tales of horrible professors. Ethan continued to smile around the beat of his swollen and wounded heart.

Afterward the two brothers cleared the table. The women remained under the veranda's extended roof, safe from passing storms.

As he made coffee, Adrian asked, "What did you two talk about before dinner?"

"Sonya told me a little about her past." Ethan finished loading the dishwasher and shut the door, and as he straightened he saw his brother was staring at him. "What?"

"She never talks about that." Adrian resumed putting coffee in the filter. Slow, deliberate motions. "Once in a blue moon I'll catch her sad, almost hiding in a corner. I have to squeeze it out of her."

Ethan leaned against the counter, uncertain what to say.

Adrian closed the lid, hit the switch, and stood watching the coffee percolate. "It really is you, isn't it?"

"Yes."

"I mean, I know it. But accepting it down deep where it counts . . ."

"I know what you mean."

"I'm still struggling to fit my head around it." He studied the coffee maker like it wouldn't work if he took his eyes off it for a second. "How old were you then?"

"Just past fifty-five."

"Not that old."

"I guess you could say I'd lived a pretty hard life."

"But full, right? You traveled the world, you surfed. Was it worth it, Ethan? Did you find what you wanted?"

"Does anyone?"

Adrian watched the coffee drip through. "I have."

"I see that now. I missed it before." Because it was Adrian, he went on, "There were some beautiful moments. But looking back . . ." Ethan was spared the need to find an answer because Gina stepped through the rear doors.

"How long does it take two guys to make coffee? We're getting lonely out here."

"Coming right up." When she returned outside, Adrian asked, "Did you and she—"

"I don't want to talk about that." It hurt too much just to think about it. "Let's go join the ladies."

―――

A bit later, Gina excused herself and entered the house. Sonya waited until they heard a door close, then asked, "Have you told her?"

"Only that I don't have long to live."

Adrian winced. "Bro, the way you say that . . . Like we're discussing a hurricane that won't reach land."

"You forget, I was on the way out back then."

"How long did you have?"

"A couple of months tops. And there was pain. A lot of it."

"Back to my question," Sonya said.

"What do you want me to say?"

In the candlelight and the pool's soft glow, Sonya's blue eyes glittered like the deep Atlantic. "She loves you, Ethan. Very much."

He nodded. "You're saying I should tell her everything?"

Sonya's response surprised him. She turned and looked at her husband. And softly said, "Yes. Definitely yes."

"Absolutely not," Adrian said, meeting his wife's gaze.

Sonya continued to observe her man. "How can you say such a thing? Gina *loves* him."

"All the more reason." Adrian looked at his brother. "I know you said you didn't want to talk about it. But Ethan, it's the elephant on the veranda."

"Gina waited for me to come back from surfing my way around the globe. Four years, almost." Every word was a new conviction. "We married. And divorced seven years later."

"That's so sad," Sonya murmured.

"I rest my case," Adrian said.

"There is no *case*." A hint of Sonya's potent rage resurfaced. "This is a woman's *heart*."

"All the more reason." Adrian pointed at Gina's empty chair. "She loves him *now*."

"What on earth is that supposed to mean?"

"I understand him," Ethan said. "And my gut says Adrian's right."

"Ethan is doing his best by her *now*." Adrian paused, almost as if he wanted to offer his wife an opportunity to object. "He is honoring her *now*."

"She needs to know." Sonya's voice was almost a whisper, as if she was speaking to herself more than the two men. "She needs to be a part of this."

"She is as much a part as anyone," Ethan replied. "On the one hand, I want to tell her. And ask her forgiveness. And apologize."

"You should," Sonya said. "You must."

"On the other, I'd rather just let her see me as I am now and hold on to this when I'm gone."

Adrian's wince was so deep, the creases turned him ancient. "Are you sure you only have a few weeks?"

"That's what Sonya told me." Then he amended, "You know, the other Sonya. Before she shot me back."

Before Sonya could shape her response, a door opened somewhere in the house and footsteps clipped across the wooden floor. She whispered, "This is terrible."

Adrian nodded. "At least on that we agree."

CHAPTER
TWENTY-EIGHT

Ethan slept so well he woke up feeling an odd sense of guilt, as though everything he was putting in place required him to be stressed and fretful. The clock read a quarter past six. He was not due to meet Gina until eight. He didn't feel up to a run. The jouncing motion would no doubt carry a price he would pay all day long. He donned swim trunks and walked down to the shore. A chest-high swell was piling in, and the outside break was dotted with surfers taking advantage of the windless conditions. The air felt dense to Ethan, as if he could sense the day's coming heat. And something else. There was a major storm beyond the horizon—he was more certain with each passing day.

As Ethan walked into the foamy shorebreak, he recalled a group of old-timers he had befriended in some distant land. Malaysia, he thought, but perhaps it was one of the Indonesian islands beyond the tourist havens on Bali. Each dawn these old fishermen gathered at their appointed spot on the beach, where untamed palms leaned in close and formed a living shelter against the sun. They would discuss the weather five days or a week out. They would gesture to the storm's incoming direction, their hands laced with ancient wounds and curled into permanent half-fists by the fishing lines they could no longer hold. Some of the surfers like Ethan had gained the habit of stopping and asking their advice. Occasionally they would respond, warning them of storms or rip currents or dangerously large waves. Almost always the threat arrived on the day and tide they predicted. It was remarkable how often the old men had been right.

Ethan reached chin deep, where he had to take little jumps to stay clear of the incoming shorebreak. The exercises that the hospital's physical therapist had assigned him were pretty lame. But doing them here, where the currents demanded a constant adjustment for balance, was something else entirely. He worked through all nine exercises twice.

As he started back toward the shore, he studied the lovely old hotel he was now calling home. The drapes still covered Gina's window. He imagined her sleeping with easy grace. He recalled how it once had been, when she woke to find him watching her. The eyes of love that she showed in the soft light of another day they were destined to share together. Her heart was there in her gaze, the door she invited him to enter through simply because she had wrapped her life around his. Her arms were soft and warm and formed a shelter for his angry, restless spirit. He remembered how it felt to allow himself to be calmed and gentled by her embrace. As if he had been born to love this amazing woman. As if this was the haven he never thought he would know, and one he most certainly did not deserve.

Breakfast was a Spanish omelet delivered to his room. Ethan ate alone, then rested a bit. He wrapped his morning meds in a Kleenex and stuffed them in his shirt pocket. His head was definitely on the mend, but the wound to his shoulder hurt quite a lot after the workout. Even so, it felt good holding off on the meds. His mind was clear, the day ahead etched in sharp lines.

Gina was ready when he knocked on her door. Today's outfit was a pale linen blouse with thin lavender stripes over cotton khaki-colored slacks and coral sandals with a cork heel. All he could think to say was, "Wow."

She smiled. "Nothing beats the wow factor in my book."

She didn't start complaining until they pulled into the bank's parking lot. The reason was, Ethan hadn't told her where they were going. "I thought you said we had to meet with the police."

"This won't take long."

"Ethan, no. You can't—" She stopped because he had already risen from the car and was in the process of shutting his door. She rose and hurried to catch up. "I don't want your money."

"You really look lovely today. How many outfits did you buy?"

"Four. Ethan—"

"We need to go back and get you a couple more. Four's not enough, especially in this heat."

She planted herself on the bank's bottom step. "Ethan, I am not going in there."

He returned to where she stood. There was a frantic

defiance to the way she watched him. Her chin jutted out like she was barely able to keep from pouncing on him with everything she had, which was a lot. Her left hand was curled around the base of the purse slung from her shoulder. It was either that or take a grip around his neck.

"Gina, please let me do this."

"Ethan, *no*. It makes me feel cheap, having you give me money."

"I understand."

"Really?"

"Yes."

"You're not just saying that so I'll let you drag me in there?"

"I'm not dragging you anywhere."

"Then let's go." But she did not turn away.

"If you insist, we'll go. But will you at least hear me out?"

"It won't change my mind. Nothing will." When he did not press, she relented, "Go ahead then. Say it."

"Your mother is right. Accepting payment for your work will make your taking time off from school look a lot better."

"That doesn't change how I feel about this."

He shifted around slightly so as to block their discussion from a pair of businessmen entering the bank. "You know what I'm going to say next."

"Don't you dare. You are *not* going to make me cry in public."

He nodded. "Just the same, it would be so very good if you would let me be part of what you do afterward. It's my gift to your future."

She took a double-fisted grip on her purse and did not reply.

176

"This is what friends do, Gina. You're helping me through something I can't do alone. I want to help you after. Please."

They left the bank twenty-one minutes later. Gina had not spoken a single word during the entire process of opening an account and signing a deposit slip for sixty thousand dollars. She had given no sign of even hearing when Ethan had explained that he wanted to pay for twelve weeks in advance. What he didn't say was how he wanted her to continue this work after, making sure his brother and sister-in-law stayed safe, even when Gina had to work on her own. If the bank clerk who handled the transaction found anything odd in Gina's stone-like demeanor, he gave no sign.

The Jacksonville central police station was located on East Bay Street, three blocks from Metropolitan Park on the river's north side. Jacksonville's law enforcement was a throwback to its early days, when the city and the port were both classed as small time. With Savannah less than a hundred miles north, Jacksonville was fated to remain its unimportant southern sister. Or so everyone assumed in the town's early days. As a result, the city's police department operated under the direction of the county sheriff. This joint city-county agency worked surprisingly well, and as the city had grown into a regional powerhouse, its leaders had seen no need for change.

The sheriff's office ran law enforcement, investigation, and corrections in both Jacksonville city and Duval County. The cheerless building occupied the better part of an entire block. Ethan pulled into the neighboring lot and spied Gary waiting just inside the glass-fronted entrance. By the time he cut the motor and slipped his arm back inside the sling, Gina had left the car and was halfway to the entrance.

Gary greeted them with, "There's been a delay. Hello, Miss Devoe. You're looking lovely as usual."

Ethan asked, "Is there a problem?"

"No idea. All they'd say is 'urgent developments in an active case.' Which is exactly what I heard yesterday."

"I'm due at Sonya's lab in an hour. She wants to run more tests."

"That is one lady I wouldn't want to keep waiting. Can you put her off?"

"I suppose we can ask." Ethan turned to Gina. "Would you see if you can reach her?"

She cast him a single cold glare, then turned away.

Gary watched her walk to the duty sergeant, who handed her the phone. "You two have a spat?"

"I have absolutely no idea."

"Man, does that ever sound familiar. I'll go see if we can speed things up."

Eventually Gina passed the phone back and thanked the sergeant. Ethan saw how her molten gaze flashed angrily everywhere but directly at him.

He said, "Gina, if the money makes you so upset, I'll take it back right now."

In response, she walked over to the long wooden bench running down the side wall. There was one other occupant, a sullen youth with a tall pompadour and what appeared to be a massive hangover, cuffed to the opposite end, directly across from the duty sergeant. Gina planted herself as far from the youth as possible. She crossed her arms over her purse and glared at nothing.

Ethan walked over and said, "Whatever I've done, I apologize."

"Really, Ethan?" She lifted her gaze, showing unshed tears. "Really?"

He remained standing, watching her, trying to understand exactly what was going on.

As if in response to his unspoken question, she whispered, "Why won't you trust me?"

He lowered himself slowly, giving her a chance to deny him the right to join her.

Gina's internal cauldron mangled her softly spoken words. "I know you're hiding something." When he did not speak, she said, "Thank you for not denying it."

This attitude was new. No boiling rage, no acidic biting tone. Instead, she revealed to him a severely wounded heart.

"Gina . . ."

"Do Adrian and Sonya know?"

Ethan sighed.

Her face crimped in the effort not to cry. "That's what I thought."

Gary chose that moment to emerge through the security door and say, "We're on."

―――

The detectives' bullpen contained twenty cubicles, with about half of them staffed. Almost all the heads rose up far enough to watch them proceed to the conference room in the far corner.

A dark-skinned man built like a block of solid cobalt stood in the doorway. "Not every day we have a real lifesaver in here." He offered Ethan his hand. "Stan Lauder. That's usually our job, Mr. Barrett. Running toward trouble, taking a bullet in the process."

"I might have done it," Gary said. "Only I was looking in the wrong direction."

Ethan knew he probably should say something—tell the detective to use his first name, make a joke of his injury. But there was a faint buzzing in his brain, remnants of hearing that Gina was all too aware of his secret. Sooner or later he needed to tell her everything, but he had no idea what to say or how to say it.

The detective introduced himself to Gina, then led them into the windowless room. An empty whiteboard ran down two walls, streaked and smudged from whatever investigation was no longer there. A heavyset Latina in a rumpled navy business suit sat in the far corner. She watched them enter with a dark, unblinking gaze.

Stan said, "Estelle Rodriguez, US Marshals Service." When everyone was seated, he went on, "Gary was my partner for his last four years, which means I can cut you some slack. Some, mind you. Not a lot."

Ethan heard the words, but had no desire to respond. He felt disconnected from the outside world, shrunk down to some internal space by Gina's revelation. The fact that she knew suggested some connection beyond logical thought. She was welded to him at some far deeper level. As if their married life and the love they once shared had managed to transcend whatever barrier he had crossed and was still with them. In the new here and now.

The woman from the marshals' office demanded, "What role does Ms. Devoe play in all this?"

"Funny," Gary replied. "I was about to ask the very same thing about you."

"Officer Rodriguez is now attached to our investigation," Stan replied. He slipped into the seat two away from the marshal.

"Which tells me nothing at all."

Rodriguez said, "Answer my question."

"Ms. Devoe serves as Mr. Barrett's researcher."

She turned to the detective. "Why are we hearing from this gentleman and not Mr. Barrett directly?"

"Because we're waiting for you to ask the question they won't answer," Gary replied.

"Which is what, exactly."

Gary just smiled.

Rodriguez's expression tightened a notch. "Ms. Devoe wouldn't also happen to be your source, would she, Mr. Barrett?"

Ethan's reply was halted by Gary lifting one finger. "No, she would not."

"Who is your source, Mr. Barrett?" When Ethan did not respond, the marshal's tone hardened. "This is me asking nicely for the last time."

"And this is the only response you will be getting." Gary continued to smile across the table. "I have been instructed by Ethan's attorney of record to say that if you insist on inquiring any further into the matter of a *confidential source*, this meeting is concluded."

"That is not for you to say."

"The meeting will resume when said attorney is present, at which time he will be the *only* person who speaks." Gary swept his hand toward Ethan. "Forget pressing Mr. Barrett any further about his confidential source and we can continue the conversation. Otherwise, have a nice day."

Stan watched the marshal for a long moment. When the woman remained angrily silent, he asked, "What line of work are you in, Mr. Barrett?"

"Investments."

"Did you meet this confidential source of yours through your investment work?"

"Nice try," Gary said. "Moving on."

"This is ridiculous," the marshal said.

Stan asked, "Will you tell us what happened in the run-up to the assault?"

"Yes."

Stan reached under the table and came up with a cheap cassette deck. "Can I record this?"

Ethan nodded. "If you want."

Ethan found himself marginally rejoining the group as he repeated the events. The detective stopped him several times, shifting back and forth, clearly trying to have him reveal the source's identity. When they reached the point where Ethan attacked the shooter, the images flashed crystal clear once more. The sunlight glinted off the gun barrel. The drugstore bag dropped to the step. The shooter lifted his weapon.

Ethan was sweating hard by the time he said, "My head must have hit the step. I blacked out."

All through Ethan's description, the marshal continued to shift her glare from Ethan to Gary to Gina and back again, as if she could not decide who to arrest first. A professional distaste radiated from the woman.

When Ethan finished and the silence had lingered for a time, Gary asked, "Can I ask a question?"

"You can certainly ask," the detective replied. "Absolutely."

"We're clearly missing something here," Gary said. "A US marshal doesn't fit into the case as I know it. What is Ms. Rodriguez doing here?"

Rodriguez demanded, "What exactly do you know?"

"That's simple enough. A shooter was apprehended and arrested." Gary spread his hands over the scarred tabletop. "See how easy that was?"

Stan told Gary, "We've had a development."

"Don't say anything more," Rodriguez snapped.

"See, ma'am, here's the thing." Stan continued to aim his words across the table at Gary. "I don't take orders from you."

"This is an ongoing investigation handled by the US Marshals Service."

"You go right ahead and investigate whatever you want." Stan gestured to the trio seated across from him. "I will continue to handle *my* investigation exactly as *I* see fit. And right now, I'm getting a lot more willing assistance from these three than I am from you."

Ethan studied the Jacksonville detective, more certain by the minute that all this was a show. Not for the marshal or for Stan's former partner. For him.

Rodriguez rose from her chair. "I will be seeking a federal injunction to pull you and your entire department from this case."

"You do that." Stan watched her storm to the door. "Have a nice day, now."

When the door slammed behind her, Gary asked, "What just happened?"

Stan tapped his pen a couple of times. He then realized

they were still recording. He cut off the tape deck and popped out the cassette. "Hang on a second."

When he had left, Gina asked, "What is going on?"

"Something big enough for Stan to need the lieutenant's permission." Gary leaned back and laced his fingers across his middle. "When do you need to leave for Sonya's lab?"

Ethan checked his watch. "We've got another ten minutes."

"I suggest you hang around." Gary smiled at the door. "Whatever this is, it should be good."

TWENTY-NINE

As soon as the door closed behind the detective, Ethan said, "That argument we just saw, I'm pretty sure Stan set it up for our benefit."

Gary did not merely turn to Ethan. He shifted his entire bulk. "Now that's an interesting thought."

"You disagree?"

"Not at all. Matter of fact, I was wondering why they felt a need to air their disagreements in public." Gary stared at the closed door. "Stan deals with the feds often enough to know getting them riled doesn't pay off in the long run."

"He wanted to show us he's on our side," Ethan guessed.

Before Gary could comment further, Stan returned. With him was an older man, lean as a greyhound and completely bald. He wore a white button-down short-sleeve shirt, a clip-on tie, and a gold badge attached to his belt.

Stan did not bother to introduce the newcomer. He re-seated himself and said, "Rickie Schofeld. Know that name?"

"The shooter," Gary replied.

"Right. Until this week, Rickie was in his second year of ten to twenty at Raiford. His third count of armed robbery. If anybody had asked me, I'd say the guy was going nowhere in a hurry."

"Except maybe to court for an appeal that wouldn't fly," Gary said, nodding.

"Rickie got himself released on early parole," Stan went on. "And nobody can tell us why."

Gina asked, "Is that normal?"

"Early release from Raiford for a three-timer," Stan said. "Would you class that as normal, partner?"

"Not in a million years," Gary replied.

"And yet nobody can tell us how it happened. Raiford points to a federal judge's order, the prison board ain't responding to my questions, and the judge is on vacation and can't be reached."

"How does a federal judge have jurisdiction over a burglary?"

"We plan on asking him that very same question," Stan replied. "Soon as the judge gets back and unseals the court records."

"What do you know," Gary said.

"Hang on, I'm just getting started." The detective glanced at the older man standing by the door. He must have received what he needed, for he turned back and said, "Day before yesterday, Rickie Schofeld was checked out of the county jail for a psychiatric evaluation requested by his attorneys. At arraignment these same lawyers informed the judge they intended to enter a plea of temporary insanity."

Gary said, "Tell us what happened."

"The plaintiff never arrived at the hospital." Stan gave

that a beat, then went on, "We know this because four and a half hours later the doctor phoned and said he couldn't wait any longer, he was late for his rounds."

Ethan asked, "Who checked him out of the jail?"

"That's another interesting question. The answer is, we don't know, on account of the page is missing from the record book. There's been an almighty ruckus. The sheriff handles all the county lockups. He's been on some kind of tear, I tell you what. Two people arrived during the visiting-hour crush and showed the duty officer US marshals' badges. One of them wore a cap that masked him from the camera, but we got a good shot of the other. She's definitely not one of their current officers. They checked thoroughly. That's why we couldn't meet yesterday. They were still checking."

"The Marshals Service suspects somebody on your staff of being behind the escape," Ethan said. Which explained the marshal's hostility toward the local detective. "What about Schofeld's attorney? Did Carstairs have anything to say?"

"Another interesting question." Stan nodded. "That lawyer either knows nothing or deserves an Emmy for his act."

Ethan looked at Gary, who responded with a single nod. *Go for it*. "Carstairs represents the investors in Sonya's company," Ethan said. "They hold a majority share and now intend to buy her out."

Stan lifted the recorder and made sure it was running. "This would be Dr. Sonya Barrett, your brother's wife."

"Correct. She has vowed to leave the group the instant she loses control. But they're still pushing for the buyout."

Stan took a pad and pen from his jacket. "What is she working on?"

"Pain management through brain waves. That's all I know. I'm due to meet with her as soon as we finish here."

The lieutenant spoke for the first time. "You think there's a tie-in between the attack and these investors?"

Ethan said, "My brother is fighting them tooth and nail."

Gary pointed out, "He doesn't think he's got a Florida snowball's chance of winning."

Ethan looked at the PI. "What if they know there's a weakness, something they see but we don't? What if they're worried the longer this case drags on, the greater the chance we'll discover it and force them to back off?"

Stan said, "There's a lot of empty spaces in that conjecture."

"And a lot of coincidences to back Ethan up," Gary replied.

"Man's got a point," the lieutenant said. He asked Ethan, "Gary told us your source said something about the getaway ride."

"Right. A stolen minivan. That's all I know."

Stan asked, "Driver?"

"No idea."

The lieutenant said, "A dark-grey Dodge minivan was reported missing yesterday from a Walmart parking lot. It was found burned to a hulk down a Duval County hunting trail."

Stan said, "Cameras outside the courthouse don't show much of the street. We haven't spotted it, and nobody remembers seeing one around."

"Still," Ethan said, "it's another coincidence."

"I need something concrete," Stan said. "Some shred of hard evidence. Bring me that and we'll be on it like a dog on a bone."

THIRTY

During the drive from the police station to Sonya's lab, Ethan outlined the questions he needed Gina to ask. He was resigned to the lab tests and did not want to spend a moment longer in the place than absolutely necessary. Gina spoke only to acknowledge his requests. When Ethan pulled into a visitor's spot in front of Sonya's building, he felt like a pet dog being hauled into the vet's office against his will.

He gave their names to a uniformed woman with the security company's logo on her jacket pocket. Sonya arrived two minutes later, followed by an attractive Asian woman in her early thirties.

Sonya motioned them through the lab entrance, waited for it to click shut, then launched straight in. "One of your security details spent the night parked in front of our home. They followed me to work. Now I've got another team who's taken over the receptionist station. The group who tracked me here is out there somewhere doing foot patrols." She crossed her arms and took a tight grip around her middle.

189

"I don't care what Adrian says. We're doing important work here, and I don't want this sort of interference."

Even now, when she was upset with him, Sonya lacked the heat Ethan had always known before. He replied, "Gary and I are becoming increasingly certain the shooter did not act alone. The police don't think it's definite, not yet anyway. But they're treating this threat as real. You need to as well."

Sonya and the other woman exchanged a wide-eyed look. When neither spoke, Ethan pressed on. "Adrian's told me to handle this. I'm doing my best here, and part of this is keeping you safe."

"I can't come up with an argument to that," Sonya reluctantly allowed.

"Thank you, Sonya."

"Don't thank me. I'm not feeling particularly agreeable. And I may change my mind."

He risked a smile. "I'll tell the teams to keep their distance."

Sonya gestured to the other woman. "This is Dr. Madeline Wang, the head of my lab. She is up to date on all my work."

"This is Gina Devoe. She's working the case with us."

"Tell Gina everything," Sonya said to her associate. "Ethan, come with me."

Sonya's lab was a series of large glassed-in chambers about forty feet square. Ethan could see Gina and Madeline enter a room two over from where he sat with Sonya. The two women sat by a narrow white desk with two whiteboards flanking the opposite glass wall. Their room was filled with desks and clunky computers and stacks of journals and printouts. Gina held his gaze for a long moment, then turned her chair so that her back was to him. Ethan sighed.

Nothing escaped Sonya. "Did you tell her how you came to be here?"

"No. But she knows I'm withholding something."

"Of course she does. She might not know what it is, but she can see there are pieces missing to what you're saying." Sonya seated herself on a padded lab stool, pointed Ethan to one on the other side of a table set on rollers, and began laying out syringes and empty ampuls for blood. "Adrian was absolutely wrong to say what he did. As wrong as you are not to tell her. Roll up your sleeve."

"I don't have any idea what I should do."

"Make a fist." Sonya fit a tourniquet around his upper arm, then wiped the vein that appeared in his elbow. "Adrian made me promise to say that it is your decision. I feel like I spent the morning in court, arguing a case against my husband."

"Ow."

"Hold still." She filled the first vial, pulled it off, and inserted a second. "Will you tell me why you think the attack on Adrian is connected to this case?"

"Of course. But I'd rather wait and talk to you both together." He pointed with his free hand toward the two women. "And I need to hear what Madeline is telling Gina. I'm still trying to fit the pieces together myself."

Sonya did not press. "Adrian had nightmares. He doesn't say it, but I think he blames himself for you not having long . . ."

"You can go ahead and say it, Sonya. To live."

She extracted the second vial and inserted a third. "I was really so definite?"

"Yes. You and Delia both."

She froze momentarily, then inserted the fourth and final vial. "We got the results back yesterday from the pregnancy test. I think that's why Adrian slept so poorly. I've had two miscarriages."

"I'm sorry, I didn't—"

"This should be such a moment of joy and anticipation. Instead, my husband is sobbing in his sleep." Sonya's entire body clenched up tight. By strength of will alone, she relaxed, then extracted the needle and released the tourniquet. "I'm so sorry, Ethan."

"You have nothing, absolutely nothing, to apologize for." The force behind his words caused her to look up. "Can I ask you a question?"

"Of course you can. And don't feel like you need to ask permission. Not ever again."

He shook his head. "Wow."

"What?"

"This is not the kind of relationship you and I had before."

Sonya wrote on the vials with a felt-tip pen. "What do you want to know?"

"The investment group that's buying you out—"

"*Trying* to acquire my lab," she corrected. In a more sullen tone she said, "All right. Yes. It looks increasingly definite that my life's work will sooner or later be stolen by Cemitrex."

"Are they involved in brain-wave stuff?"

"*Stuff*? You call my life's work *stuff*?" She laughed. Or tried to. "To answer your question, so far as Adrian has been able to determine, they have never invested in a medical-research group of any kind before. But they are like the mythical giant squid of the deep. You have heard of them, yes?"

"Sure. Big enough to drag ships down."

"That is Cemitrex." She continued labeling the vials. "Six billion dollars in assets, and they are everywhere. When they made their investment, they bragged about their reach. They claimed . . ." She set down the pen and last vial. "I was very foolish to agree to their terms. Adrian blames my attorney. Perhaps it was partly his fault. But I was the one who listened to their promises of complete scientific freedom, and I was the one who signed."

Ethan gave that the pause it deserved, then asked, "Is there anything in your current research that might make them think this time-travel concept is possible?"

"Absolutely not." Her response was unequivocal. "Since this episode began, I've gone back through all my notes. Right back to the very beginning, Ethan. Now that I know what to look for, I'm finding elements that suggest this temporal transfer of consciousness is feasible. But I am years away from making this an actual foundation for experimentation. Perhaps . . ." Abruptly she stopped and smiled. "I was going to say, perhaps never. But you've made a hash of that, haven't you."

For a woman who smiled so seldom, it had a transformative effect. "Then maybe I've got it wrong. Maybe Cemitrex is just greedy."

She lost her good humor. "My pain-control work is far from completed. But it does hold huge potential." She hesitated. "Adrian thinks you're onto something."

"He didn't tell me that."

"Adrian said it was his gut talking and not his head. But his gut is often right. So you will keep on searching?"

"You bet."

"Thank you, Ethan." She gripped his upper arm. "I am so very glad you are on our side."

As Sonya began fitting his chest and neck and forehead with electrodes, Ethan said, "So there I was, thirty-five years from now, minding my own business. And up you pop with your daughter." He pretended not to see the flood of emotions that threatened to overwhelm Sonya. "Then the two of you shoot me back to now. What I want to know is, how can that happen since by the time we get to the future, I will be long dead, and you won't be the same person?"

"The million-dollar question." Sonya's gaze went from intense to farseeing. "The answer is, all the physical and observable elements of the macro universe do not represent the full scope of reality."

"Okay. Now break that down into bite-size grammar-school segments."

She resumed plugging his electrode cords into the EKG machine. "Have you ever heard of the quantum universe?"

"Oh, sure. Where I come from, everybody is talking about it. Some people even claim to understand what it means."

"Hold still, please." Sonya watched the machine spin out the narrow graph paper. "Quantum entanglement may be the true answer to what you have experienced. And you in turn might be the first physical proof of its existence. The issue, Ethan, is that no one can define human consciousness. You can't bottle it, you can't find it on a map of the brain. It's been a hotly debated issue for almost five hundred years.

The more we study the human thought process, the less we understand."

The machine beeped. Sonya tore off the strip, studied it intently, then rose from her stool and pointed toward the next room. "There are recent studies that indicate thoughts do not take any time at all. One study in particular suggests resolution to some problems occurs simultaneously with the right question being posed. All of which point to thought and consciousness actually being governed by the laws of the quantum universe."

Ethan liked the way she spoke. She was fully engaged now, the brilliance on full display. What was more, she included him in the process. He was not some outsider knocking at the gates. She revealed herself. He did not understand most of what she said, but he didn't care. "Back to my question."

"We never left it. Do you mind if I take a scan of your brain while we talk?"

"Not at all."

She pointed to a windowless cubicle at the lab's other end. "Please undress and put on the sterile hospital gown and cap I've left for you."

When Ethan stepped behind the barrier and was out of sight, it seemed to release Sonya. She began talking as she would to a colleague. Or like they were equals. Ethan listened and marveled at everything she knew and he never would.

"Quantum entanglement is a physical phenomenon that occurs when pairs or groups of particles interact and share spatial proximity in ways such that the quantum state of each particle cannot be described independently of the state of others. Distance between the particles changes nothing. Time . . ."

Ethan pulled the gown free of its plastic covering and slipped it on. The cotton felt cold against his bare skin. "Go on. Time . . . what?"

"Three years ago, two physicists, one of whom is a close personal friend, suggested that time is nothing more than an emergent phenomenon, a side effect of quantum entanglement."

Ethan stepped from the cubicle and turned around so she could fasten the cords of his gown.

"I can get you a pair of slippers if the floor is cold."

"I'm okay. Go on."

"Don Page and William Wootters have developed a theory that time as we know it is nothing more than a result of observing a quantum event under Newtonian conditions."

Ethan turned and just looked at her.

She smirked and translated, "The concepts of past, present, and future are all merely side effects. They are part of our physical existence. Like how gravity holds us to the earth but can't be defined until we reduce it to the level of the very large or the extremely small. At those junctures, gravity becomes a component of space-time entanglement."

As she led him into the MRI chamber, Ethan said, "Back to my question."

"If Don and Bill are correct, time is a map. All points coexist." She guided him down onto the sliding gurney and fit a strap across his chest. "This machine is very noisy. Do you want earplugs?"

"No. So I've changed a point on the map."

"Precisely." She beamed down at him. "Isn't that exciting?"

"Confusing, more like."

"Welcome to quantum mechanics." She continued to smile. "There are any number of possible answers. Does a new secondary map branch off now? Have you merely shifted lines on the current map? Can you alter one component of a future 'now' and have this resulting change merely be absorbed in the present 'now'? Your transition opens up a whole new universe to explore."

"That's what you called it."

She stopped in the process of rolling him inside the machine. "I'm sorry, what?"

"Transition. That's the word you used when you and Delia shot me back here."

She studied him a moment. "Every time you say my daughter's name, I want to weep."

For the first time, Ethan found himself filled with a bone-deep affection for his sister-in-law. "Delia is as smart as you, and as beautiful."

She rolled him all the way inside, locked the gurney in place, then set a hand on his bare ankle. "I never thought I would say this to you. Never, never, never. You dear, sweet man."

The good feeling stayed with Ethan as the machine began warming up. It was far louder than he expected, something he assumed was the result of it being an early version of what had become a standard part of every medical exam. The initial hum grew louder and was joined by a rhythmic drumming.

Sonya's voice asked, "Can you hear me?"

"Barely."

"We are beginning the scan in just a—"

Then the world fractured, and his skull felt like it split apart.

THIRTY-ONE

The machine's hum was joined by a screeching that grew inside Ethan's head. The clamor rose until it felt like it was shattering his brain.

And then it did precisely that.

For Ethan, it seemed as though the noise actually took on a visual form. He saw himself back on the other gurney, the one in the truck's rear hold. He saw the other Sonya lean down over him, her face aged beyond her years, her gaze filled with bitter struggle and loss. He saw . . .

Ethan was back on the crystal-blue wave. The sun appeared at the far end of the tube. The same white light grew until it blanketed everything. Only this time the light seemed to swallow him whole.

And then his body convulsed as a fist slammed into his chest.

Suddenly all the horrible intensity was gone. The savage light, the noise—all of it vanished.

He was once again seated on his board. Out to sea, massive waves rose up and marched toward him, big as mountains. Closer to shore, everything was a maelstrom of fury and foam. But where he sat, it was calm. Ethan was filled with an immense sense of peace. He had never imagined anything could look quite so, well . . .

Perfect.

Then he realized he was not alone.

Another man was seated on a board not far away. For some reason, Ethan had difficulty seeing him clearly. He found it very difficult to shape his words. "Am I dead?"

Then he was back. Sort of.

Quick flashes came and went in the space of a single heartbeat. Faster.

Madeline Wang straddled him and pummeled his chest while Sonya screamed into a phone.

He blinked, but it seemed like he left and came back again. Gina shouted at him to *stay with them*.

Another blink, and Sonya called to unseen people that they were *back here*.

A third brief separation, and a man and woman in pale red uniforms lifted him onto a gurney. Gina held his hand and called his name.

He might have left again. He probably did. Then lights flashed through ambulance windows and someone shouted, "Clear!"

———

Ethan woke up back in the hospital. Gina still held his hand.

Turning his head required some immense effort. He did it just the same. She was stretched out in a seat where a footstool extended when the chair went prone. A purple blanket was tucked up to her chin. He listened to her breathe and knew he was going to tell her. No holds barred. Then his eyelids started sinking of their own accord.

Ethan managed to whisper only two words. "It's time."

CHAPTER
THIRTY-TWO

The next day he mostly slept. Sonya came twice, both times to apologize. When Ethan insisted she had done nothing wrong, she smiled in the manner of someone being forgiven for a great wrong.

Madeline, her associate, was a licensed medical doctor. She and Sonya together kept an almost constant watch. Ethan was subjected to half a dozen EKGs. All of them came back completely clear. Once Gina was assured that Ethan was definitely on the mend, she allowed Adrian to drive her back to the hotel and rest.

By the next morning, Ethan's chest had mostly stopped aching. His head and shoulder were also much improved, as if what he most needed was a day and a half of enforced bed rest.

Soon after breakfast, they all crowded in—Sonya, Adrian, Gary, Beth Helms, Madeline, Gina, the doctor, and two nurses. The doctor insisted that Ethan be held over for a full range of tests. Sonya and Madeline both refused outright, waving the EKG tapes in his face. The doctor grew irate at having his authority challenged. Adrian then added his own brand of force, claiming to be his brother's legal representative and insisting the doctor stop responding with knee-jerk measures to what was clearly a medical issue beyond his control and his understanding. That made the doctor so furious, the men might have come to blows had Gary not stepped between them.

When he finally accepted that he was not going to get his way, the doctor scrawled his signature so hard it tore the release form. He then told Adrian and Sonya, "Don't even *think* of ever coming here for care." He could not slam a door on pneumatic hinges, but he tried his best.

When he and the nurses were gone, Beth said, "I'm glad neither of you were armed."

Gary told Ethan, "I think you better make this the last time you ever set foot in here, even for aspirin."

Sonya looked at her husband. "In case you were still wondering why I refused to go for a medical degree, he just left."

Gina said, "Maybe that doctor should get himself checked out for cardiac arrest."

"Everybody take a good look for gunshot wounds," Beth said.

Adrian said, "I sure hope I don't have a medical case where the opposing counsel get hold of that guy."

Ethan lay there and watched the exchange.

Friends.

———

Adrian and Sonya expected him to come live with them. They didn't even invite him. They simply stated it as fact, as though there was no way he could possibly consider residing anywhere else. When Ethan said he was going back to the hotel, all the wrath they still had left over from the confrontation with the doctor resurfaced.

Before they could unload on him, Ethan said, "Gina and I need space."

The words caught everyone by surprise. Especially Gina.

Sonya said, "You can have the bedroom annex."

"Absolutely," Adrian said. "We'll shift upstairs into my office."

"The upstairs has a full bath," Sonya said. "We'll be fine."

"That's not the issue and you know it." Ethan could see from their expressions that they didn't, so he went on, "We need a place that is ours—sort of. Independent of the investigation and everything that's going on. A place where we can step back and just be together."

Adrian protested, "That doesn't make any sense."

"Actually, it does," Sonya said.

"They can have that just as well at our place."

"You just said it, hon." Sonya kept her gaze on Ethan. "*Our* place."

Adrian opened his mouth, but all he said was, "How am I supposed to argue with that?"

Sonya offered Gina a small smile. "Despite everything you've heard to the contrary, men are trainable."

Beth laughed. "Yeah, but is it worth the effort, that's what I'd like to know."

"Some are," Sonya replied, still smiling at Gina. "Sometimes."

Adrian continued to watch Ethan, his expression sad, resigned.

Finally Ethan said, "Somebody call the nurse so I can get unhooked and out of here."

———

Gina insisted on pushing Ethan's wheelchair out of the hospital herself. After the confrontation between Adrian and the doctor, the dispatching nurse did not offer a peep in protest.

The others stood there on the sidewalk and watched as Gina helped him out of the chair and into the BMW's passenger seat.

Sonya made a process of fastening his seat belt, but only so she could whisper, "I am so very, very sorry."

"You didn't know," Ethan said once again. "You couldn't have."

There was a great deal more she wanted to tell him. Ethan could see it in her gaze. But she merely straightened and stepped back far enough for Adrian to settle his arm around her shoulders. They all stood there and watched Gina drive them off. No one waved.

They drove through central Jacksonville in complete silence. Ethan kept his eyes shut most of the way. He was content to wait, to enjoy the freedom and the salt-laden air flowing through his open window. He knew Gina was watching him. He knew what she was not saying.

He knew it was time.

THIRTY-THREE

When they crossed the inland waterway bridge and stopped at a red light, Gina turned to him, her gaze a silent plea.

Ethan took a breath and started talking.

The sun was a tight sliver over the western skyline when they arrived at the hotel. Gina pulled into the lot and sat there, staring out the windshield, her hands keeping a tight hold on the wheel. Motionless.

Ethan was grateful for her remaining where she was. He knew he had to tell her how they ended. But after that he needed to be able to walk away from the memories. Rise up, shut the door, leave it all behind.

If only.

"We divorced seven years after we were married." He felt like the words emerged with the emotionless beat of a metronome. "By that point, there really wasn't anything much to salvage. You needed to be there for your mother. I let you go."

She released the wheel and wiped her face. Her hands were as unsteady as her breathing.

"As far as my own life went, nothing was ever as good as it should be after that. I didn't try to get you back, mostly because I didn't feel like I deserved you. Plus, well . . ."

Her voice was almost as deep as his own. "Tell me."

"I knew you were right to go. And I was afraid if I asked you to come back, to try again, I would only bring you more hurt and harm." He could no longer bear to watch her, so he turned to the window. "Right to the end, I woke up too many nights, feeling this great void in the middle of my life. The day I learned about the cancer, I just sat there in the doctor's office thinking this was exactly what I deserved for having gotten it all so wrong. And hurting you—"

Ethan stopped when she wrenched open her door and started for the hotel. He sat and watched her hurry along the front walk. Not running. But close.

He breathed in and out, thinking she was right to leave him. Again.

But when she reached the front step, Gina just stopped, staring at the doors ahead of her, captured by the sunlight and her sorrow.

Ethan emerged slowly from the car, straightening in stages, then walked up to her. Gina stood motionless, blinking slowly, releasing tears she probably was not aware she shed.

He started to reach for her arm, then hesitated and asked, "Can I help?"

She nodded, and a crystal drop of sorrow stained the sidewalk by her feet.

When she reached over and took hold of his hand, her fingers still wet from her tears, he felt his heart crack wide open.

The nice young lady behind the reception desk watched them enter but did not say anything. A young family with two toddlers laughed and played in the lobby area.

Ethan started to guide Gina toward the stairs, but she stopped him by the bottom step and demanded, "Is there more?"

"Only if you want," he replied. "I've told you Sonya brought me back. But not how it happened, or . . ."

She released his hand and headed down the rear corridor. Ethan watched her push through the doors leading to the pool and veranda. He felt eyes scrutinize him as he followed. The attention made him feel ashamed. As if no one as beautiful as Gina should be brought so low.

He was exhausted, and he was more hungry than he was tired. Even so, he was glad to be out here on the sunlit deck. He wanted to finish his telling, give her a chance to ask any questions she might have, and then leave her to decide. Now that it was out, he knew there was a very real chance she would just walk away. Close the door on all this sorrowful confusion. Erase him from her life before he could cause her any more pain.

The rest of the telling did not take long. He related his final paddle-out, meeting Sonya and her grown-up daughter, their invitation. He described the alternative he faced, the constant pain, the approaching end. His chest ached throughout, but he could not tell whether it was from his recent ordeal or the words and their impact on Gina. His shoulder and head hurt almost as badly as his chest. The two new prescription bottles made a lump in his right pocket, but he was not tempted. The pain had a rightful place in this hard hour.

Ethan finished the telling by describing his return. The days before he met her had formed a counterpoint to the hard truths. He described the contest, the bet, the struggle to make sense of his next steps. Then he stopped.

He sat and reveled in the sense of release. Sonya had been right, he knew that now. Gina loved him. She deserved to know.

Finally she turned and looked at him. Tears hovered on her lower lids, like sobs poised to break open the evening.

He rose and made his way to the empty outdoor bar and returned with two napkins. "Here."

"Thank you, Ethan." Her voice was soft. Ancient. She wiped her face. "I knew it had to be something terrible. Like maybe you had gotten married while I was gone. Or you had a child or something."

"You believe me." It was not a question.

"All of these things that haven't fit together right, now they form a picture." She bundled the napkins in her hands. "I suppose it's better to say I don't *not* believe you."

He breathed in and out. Until that moment, he had not realized how important it had become for her to accept that he was telling the truth. "I want to apologize."

"For things that never happened?"

"They have to me. So much of what we went through comes down to how selfish I've been. I caused you a lot of pain, Gina. You didn't deserve that. I see you now, how beautiful you are, how genuine, how much in love . . ."

She rose from the chair and rushed from the veranda. She almost collided with the family bringing their tod-

208

dlers out for a sunset swim. Ethan doubted she saw them at all.

He slowly made his way upstairs and ate a solitary meal with the gathering night for company.

Gina did not call.

THIRTY-FOUR

Ethan was woken twice by nightmares. Both were tangles of two fractured sets of events. In the first, he retold his story, only this time to the old Gina at her mother's funeral. In the second, he watched helplessly as Adrian was shot on the courthouse stairs. Only now it was Jimmy Carstairs, the opposing counsel, who fired the bullet.

Strangely enough, he woke up feeling both better and refreshed. He left the hotel and watched the morning strengthen while doing his physical therapy exercises in chest-deep water. He returned to the hotel and showered, and as he was dressing he had the first glimmer of an idea. Something that might, just might, begin to make a difference in the courtroom. As he went downstairs for breakfast, he wondered if perhaps the idea had been there all along, only it needed him to clear his mind and heart through the retelling before he could see.

Ethan kept hoping Gina might appear. He was tempted to call her room but was halted by the simple fact that he had no idea what to do next. He missed her terribly. It felt as though she had already left. There was nothing he could do about it this time either.

When Adrian appeared in the dining room's doorway, Ethan could have hugged him for pushing away the fears. Adrian slipped into the chair next to his and asked, "How's the patient?"

"Good."

"For real?"

"I did a half hour of my physical therapy exercises in the ocean at dawn."

"Then I guess you'll live." He pointed to Ethan's empty plate. "What was that?"

"Spanish omelet and hash browns."

When the waiter walked up, Adrian said, "I'll have one of those. Skip the potatoes and bring me brown toast. And coffee." He turned to Ethan. "Where's Gina?"

"I have no idea."

Adrian waited until the waiter had filled his cup. He added milk, stirred, and sipped. "Must have been some spat, the way your face just turned upside down."

"There was no argument," Ethan replied. "I told her every-thing."

"When?"

"Soon as we got back."

"And?"

Ethan shook his head. "I tried to apologize. She left."

Adrian studied his brother over the rim of his mug. "Was that wise?"

"She suspected. She asked. Demanded, really. Sonya was right."

"Yeah, she often is." Adrian did not speak again until the waiter deposited his plate. He took a couple of bites, then said, "Sonya asked me to tell you she had a cardiologist take a close look at all the EKG tapes from the hospital. Consistency is everything, according to her and Madeline. They are fairly certain there's no long-term damage."

Ethan decided there was no reason to point out how the event might have shortened his remaining time. Especially coming as it did on top of his being shot.

Adrian asked, "You plan on sitting around here moping all day? I'm asking because I could use your help."

"Sonya's case?"

"No, sport. *Our* case. Either you come up with something I've missed or we're as well toasted as this bread." Adrian used his fork to point at the exit. "Go get dressed for downtown. We're due in court."

———

When he returned downstairs, Ethan left Gina a note with the receptionist, saying he was in court with Adrian and she was welcome to join them if she wished. As they drove away from the hotel, Ethan watched the ground-floor corner window. The drapes were closed.

Adrian glanced over and said, "At least she hasn't taken off for Orlando."

"You don't know that."

"Actually, I do."

"You asked the receptionist?"

Adrian jiggled his eyebrows. "We're a full-service operation."

Ethan felt his band of tension ease a notch. "I'm glad."

"I figured you would be. And you'd be afraid to ask. I sure would." Adrian shrugged. "You just told Gina you're back from a future where you two were divorced. Give the lady some space."

Ethan had no idea what to say, so he remained silent. When they turned onto the inland waterway bridge, he spotted a dark Chevy SUV staying close on their tail. "Is that Sinclair's security team dogging us?"

"None other. They're on us 24/7. It must be costing you a fortune."

"Money is not the crucial issue. Speaking of which, you and Sonya need to go by and sign the documents for our investment account."

"Your banker phoned me yesterday."

"That would be Reginald Firth."

"Reggie's been sent down from Boston. He figures joining the right clubs and showing up at the right lunches make him a local." Adrian turned into the courthouse garage and rolled his window down for the ticket. "Reggie complained you were blowing all your capital on some childish investments. That was the word he used. Childish. If somebody stole the man's vests, he'd collapse like a punctured balloon. I told him to do precisely what you said, else I'd sue his sorry hide all the way back to Yankeeville."

"Thanks for backing my play."

Adrian pulled into a parking space, put the car in park, and sat staring at the wall. "Sonya and I have to leave town this evening. We won't be back until Sunday afternoon. Her mom suffers from dementia, and we've got to move her into assisted living, which means making her our ward. We have a court-appointed specialist meeting us tomorrow. The papers are all drawn up. We move her Sunday. If we get back in time, Sonya wants you over for dinner. But we won't know for certain until Sunday morning."

"I'm a big boy," Ethan said. "I can take care of myself for the weekend."

"Still, I wish we could be here for you."

"You are," Ethan said. "And it means more than I could ever say."

Adrian cast him a dark look, then resumed staring out the front windshield at the concrete wall. "There's every chance the judge is going to throw out my case today. Which means on Monday Sonya will officially hand the new owners her resignation, even though it means leaving behind the work that has been the center point of her adult life. If you've got anything to offer, now's the time."

"I do have one thing. Actually, it's only part of a thing. More like a tiny, fractured—"

"Skip the windup, bro. We're due in chambers."

Ethan found it easier if he copied his brother's position. He stared at the grimy whitewashed cement and said, "It seems to me that everything we've been doing is reacting. They make a move, you respond. But if we're really down to the wire—"

"We are."

"Then what do we have to lose? Why not take the fight to them?"

"You mean change tactics."

"To tell the truth, I have no idea what that means. You're the lawyer. But yeah, changing tactics sounds good."

"That actually makes sense." Adrian still spoke to the wall. Tense. Alert. "The problem is, I can't find a motive for

214

why they're pushing us so hard. I've been over and over this. I can't see what it might be."

Ethan's middle-of-the-night impressions were no clearer now. Just the same, he said, "What if it's because you're looking at the one big issue, the elephant in the room? Sonya's pain research."

"Which holds potential," Adrian said. "I mean, we're talking hundreds of millions, but not for years. And if they move now, they lose her, and that slows them down. Maybe stops them cold. You see?"

"Yes, Adrian. But that's not . . ."

Adrian turned from examining the wall, his gaze one shade off frantic. "Let's hear it. Warts and all."

"What if the reason they're pressing *isn't* her primary research? What if she's stumbled onto something that might, just might, hold even bigger potential? At least as far as they're concerned."

"Such as?"

"Like shooting me back thirty-five years."

Adrian was shaking his head before the words were shaped. "She's already told you. That doesn't wash. She's been over and over her research, and there is no—repeat, no—indication this is even the slightest bit . . ." He stopped talking as Ethan lifted one hand and held it between them. "What?"

"Then a different issue. Something you and Sonya have discounted because, say, it didn't work." It was Ethan's turn to be halted. Adrian's gaze flashed in the murk, like a light had gone on inside his head. "What is it?"

"Go on. Finish the thought."

"What if their motive isn't Sonya's primary research at

all? What if something else they're doing gives them a totally different perspective? Say you were about to hit a button they can't afford for you to push. Maybe it's, I don't know, a sidebar. Something that doesn't mean anything regarding her core aims. But for somebody else it could be big." Ethan felt as if his brother's intensity formed the required cohesive force to pull his thoughts together. "Say they're hiding some ulterior motive for being interested in her company. Can you use the court to uncover it? Maybe ask the judge to help find out who is actually behind Cemitrex?"

Adrian froze a second time.

"No legitimate investment group is going to come after you with a guy they've sprung from prison. Two people with fake marshals' IDs spring a guy from prison and just vanish? Please. What if Cemitrex is just a smoke screen?"

"A front."

"Whatever. They're hiding the real buyers, who have totally different reasons for wanting Sonya's company. Could the judge go for that?" Ethan felt deflated by everything he couldn't offer. "I wish I had more. Sorry."

"No, no, this could actually do the trick."

"Really?"

"Hey, we're in a better position than ten minutes ago. If I could give Judge Durnin one legitimate reason, he would help us. I know it in my gut." Adrian opened his door. "Let's go ask him to help us slay some dragons."

THIRTY-FIVE

When they entered the courtroom, Adrian directed Ethan into the pew directly behind his table.

Jimmy Carstairs and two younger attorneys, one male and one female, were already seated at the opposing counsel's table. Their chairs were turned inward so they could cluster together in a tight huddle. The young man looked up when Adrian pushed through the swinging barrier. He smirked and whispered something to the others.

Adrian ignored them. As he opened his briefcase and pulled out a pair of bulky files, a young man in shirt and tie and no jacket emerged from the door beside the judge's bench and said, "Counsels are requested to join Judge Durnin in chambers."

Ethan was left alone in the empty courtroom. The minutes passed slowly. He didn't mind in the least. It reminded him of surf sessions in huge, clean waves. There was always that crazy interim stage between paddling out and taking off on the first set. Success on big days often depended on how this time was spent. Inexperienced surfers and those dominated by the fear factor struggled to get their breathing and hearts under control. They remained overwhelmed by the sheer uncontrollable power that surrounded them on every side. When standing on the shore, beginners often thought the major challenge was simply getting out. It was only now, as they sat in the narrow space between the approaching mountains and the impact zone, that they could realize the real trial was yet to come.

Experienced big-wave surfers used this time to prepare. The larger the swell, the more dynamic the currents. Winds and tides and rips and the number of waves to each set, the structure of the bottom and how the waves would break—all these elements could only be gauged from this narrow region of calm called the lineup. Reading the situation correctly was often the make-or-break issue—the difference between being pounded in the impact zone and having a great ride.

That was precisely how Ethan felt now. He sat on the hard wooden bench and studied the terrain. There was a great deal of satisfaction in how Adrian had reacted to his suggestion. The way it had resonated. How it had offered his brother a ray of hope. This was enough to confirm that Ethan was on the right path. Maybe.

He began tracking out, seeking the unseen danger elements in this final moment of calm. He was hard at it when Gary slipped into the pew beside him and asked, "Where is everybody?"

"The judge called them into chambers."

"When?"

Ethan turned around to read the clock over the rear doors. It said a quarter to eleven. The problem was, he had no idea when they had entered. It felt as though time had become a relatively unimportant factor. Far less vital than him being ready when the next step became visible.

He replied, "A while ago."

Gary seemed to find nothing wrong with that. "I stopped by the hotel. Gina was checking out. She said to tell you she had spoken with Sonya and was moving in with them."

Ethan could almost hear another small sliver of progress being fit into place. "That's great."

"For real?"

"Absolutely. She needs . . ." He had no idea how to explain the reasons for why this was such fantastic news. "Thanks for letting me know."

"No problem." Gary studied him. "I thought you'd be, well . . ."

"I'm not. This is the best for us both."

"Okay." He stretched out the word and extended his legs at the same time, getting comfortable. "Change the subject?"

"Sure."

Gary pointed at the empty bench on the other side of the aisle, directly behind the opposing counsel's table. "The lady you asked me to check out."

Ethan needed a moment to realize what Gary meant. Then he recalled the hatchet-faced blonde. It seemed like years ago. "What about her?"

"She's a former spook."

Ethan did not rise from the seat as much as spring into action. "What?"

Gary nodded, clearly pleased with the effect his news had. "Her name is Beryl Aldain. Ever heard of DARPA?"

"The name. Somewhere. But I don't . . ."

"I had to look it up myself. Stands for Defense Advanced Research Projects Agency. They develop emerging technologies, next-generation weapons, stuff like that."

Ethan breathed in and out, taking it in, trying to figure out what precisely it meant. "Where is she now?"

"Gone. Took all this while to find somebody who'd talk to me. As soon as that happened, I went by her hotel. She's checked out. A pal at the airport shows her as having left for DC."

Another breath. "When did she leave?"

"The million-dollar question." Gary smiled. "Ten minutes after my DC source gave me the goods."

"Whoa."

"The copy of her flight itinerary cost me a hundred bucks. You'll see that in my expenses."

"No problem." He leaned across the railing and took the yellow pad from Adrian's table. "Can I borrow a pen?"

THIRTY-SIX

Ethan had just finished writing his note and replacing the yellow pad on Adrian's table when the attorneys followed Judge Durnin back into the courtroom. The judge seemed to be in his late sixties, tall and solid with features of precisely carved obsidian. Durnin's gaze carried a burning intensity. Ethan had the impression that he could slice his way through any fog of confusion and subterfuge, no matter how dense.

Ethan's attention switched to his brother. Adrian wore the same grim expression he had carried into the judge's chambers. But there was something lurking beneath the surface now, something that had not been there before. Then Adrian winked. A swift little motion, there and gone in an instant. But enough to cause Ethan to shiver.

A uniformed deputy and the court reporter entered through a side door Ethan had not noticed until then. The officer was old and paunchy and possessed a face that had slipped downward like melting wax. He droned, "All rise."

Adrian reached his table and stood looking down at Ethan's

note as the judge seated himself. His only motion was a soft tapping of one finger on the yellow pad's corner. But something in the way he held himself caused Ethan to shiver a second time.

"Mr. Barrett, you may proceed."

"Thank you, Your Honor. One moment, please." He turned and gestured for Ethan to shift forward. Adrian gripped the rail with both hands and came in close. "This is real?"

"Gary says it's absolute."

"Where is he now?"

"He said there was another contact he needed to chase down."

The judge said, "We're waiting, Mr. Barrett."

"Thank you, Your Honor." Adrian recomposed his calm mask and straightened. "Your Honor, certain new information has just come to light."

Jimmy Carstairs said, "Really, Your Honor, there needs to be an end to counsel's delaying tactics."

The opposing counsel was a massive guy in his fifties. Carstairs had to be carrying a hundred pounds of excess weight. Even so, he moved with the smooth grace of the athlete he probably once had been. He wore an expensive three-piece suit and kept his remaining hair cut so short it lay on his head like frosting. He dwarfed his two junior lawyers.

"Five minutes, Your Honor," Adrian said. "Ten at the very most."

Carstairs snorted. "Where have I heard that before."

"Proceed, Mr. Barrett. But be aware, you are on a very tight leash."

"Thank you, Your Honor." Adrian moved to his right

and cleared the desk. There was nothing between him and the judge now but his own bench. "For just a moment, I ask that we return to a question posed at the beginning of these proceedings. Why now? Why would a Washington-based hedge fund decide to acquire a company with no discernable assets and no saleable product at this specific point in time?"

The other attorney remained standing. "Your Honor, I object. We are covering—"

Durnin lifted his gavel. "It's Mr. Barrett's hanging. I will grant him the necessary rope."

Adrian continued, "Dr. Sonya Barrett is involved in cutting-edge research. Somewhere down the line, she may come up with a genuinely new and world-changing product. But that is years away. Maybe decades. And yet this group is insisting on paying twenty-two million dollars for a company that has shown no return and at this moment has absolutely nothing to sell."

The judge kept his gavel raised, poised in anticipation of the other lawyer objecting. "Where are you going with this, Mr. Barrett?"

"I return to the question I posed in our first meeting, Your Honor. They know my wife will leave as soon as the acquisition takes place. She will set up another company and continue with her research. They cannot stop her. They've tried, and they've failed." Adrian turned and faced the massive lawyer. "They're hiding something."

"Your Honor, this is ridiculous," Carstairs said.

"I think it is in the court's interest to ferret out what they don't want us to know."

Carstairs rolled his words with the force of a professional actor. "My clients, Your Honor, claim the scientists have changed direction. Dr. Barrett and her team have thrown out the original intents of their agreement. She has completely altered course. The rule book we legally set in place has been trampled on."

"Give me one example of these supposed transgressions," Adrian said.

Carstairs continued to address the judge. "My clients feel they have no choice but to buy the company outright."

"Once again, Your Honor, the opposing counsel refuses to answer my question."

"Because your objections have no legal foundation," Carstairs snapped. "We are not legally required to grant you *any* reason. The contract clearly states we can acquire your client's property whenever we want, for whatever reason we deem valid!"

Adrian looked at the opposing counsel for the first time. "Who is this 'we'?"

Ethan saw something flicker in the other lawyer's gaze. There and gone in an instant, but he saw it. And he was certain Adrian did too.

"Different question, same answer, Your Honor." Carstairs settled his ample bulk against the table's edge. "My clients' identity beyond the corporate structure that initiated the investment is not in question."

"Ah, but it is," Adrian replied. "As we have already pointed out, Cemitrex's shares are held by two Bahamian corporations."

"Legal entities, with full rights to own American companies. Your Honor, we've been all through this. It's time—"

"But what are these Bahamian groups hiding?"

"Asked and answered. They have every legal right—"

"And exactly what role does an agent of DARPA play in all this?"

Ethan saw the lawyer wince. Like the man had been struck hard and tried not to show it.

Judge Durnin said, "I'm sorry, what?"

Adrian pointed to the empty place behind the opposing counsel's table. "For the first week of this case, Your Honor, my esteemed associate's every step was dogged by an agent of our defense department's most secret entity."

"Mr. Carstairs, is this true?"

"Your Honor, the employment records of every executive hired by my clients is hardly of concern."

"But I say it is of the highest possible concern," Adrian shot back. "I ask you again. Who are your clients?"

Carstairs turned red. "Cemitrex is controlled by two trust groups in the Bahamas. Under Bahamian law, all trustees are confidential. There are numerous legal precedents in Florida court upholding this confidentiality. For me to disclose their identities would be a serious breach of my duties."

"Confidentiality has already been breached. This employee was here, taking part in our case, for over a week." Adrian turned to the judge. "Your Honor, I formally request the right to interview one—"

"Your Honor, I object in the strongest possible terms!"

Adrian pretended to have difficulty locating her name. "Yes. Here it is. One Ms. Beryl Aldain, agent of DARPA."

"*Former* agent!"

Judge Durnin said, "Granted."

"Your Honor, this is *outrageous*," Carstairs said.

"Noted."

"I have no idea where this executive is or what duties called her away—"

"The moment my investigator uncovered her identity," Adrian said, "she vanished into thin air."

Durnin raised his gavel, halting Carstairs before he could object. "What precisely do you mean by that?"

"My firm has employed Gary Holt, a former detective with the city's force, to investigate elements related to this case. This morning he finally discovered Ms. Aldain's connection to the defense department's secret operations. That very same hour, Ms. Aldain boarded a plane for Washington."

Judge Durnin turned his attention to Carstairs. "I hereby order your client's employee—what was her name again?"

"Beryl Aldain, Your Honor," Adrian said.

"—to appear before this court and offer testimony under oath." Durnin checked his diary. "I have a hearing scheduled for first thing Monday morning. It shouldn't take more than two hours. Is ten thirty acceptable to both parties?"

Carstairs rubbed unsteady fingers across his forehead. "Unfortunately, I am due in Atlanta, Your Honor."

"This being Friday, you have all weekend to make adjustments. Mr. Barrett?"

Adrian said, "Works fine for me, Judge."

"Your Honor—"

"If need be, Mr. Carstairs, surely one of your associates can accompany your client's employee." He rapped his gavel. "Court is adjourned until ten thirty Monday morning."

THIRTY-SEVEN

As soon as they returned to Adrian's office, Ethan's brother was asked to field an urgent call. The receptionist waved Ethan over and passed him two messages. The first was from Gary. The investigator said his lead was taking longer than expected to develop, he was away, and he wouldn't be available until Monday morning.

The second was from Gina and basically repeated what Gary had already passed along. She had spoken with Sonya, had checked out of the hotel, and was staying at Adrian's for the weekend.

Ethan seated himself in the waiting room and found himself thinking back over the massive sweep of recent events. Starting with that first dawn, waking on the end of the pier, driving his brother's wretched Wagoneer to the beach, the contest, the win. So much had happened. A lifetime of changes. It was all so vivid, these new recollections, the events that had not happened before. He could still feel himself sweeping through that last magnificent ride, greeting

Hennie Bacchus there on the beach, laughing together over the incredible energy they shared . . .

The idea came to him then. As he rose from the sofa and crossed the waiting room, it felt better than good to ask the receptionist if he might use her phone.

He did not have the slip of paper Hennie Bacchus had handed him after the contest. But the agency Hennie had told him to use as a contact point was certainly easy enough to recall. He called information, got the number, and dialed.

"Champion Agency."

"Hi, uh, I was told I could reach Hennie Bacchus through you."

"Who is calling?"

"Ethan Barrett."

The receptionist on the other end brightened. "Oh yes. Mr. Barrett. Hennie asked us to contact him immediately when you called. Is there a number where he can reach you?"

Ethan gave the receptionist his hotel number. As he passed back the phone, Adrian rushed up. "You're still here. Great. You know about Gina?" He nodded when Ethan showed him the message. "Sonya insists we'll be done in time to host you for dinner on Sunday. In the meantime, who knows, maybe this is best."

"Like you said, at least she hasn't gone back to Orlando."

"Right." Adrian turned to the receptionist. "Sonya's due downstairs in five minutes. All fires are hereby put on hold until Monday."

———

Ethan joined the Friday afternoon crawl toward the beach. The trip from Adrian's office to the final bridge took over an hour. He swung three times through the hotel lot before he could find a vacant space. It was almost four when he finally reached his room. He stripped off his downtown clothes, took his time through two more sets of the PT exercises, showered, and was headed downstairs for an early dinner when the phone rang.

Hennie Bacchus greeted him with, "It was great hearing you'd called, mate. How're things?"

Ethan stood in the center of his hotel living room. A gentle breeze blew through the open balcony doors. Standing there with Gina's note in his pocket and her absence resonating at the level of bone and sinew and heart, he found himself surrounded by the unknown.

"Ethan? You there?"

He swallowed hard. "To tell the truth, I have no idea how things are."

"You want to talk about it?"

"I don't know if I can find the words. But I'd like to try."

"Listen up. My sponsors have me in Arizona for a photo shoot. I'm working till late tonight and I'm due on set again all day tomorrow. It's dry here, man. Dry. Six days I've been stuck out here in the desert, and I'm seriously into withdrawals."

"It also sounds like you're seriously busy. I don't want—"

"You just stop right there. I'm still thinking about what you told me out there in the lineup. This is payback, mate. Where and when can I reach you Sunday morning?"

They made arrangements to talk at nine, then Ethan headed down to the hotel restaurant. There was a distinct flatness to the atmosphere, as if Gina's absence had robbed his existence of some unique flavor.

Most of his lonely meal was spent reviewing his time with Adrian. He recalled each event with a singular clarity. Talking in the car while his brother's laser-tight gaze burned a hole in the concrete. Watching his brother stand before the judge, his every action designed for the audience of one. Each gesture, the modulation in his voice, the timing of his words—all intended for maximum impact.

Adrian was a frontline officer, Ethan saw now. It was something that had escaped him until that very moment. Adrian was the legal equivalent of a battle-hardened general. He could marshal his troops and attack the enemy with a brilliant eye to tactics.

As he climbed the hotel stairs, Ethan remembered something his brother had often said after their parents were gone. *"The Barrett brothers against the world."*

The pleasure of having a role to play in Adrian's future created a soft melody that carried him off to sleep.

———

Ethan slept well and was awoken by gulls complaining from the balcony railing. He decided to eat breakfast first, then go for a long beach walk and fit the PT exercises into his turnaround point. All that changed, however, when he arrived downstairs.

A television in the lobby and another in the bar were both tuned to the weather channel. The volume was not loud, but even so the screens drew every eye like magnets. Ethan entered the restaurant and waited until the receptionist turned away from a third screen above the buffet table.

She smiled apologetically. "Sorry to make you wait."

"No problem. What are they saying?"

She looked at him more closely. "You're a local, right?"

"Cocoa Beach, born and raised. You?"

"Been here my whole life." She shifted her reply to suit someone in the know. "It's just a cat 1. They're expecting it to strengthen, but you know how it is."

"I do indeed." Winds of a category 1 hurricane topped out at ninety-five miles per hour. Locals generally didn't break a sweat for less than a cat 3.

She said it anyway. "Eleven months of the year, when the weatherperson comes on, most people go see what they can find in the fridge. I mean, how much drama can you get from Florida weather?"

"Hurricane season is the weatherman's one chance to shine," Ethan said, following her across the room.

"Tell me about it. So reading between the hype, I'd say there's less than a fifty-fifty chance it will make landfall, and if it does, the eye will be somewhere above Savannah." She stopped by the doors leading to the veranda. "A table just opened up in the shade."

"I'll take it." He followed her outside. "You know your stuff."

"Hey, storms are like most guys I meet around here. They come, they make a lot of noise and maybe a little damage, they go." She filled his water glass and handed him a menu. "That's the price a girl pays for living in paradise."

Ethan was the only person in the hotel restaurant eating alone. He was surrounded by families and couples chattering and happy and thrilled to be sharing a beautiful morning in such a lovely setting, the storms of life all kept at a safe distance. Ethan minded being on his own, but not as much as he might have expected.

Gina's note was still in his pocket. As he ate he replayed the events and came back to the same decision as before. He had done what he was certain was the right thing. For her, not for himself. The knowledge offered a remarkable comfort.

He was heading down the hotel's front steps when the idea took hold.

From his position on the steps, he looked out over an utterly pristine sea. Days and sometimes weeks leading up to a big blow, all the bad weather was sucked up, like nature's massive vacuum cleaner went hoovering along the coast. There was not a breath of wind. Out to sea, the first of the storm's waves were marching in. Not huge surf, not yet. Chest to head high, perfectly formed. What was more, because the waves were breaking everywhere, no spot along the beach was crowded. Ethan watched a pair of ratty surf mobiles with South Carolina plates pull into spots just down from the hotel. It was like watching a circus clown act, all these young kids scrambling out, more and more of them gathering on the boardwalk and screaming at the sight on display.

Ethan had to smile at how he considered them kids. They were all his age, at least physically. So many days he'd done the same thing, poring over charts and marine forecasts, arguing with fierce abandon about where the waves might break best. Especially if the surf arrived on a weekend, like now. Back in the day before the internet made such decisions a cakewalk, these conversations could last all week. Just so he and his buddies could arrive here, at this very spot, and scream with joy over having gotten it right.

Ethan watched them unlatch their boards and go flying down the beach and thought, *Why not?*

The surf shop two blocks north of the hotel was doing a booming trade. Ethan purchased a new tri-fin, wax, leash, board shorts, and a Lycra T-shirt for protection against UV. He was checked out by a smiling young woman clearly operating on a commission. She treated Ethan as just another rich young tourist. She didn't say anything, but the knowing smirk said everything. Days like this, the waves were known as a ground swell, meaning they were generated far out to sea. This also meant there were long pauses between sets, making the paddle-out easy enough for beginners. These same beginners would make it outside, only to be greeted by waves they couldn't handle. If they were smart, they'd turn tail and take the first smallish wave back to shore. Most were not that smart.

He chose a spot where there were no other surfers. He took his time, pausing every couple dozen strokes, using the paddle-out as a slow warm-up, being very sensitive to how his shoulder felt. Ethan had never been shot before, but he had recovered from his share of injuries—landing wrong on a rocky shorebreak, being hammered by waves heavy enough to break his board, twice being hauled across coral atolls by sets that just would not stop pounding. He knew the routine.

There was a singular joy to arriving outside. He sat by himself and let the first set roll under him, utterly captivated by how good it felt. Ethan had the sense of a brand-new experience. Not so much that he had never done this before. Rather, that all of the previous sessions paled in significance. He knew it was probably due to how this could well be his last surf session. If not today, then tomorrow, or next weekend . . . He knew the finale was within reach. Even so, this awareness could not dim the wonder of being here.

The sun baked his neck and shoulders, and the ocean was an almost perfect temperature. Gulls sang, and distant surfers finished their rides by singing back. He wished there was time for everything.

Adrian had never much cared for surfing. He had done it as a young kid basically because everyone they knew surfed. But fishing was always his thing. Gina had gone out occasionally, but the big-wave locations always terrified her. It required a madcap passion to paddle into waves large enough to kill. Whenever she had flown to meet him, she always refused to even approach the beach on such days. Because she loved him.

Sitting there straddling the board, Ethan cupped his hands, filled them with water, and lifted the shimmering gift up to the sky. Wishing only joy to this woman who had cared for him so deeply. Wishing her a full life. Wishing her all the wonder of such days. For her and her alone.

Saturday afternoon Ethan lolled on the beach like a tourist, staying mostly under a rented umbrella. He watched the scene a little. Occasionally he followed a surfer carving a nice line. Now and then he missed Gina. He came up with a few more ideas about the coming week's legal events. But mostly he just drifted. It was only now, in the first free hours he had known since his transition, that he really had time to reflect on what he had left behind.

Death was no further away now than then, if Sonya's and Delia's calculations were correct. He had no reason to suspect otherwise. Even so, this day, this hour, was a gift beyond measure.

The next morning he woke up with a bit more discomfort in his shoulder. But his body's ability to heal itself with youth's swiftness continued to amaze him. He stretched and went downstairs for breakfast and was back in his room at ten minutes to nine.

Sitting there by the open balcony doors, waiting for Hennie's call, Ethan watched a trio of pelicans sweep past his window and found it strange that he had never felt an urge to follow Hennie's example. He had admired Hennie as a man and a surfer, how he had risen from awful beginnings to become one of the greats of a free South Africa. And yet . . .

He recalled walking the rutted streets of Hennie's township and marveling that such a leader in the surfing world could have come from such a place. He loved Hennie's style in the water, admired how no measure of fame had impacted the gentle and caring manner with which he met the world. And yet . . .

As he sat there, the terms Ethan had used to define his former existence echoed through his mind. Being his own man. Going his own way. Surfing the world and living on his terms. Just like Hennie, he had thought at the time.

How blind he had been.

When the phone rang, Ethan answered with, "Good morning, Hennie."

"How's your weekend been, mate?"

"Good. No, better than that. Mind if we jump straight in?"

"Fire away."

"I want to talk with you about things. But for you to understand, first I need to tell you what's happened to me."

"That's why I'm here."

"It's going to sound crazy."

"Mate, you don't know crazy like I know crazy."

"Prepare to be amazed."

The surfer huffed a laugh. "No offense, mate, but you'd have to know my homeland to understand just how crazy life can get. America's got some weirdness all her own, I'll give you that. But nothing like what I grew up with."

"I've visited your township," Ethan replied. "I understand what you're saying. And I'm telling you the absolute truth, you better be sitting down."

Hennie's voice grew skeptical. "You've been to Port Elizabeth?"

"I've been to Kwazakele," he replied, naming the highly dangerous Port Elizabeth township of Hennie's birth. "Twice."

"When was that?"

"The first time was . . . let's see. Twenty-five years ago. Sort of."

Hennie went silent. "How old did you say you were?"

"Twenty. Sort of."

Another long pause, then, "Okay. I'm sitting down. Let's hear it."

The telling became far more than simply recounting the events around the transition. Ethan continued straight into the contest, and from there to the courthouse shooting and then to the conversation with Gina, the MRI scan, the seizure, dreaming that he was out there in the lineup again, helping his brother, and realizing he had to make this call.

He finished with, "I'm doing my best not to count down the days I have left. I suppose what I'm feeling is just a holdover from before, back when the docs gave me a few bad weeks before checking out. But I think it's more than that.

I feel the end out there, just beyond reach. You know how you can sense a storm before it shows up?"

Hennie spoke for the first time since Ethan began his telling. "I know."

"It's like that. I can tell you without the slightest shred of doubt, the end is not far off."

The silence lasted quite a while after Ethan finished. He did not mind in the least. He sat by the balcony doors, feeling the rush of salt-laden air. The warm breeze anchored him to the here and now, however impossible that was. He sat and watched the gulls and the shimmering blue sea, and waited.

Finally Hennie said, "Okay, so here's what I want to tell you. I'm hearing a number of questions in what you've said. And I have just one answer to all of them."

Ethan nodded to the morning beyond his window. He liked how Hennie felt no need to doubt or act amazed. He felt as linked to the South African as he had that incredible day, standing on the beach with their arms around each other, reveling in the joy of having shared those waves. "I'm listening."

"First, nothing has changed." Hennie spoke now in a measured cadence. His tone had become more musical, as if speaking with Ethan about the transition had taken him more deeply into his African roots. "You are facing the same challenge you were before. The same challenge we all face. You know what that challenge is?"

"Not that I can put in words."

"The challenge is this, my brother. You must decide how you are going to face the day. Before the . . . what did you call it?"

"Transition."

"Before that happened, you lived only for yourself. You used those exact words, and it's beyond good that you have recognized this. A thin life, my people would call it. Now, since your transition, what are you doing?"

"Trying," Ethan said. "As hard as I know how."

"And that's the key here. Not that you *do* but that you *try*, and you give this everything you have. Which you are."

There was no reason why Hennie's words should make his eyes burn like they did, or blur his vision to where all Ethan saw was a sparkling pastel blue.

"The question I'm hearing you *not* say is, how do you *keep* trying? How do you know you're taking the right aim, following the right course?"

Ethan managed one word. "Yes."

"Straight up, mate, there's only one way I know how to do that. Because it's hard. So incredibly difficult. Life throws so much at us, all these reasons to change course. Tell me I'm wrong."

"You're not wrong."

"The answer, brother, is to aim for the eternal. Long as you do that, you're good to go. Even if you miss your target, even if you fall flat on your face, you know you've given it your best. You *know*. Because it's not for you. It's . . ."

Ethan breathed in and out, feeling a link to the man and the power of that lone word. "Eternal."

THIRTY-EIGHT

Later that morning Ethan returned to the water, surfing closer to his limits, pushing himself harder, testing his shoulder between each set. The waves were bigger now. They carried a muscled punch that was rare for Florida surf. There were far fewer surfers in the lineup. Getting out was tricky. The currents were rough. The wind was stronger as well, blowing from land out to sea. This offshore flow caused the waves to jack up tighter and fall faster, creating deep tubes, another rarity for Florida. The hurricane was on its way, the surf seemed to say. This was merely a foretaste of things to come.

When his shoulder began throbbing, Ethan rode the next wave to shore and returned to the hotel. He entered carrying his board and exchanged hellos with a number of the staff. One of the receptionists walked over, handed him a message, and asked about the waves. Ethan was becoming a sort of local now. The oddball kid who lived in a corner suite, who put up his girlfriend in the hotel's opposite corner, at least until she dumped him and checked out. Which was after her mother showed up and woke the hotel with their quarrel before joining the rich kid for breakfast. Oh, and all this was after the guy saved his brother from getting shot on the courthouse stairs. Sure, it had been in all the news . . .

Ethan climbed the central staircase, thinking they had every reason to give him the eye.

The message was from Adrian, confirming they were on their way home and telling him to come over for an early dinner. Ethan showered and stretched and ate a room-service sandwich. Then he lay down with the balcony doors open. He bunched up pillows so he had a prone view of the beach and the surfers and the sunlit sea. He found himself thinking about Hennie's words and how they fit around everything that had happened since his transition. As he dozed off, he imagined touching Gina's cheek, framing her love-filled gaze with his hand, speaking to her that one potent word. *Eternal*.

———

Ethan pulled into his brother's drive an hour or so before sunset. The front door was partly open to the heat. As he rose from the car, Ethan heard a deep bass rumble of thunder. The sky overhead was a porcelain blue, just slightly veiled with very high clouds. The offshore wind had continued all day, sucking up all the humidity, turning the afternoon bone dry. The thunder growled a second time as Ethan climbed the front steps, as if nature mocked the day's pleasant tone.

As he started to knock, Adrian pulled the door farther open, drew his brother inside, and put a finger to his lips. A briefcase rested on the side table. Adrian wore an ironed Izod shirt and pleated cotton dress trousers and tasseled loafers. Ethan stepped in beside his brother and heard the two women talking just out of sight.

Gina said, "How am I supposed to accept what he's told me?"

Sonya replied, "It's very difficult, I agree."

"It's impossible!"

Adrian smiled at his brother as Sonya asked, "Are you saying you don't believe him?"

"I don't know what to believe!"

"Hard as it is for me to take this step, I for one have found every conceivable reason to accept Ethan is telling some version of the truth."

"What do you mean, 'version'?"

Ethan heard a soft hammering and assumed one of the women was using a knife and a chopping block. Sonya said, "It's a term from my research. When we work with human subjects, we must accept that their responses are not always in line with their experiences."

Gina remained on the verge of anger. "I have no idea what you're talking about."

"We can control a subject's experience. That is what establishing protocols are all about. What we can't control is how the subject *views* the experience or what their *reaction* might be. Sometimes the way they emotionally respond to our experiment completely skews what they perceive. So right now, all we can say for certain is, Ethan has experienced something remarkable."

"That's not good enough!"

"No. If I were in your position, I would probably feel exactly the same way." Sonya continued speaking in a calm, almost detached manner. The scientist doing her best to hold to the facts. "Which is a case in point. What you *perceive* about Ethan's sharing his experience is colored by how it impacts you. How it makes you feel."

Gina remained silent.

"Ethan has told us his version of the truth. And our natural reaction is to reject what he is telling us as impossible."

"Exactly!"

A pot rattled. The water turned on. "I started studying the human brain as an undergraduate. That was seventeen years ago. And all I can say for certain is, I know so very little about what makes us who we are. We use terms like consciousness with such ease. But what is it really? Do you know that for over a thousand years, the most learned authorities insisted that human consciousness was housed in the stomach? Another thousand, the heart! Thanks to all the new technologies that I and other researchers can call on, we can now actually watch thoughts take form in the brain. We have finally begun to map the physical process of a mental response taking form. But what does it mean? Is that all there is to the concept of an individual human being and their individual reality?"

"You're not helping."

"What do you want me to say?"

"That I'm right to leave."

The water turned off. A pot was set down on a metallic surface. Sonya took her time responding, and when she did, her voice had gone flat. Toneless. "Of course you must do as you see fit."

"My mother would say it's time to go. Past time!"

"Your mother is not here. Nor is she in love with Ethan."

"A man who is dying."

"And now we come to the true crux of the matter. Remember what I said before. You *perceive* what Ethan told you through the sorrow you were already feeling. Very recently his heart went into atrial fibrillation, and it frightened you terribly. We were all terrified that we might have lost him. And when he returned, when you could be there with him again, you were faced with the fact that sooner rather than later, we are going to lose him for good." Sonya's voice cracked slightly. She paused, then went on in a calmer voice, "And it's at that point, your weakest and most vulnerable moment, that he tells you of this impossible journey his consciousness has taken."

"You're breaking my heart."

"All of this is so very hard. Do you know I detested Ethan? Before, I mean. I hated being around him. And now it breaks my heart as well to think that someday very soon . . ."

Adrian's calm demeanor melted. He gripped Ethan's arm and silently drew him back out on the front step.

Ethan was left both uncomfortable and helpless by the emotions he saw playing over his brother's face. Adrian eventually cleared his eyes and said, "You hear the latest report?"

"About what?"

"I take that as a no." He wiped his face a second time. "The storm has changed course. It's headed straight this way." When Ethan did not respond, Adrian pushed open the front door and called with false cheeriness, "Look who I found lurking outside!"

As Ethan entered the kitchen, Gina slipped out the rear doors and stood by the pool, staring at the night, her arms wrapped tightly around her middle.

"Give her time," Sonya said.

Ethan said, "I should go."

Adrian glanced out the rear doors and nodded once. "Might be wise."

Sonya offered, "You could sleep upstairs in Adrian's office. I'll even bring your meal up on a tray."

Truth be told, Ethan would much rather have stayed. All the reasons he once had for maintaining his distance were fading. The surge of events was pressing down, revealing one vulnerability after another. The love he saw in their faces, the concern, drew him ever more tightly into the fold.

Even so, he said, "Gina left the hotel to put distance between herself and me. I need to respect that until she says otherwise."

Sonya pursed her lips and breathed out. A long release of all the arguments she would not use. She set down her cooking spoon and wiped her hands on a kitchen towel. She walked around the central counter, opened her arms, and embraced Ethan tightly. Then husband and wife walked him out into the night.

THIRTY-NINE

Monday morning, Ethan was awoken around five by great claps of thunder. The lightning flashed so close it illuminated the boundaries of his curtains like they were on fire. He lay and listened to the lashing rain. A bigger storm was out there, just beyond the horizon. He could feel it.

He dozed on and off for another hour, then rose and slipped into swim shorts and walked down to the ocean. The passing storm had not eased the heat or humidity, which were already intense at daybreak.

Ethan had come to love this season as a child. Mid-September to mid-October was the height of Florida's hurricane season. His father used to say it was the tropics' way of arguing with the changing weather tides. That was how he put it—tides in the atmosphere, just as they were in the sea. His father used to make up stories for his younger son, where the summer tide fought a long battle with the autumn tide. The summer tide always thought he was strong enough to keep the autumn tide from taking his place. But the autumn tide was wise in the way of an experienced woman, his father said. She let the summer rage and struggle and vent his fury. And in the end, she won. She always won.

———

Adrian phoned just as Ethan emerged from the shower. "You hear from Gary?"

"Not a word. You?"

"He phoned the house yesterday, said he was onto something solid. Couldn't or wouldn't discuss it on the phone. The line was awful. I'm thinking he might have been down in the islands."

Ethan pondered that for a moment. "What does that mean?"

"Hard to say. I'm hoping he might have a lead on the missing Defense lady." Adrian's voice was courtroom tight. The words carried a clipped quality, like each was carefully measured before being allowed to emerge. "You coming to court?"

"Leaving in ten minutes." Ethan hesitated, then asked, "How is Gina?"

"She's good. No, better than that. I have to tell you, bro. Having her around here has been a really good thing. Sonya's been on a tear ever since I asked her to take the stand. I don't know what I would've done if Gina hadn't been here. Taken a room in your hotel, most likely."

"Sonya is going to testify?"

"It came to me on the drive back. All the fragments are beginning to knit together, thanks to you."

"I thought you were going to grill Beryl Aldain."

"Not a chance. I'd give you hundred-to-one odds that lady never shows."

"But why—"

"Pressure, kid. It's all about screwing the lid down tight, then bringing Jimmy Carstairs to a boil. I'm still banking on the fact that Judge Durnin is on our side and as curious as I am over what the Cemitrex folks are up to."

"So asking about the DARPA lady . . ."

"It's a means to force Cemitrex to tell us what's going on. My guess is, Cemitrex is serving as a front for the Defense research group. But that still doesn't explain why they're so hot to take over Sonya's company." Sonya's voice called from somewhere distant. "We're leaving now. See you in court."

The three opposing counsel were already clustered behind the left-hand table when Ethan walked in. Adrian was seated across from them, making furious notes as Gary leaned over the wooden barrier and spoke softly.

Gina and Sonya were in the right-hand pew, one row up from the entrance. Sonya watched Adrian and Gary with a gaze that reminded Ethan of a frightened deer. Eyes wide, skin taut, motionless. Gina held one of Sonya's hands with both of hers.

Ethan remained standing in the aisle, watching the two women. Finally Gina glanced over. She gave him a long look with those amazing eyes of hers, all the fire and passion on dark display. Finally she mouthed, *Join us.*

He breathed a silent sigh of relief and seated himself. "What's going on?"

"Gary just showed up. That's all I know."

He kept his voice in the faintest of whispers, just breathing the words, "Sonya, you okay?"

"I hate speaking in public." Sonya turned his way, showing him a near-panic expression. "No. Hate isn't strong enough. What's a more powerful term?"

"You'll do fine," Gina said.

"There should be another word with an exponential force, hate multiplied by a factor of millions." Sonya glared at her husband's back. "I can't believe I let him talk me into this."

The grip Sonya had on Gina's fingers turned them bloodless. If she minded, Gina gave no sign. "You heard what Adrian said. All you need to do is focus on him and talk about your research. It'll be over before you know it."

Sonya rocked back and forth, tight little motions.

"You're doing this for him," Gina said. "And for your company's future. And for your years of research. Focus on that."

Sonya gave no sign she even heard, but gradually she stilled. It seemed to Ethan that she might have breathed a little easier.

Then the front door opened, the judge walked in, and the uniformed officer said, "All rise."

FORTY

Once the judge was seated, Jimmy Carstairs remained on his feet behind the table. To his left, the two minions sat up straight, on full alert. Ethan had yet to hear either one speak a single word. Carstairs stood around six foot five, his barrel gut wrapped in a finely tailored pin-striped suit. But the arrogant demeanor was gone today, or so it seemed to Ethan. Prick the guy with a needle and he'd flutter around the ceiling until all his hot air escaped.

The judge was apparently in no hurry to begin. He ruffled the pages of his diary, searched his desk for something, then motioned for the court reporter to come over. They had a quick discussion, the reporter resumed her seat, and finally Judge Durnin looked up. "Nice to see you managed to join us, Mr. Carstairs."

"This case is of paramount importance, Your Honor. I had no choice in the matter, even though it inconvenienced my firm quite considerably."

"Did it. How tragic." Judge Durnin searched the room.

"And yet I fail to see the witness the court instructed you to produce. What was her name again?"

Adrian spoke for the first time. "Beryl Aldain, Your Honor."

Only then did Ethan realize that Carstairs had been continually clearing his throat. It was a small sound, a single cough, easy to overlook. He did it again. "Your Honor, I regret to inform the court that this particular employee has resigned from her position."

Judge Durnin folded his hands on his desk. "Has she now."

"Indeed so, Your Honor." Another cough, so quick it seemed to Ethan that it happened against the lawyer's will. "Ms. Aldain has a contractual right to terminate her employment at any time. I know because I personally reviewed the relevant documents."

"Oh, I'm sure you have." The judge turned to Adrian. "Mr. Barrett, do you have any response to this news?"

"Two points, if it pleases the court. First, I formally request that Cemitrex identify a different executive, and that you require this individual to appear before the court so that he or she might be deposed."

Carstairs began, "Your Honor, that is utterly without precedent—"

"Hold that thought, Mr. Carstairs. Go on, Mr. Barrett. Your second point?"

"I ask that Dr. Sonya Barrett be permitted to testify."

"Is that her I see at the back of the courthouse?"

"Indeed so, Your Honor. Although her research has reached a crucial stage, she has joined us today so as to shed light on what we now think might actually be behind this attempted acquisition."

"There is no *attempt*," Carstairs sputtered. "My client has every right—"

"Mr. Carstairs, interrupt these proceedings one more time and I will hold you in contempt." Durnin gestured with the hand not holding the gavel. "Mr. Barrett, I will withhold decision on your first request until after your witness has testified. You may proceed."

Ethan rose from the pew and stepped into the aisle. Sonya released Gina's hands and rose to her feet. She walked forward, then froze where Adrian stood holding the wooden gate open for her. For an instant, Ethan feared she had locked in panic. Then he realized she was staring at the opposing lawyers. He settled into the seat next to Gina and watched Sonya's features tighten with rage and loathing until her face went as bloodless as Gina's fingers.

Adrian touched her elbow and eased her forward. Sonya allowed herself to be guided into the witness stand. All the while, though, she continued to visually blast Carstairs and his minions.

As she was sworn in, Adrian moved back behind his table. He asked her to state her name for the record. He then led her through a brief summary of her professional background. Gradually she released her molten grip on the lawyers and focused on her husband.

Adrian held to a quiet, conversational tone as he asked, "What are you and your company currently working on?"

"The same premise I've been involved in since graduate school. Defining and mapping electromagnetic elements of human mental activities."

Adrian widened his eyes in mock surprise. "But the

attorneys representing Cemitrex accuse you of moving away from your contracted direction."

"That's absurd."

"What makes you say that?"

"They receive regular status updates. We have monthly conference calls. They have also hired an outside micro-biologist who spends a week with us twice each year. Their scientist is granted full access to all our records. They know perfectly well my research hasn't varied one iota."

"What precisely did Cemitrex ask you to produce?"

"Study and *hopefully* produce," Sonya corrected. "My early research pinpointed three regions of the brain associated with chronic pain."

"And these are?"

"We've known for some time that the spinal cord carries pain messages from the body's receptors to the thalamus and the cerebral cortex, where the message is processed. My team and I have discovered that there is a gradual reorganization of the brain's circuitry, specifically within the dorsal root ganglia, caused by long-term pain."

Adrian leaned over his desk and wrote something on his legal pad. "And the aim of your research is . . ."

"We have determined that repetitive signals, which we have now mapped, can alter the brain's function. We seek to in-fluence these same regions in a positive manner through the noninvasive application of various electrical and magnetic impulses, and in time, bring the chronic pain under control."

Adrian made another note. "That is the vital term in re-gard to your research, is it not? Control."

"Correct." Sonya was gradually shifting away from the courtroom and the opposing counsel and everything that was staked on her testimony. It was just her and Adrian now, focusing on her life's work. The two of them in tune. "Pharmaceutical products seek the eradication of pain. But regular intake of these medications results in severe side effects. Lethargy, mental fatigue, liver and heart failure, addiction."

"And with your product?"

"There is no *product*. We are years from bringing a product online."

He nodded slowly. "With your concept, then."

"There are no side effects."

"None?"

"Zero." She gripped the front barrier and leaned forward. "Our studies reveal that chronic pain carries three distinct elements for the sufferer. One is obviously the pain itself. Equally important are two other factors that are often overlooked."

"And they are?"

"Fear of the pain's return and loss of control over so much of the patient's life."

Adrian shifted his pad from his table to the podium stationed next to it, placing more distance between himself and Carstairs's team. "Control."

"It all comes down to this: granting the patient a risk-free means of bringing their pain under control."

"How exactly does this happen?"

"First we map the patient's brain-wave patterns. This is where our research veers away from all others in the field. We see each patient as possessing a unique pattern. Two patterns, actually. One when they are free of pain, the other when they suffer an attack. We then design an electromagnetic frequency that stimulates the brain's return to pre-attack status."

"You zap the brain."

Sonya did not smile, but she did rearrange her features for just an instant. "Correct. Using a combination of MRI and electronic impulses, we zap the brain. When we do this enough, the patient's brain reverts to its pre-pain structure. This happens at precisely the same moment their fear dissolves. We are certain the two issues are connected. How, we have not yet determined. But we will."

Adrian studied his notes, his face creased in supposed confusion. "I don't understand, Dr. Barrett. It sounds to me like your product is close to being ready."

"It's not."

"And Cemitrex could be excused for thinking that you are overplaying the research scientist role, holding back on giving them what they contracted—"

"That is ridiculous. It shows how little attention they've given to everything we've been doing." Sonya's entire stance underwent a drastic shift. Adrian's words drew her attention back to the trio seated at the other table. Her voice took on the tight edge of barely controlled fury. Or terror. Or both. "It takes us between four and seven months to map the individual sufferer's wave patterns and determine the required frequency response. We recently calculated that it is costing us three hundred thousand dollars per patient to prepare their treatment."

Adrian followed her unblinking glare to Carstairs. A quick glance, as if wanting to reveal a trace of his own rage. "Three hundred thousand dollars."

"And that's not all. Currently the only way we can apply the required frequencies is to have the patient return to our lab *during each attack*. The necessary equipment is twice the size of this courtroom."

"So in order to bring your product to market . . ."

"We must resolve two problems. No, three. First, we have to design an automated method of mapping the individual patient's brain and calculating the necessary electromagnetic response. Second, we must shrink the required machinery down to something that could fit inside a doctor's office. Or even better, be available directly to the patient. I would love to see this become something a sufferer might wear on their belt or carry in their purse. And third, we have to raise our success rate. Right now we are only able to help about half our patients."

"What is the success rate of pain medications?"

"Better than that, but not by much. Six in ten. Seventy percent with the new migraine-specific medications. But again, with huge potential risks to some patients."

Adrian's pen scratched loudly in the otherwise silent courtroom. Judge Durnin had planted an elbow on his desk and held his face in his hand. His gaze swiveled back and forth between Adrian and Sonya, and he appeared utterly captivated. Jimmy Carstairs was so still he might as well have stopped breathing.

Adrian let the silence drag out a bit longer, then said, "Has your research turned up anything unexpected, Dr. Barrett? Some angle or new direction that has caught you by—"

Carstairs sprang to his feet, a jack-in-the-box wearing a three-piece suit. "Your Honor, we request an immediate recess!"

FORTY-ONE

It appeared to Ethan that the judge was reluctant to focus on anyone else. He came around very slowly, blinked, and said, "Denied."

As he turned back, Carstairs said, "Your Honor, I am faced with a matter of the utmost urgency!"

Durnin leaned back in his seat. "Remind me whose courtroom this is, Mr. Carstairs."

"Yours, sir. But—"

"Oh, good. I was concerned you might have forgotten."

Carstairs waved his phone. "Your Honor, I *must* respond to this entreaty. It has to do with the matter in Atlanta."

The judge asked Adrian, "How much longer do you require to complete this witness's testimony, Mr. Barrett?"

"Some time, Your Honor. I believe Dr. Barrett will provide us with evidence that her company was duped." Adrian pointed at the empty bench behind Carstairs. "The woman who would rather quit than testify under oath constitutes an illegal omission of facts pursuant to who my client was—"

"Your Honor, *please*."

Durnin did not even glance over. "You were saying, Mr. Barrett?"

"I suggest we are looking at a serious case of fraud, Your Honor. I will seek the court's approval to rescind the original deal."

"In other words, we may be here for some time." He glanced at his watch. "Very well. Court is adjourned for an early lunch. We will resume Dr. Barrett's testimony in one hour. And, Mr. Carstairs?"

"Yes, Your Honor."

"Be on time."

———

Ethan watched as Sonya rose from the witness stand. When Adrian stepped over to help her, she said, "I'm okay now."

"You sure?"

"Yes. Thank you, Adrian."

"I'm the one who is grateful. You were excellent up there."

"Thank you." Sonya offered a weak smile as she passed Gina and Ethan. "Thank you all."

Adrian held open the rear door. "Shouldn't take much longer."

Gina asked, "What you told the judge, does that mean we might win?"

"I wanted to place my stated aim in the court's record. For the moment, that's all I can say for certain." Adrian motioned for Gary to join them. As they left the courtroom, he said, "We might be able to formally request a buyback. But only if we can first prove criminal negligence."

Sonya stared down the empty corridor. "But a buyback would mean we'd have to come up with the money, correct?"

"Their original investment of seven million dollars," Adrian confirmed. "Plus interest."

Ethan offered, "I might be able to help with that."

"First things first." Adrian kept his hand lightly resting on Sonya's shoulder. "For now, we need to focus on getting those animals off our backs."

"So . . . I have to testify again."

Adrian patted her shoulder. "Sweetheart, I wish you could have seen yourself up there."

"I forgot where I was for a while. Then it all snapped back into focus, and I was terrified all over again."

"You were a pro." Adrian turned to Gina. "All right if you take over from here and the two of you go grab a bite somewhere?"

"If you think that's best." She stepped up beside Sonya.

"Gary and I need to put our heads together," Adrian went on. "I need to see how his new intel might fit into the dance. And I want Ethan with us in case he comes up with another idea."

"Part of one, anyway," Ethan corrected.

Sonya asked, "Why can't we hear?"

"Because if his new information is good—"

"It's better than good," Gary said. He imitated Tony the Tiger. "It's grrreat."

"—it may help if you hear it first on the stand. Your reaction can influence the judge's." When Sonya did not object further, Adrian asked Gary, "You mind buying the three of us drinks and sandwiches from the diner?"

"No problem."

"We'll grab my car and meet you out front." He was already heading for the stairs. "Fast as you can."

───────

Adrian pulled into Lavern Street and parked where they could look out over the park and the sparkling Saint Johns River. Gary handed out sandwiches and Cokes.

Adrian unwrapped his sandwich and took a bite. "First, tell us where you vanished off to."

"Bahamas." To Ethan, "You'll be seeing that on my expense report."

The meat and relish fragrances defied the air conditioner's wash. "That's what the money is for."

"Hold it right there," Adrian said. "Did your trip involve offering bribes?"

When Gary hesitated, Adrian shook his head. "No, no, as an officer of the legal system I can't be party to that."

Gary looked to Ethan. "So . . ."

Ethan suggested, "You tell me in strictest confidence. All I tell Adrian is what we've learned. Not how we got here."

Adrian took a thoughtful bite, then opened his door and stepped into the sunlight.

Ethan said, "Go ahead."

Gary watched Adrian. "Beryl Aldain."

"The lady spook."

"She's more than that. She's an officer of the Bahamian trust group."

Ethan knocked on his window. When Adrian glanced over, he gestured and shouted, "Get in."

───────

"We can't use this," Adrian said.

"It's solid intel," Gary protested.

"I don't disagree. But I'm telling you we can't reveal that we know this. Not in court."

Ethan said, "Explain why in terms we might understand."

"Opposing counsel will demand to know how we learned this, which would require Gary to be sworn in as witness. Either Gary perjures himself, which I can't allow, or he tells them how he bribed an island attorney—"

"Secretary."

"I didn't hear that. He paid money for confidential information. Which, just so we're clear, is deemed classified by both governments. The US Congress is going to change the relevant code, and soon. But for the moment, the law is against us. Officers of a Bahamian trust may legally remain invisible." Adrian sipped from his drink. "If I divulge this knowledge, Jimmy Carstairs will shout his objection, and Durnin will have no choice but to throw our case out of court."

Gary bundled up his trash. "Sorry."

"No, no, don't misunderstand me. What Ethan has told me in strictest confidence is crucial information."

"Just not in court," Ethan said.

"The question is," Adrian asked, "how can we legally bring this information to light and place it in the court record?"

Gary said, "So, you're saying I did good?"

"I have no idea what you're talking about." Adrian started the car. "But what Ethan told me is absolutely explosive. An officer of Cemitrex and board member of the Bahamian parent-trust would rather resign than give testimony. Why? To my mind it suggests that Beryl Aldain has remained viscerally connected to Cemitrex. Perhaps she's also a full-time employee of the nation's most secretive military lab. Which means . . ."

When Adrian went silent, Ethan pressed, "It means what?"

His brother turned off the motor and just sat there, staring blindly at the sunlit river.

"Earth to Adrian."

"Something you said back in the garage."

"About going on the attack?"

Adrian bobbed his head from side to side. "That other thing. About looking at their acquisition from the standpoint of a totally different motive."

"And?"

"Something Sonya told me—it must have been a year ago or longer. They started killing their test subjects."

Gary's head jerked around. "You mean, they murdered patients and didn't let on?"

Adrian's gaze sharpened. "Of course not, you dodo. What do you take my wife for?"

"As of twenty seconds ago, I have no idea."

"They were lab animals, you idiot. And she didn't murder them. They died."

Ethan asked, "From what?"

Adrian restarted the car and backed from the space. "That's exactly what I need to ask Sonya." He accelerated into traffic. "Jimmy Carstairs is about to have himself a very bad day."

CHAPTER
FORTY-TWO

When the judge seated himself, his first words were, "Mr. Barrett, you may proceed."

Jimmy Carstairs remained standing. "If it please the court."

"What is it now, sir?"

"Your Honor, I respectfully request an adjournment until tomorrow."

Durnin took a two-fisted grip on the gavel. "And why, pray tell, would I consider giving up a perfectly fine afternoon session?"

Carstairs began clearing his throat again. Only now it was between every second or third word, as if the act of speaking at all had become a terrible strain. "Your Honor, I have been instructed by my clients that a matter of utmost urgency has arisen."

"Have you."

"Yes, Your Honor. They assure me all the required information in regard to opposing counsel's queries will be supplied tomorrow. Next week at the very latest."

"Is that so." The judge turned to Adrian. "What do you have to say to that, Mr. Barrett?"

"This only confirms my worst suspicions, Your Honor."

"Explain."

"Given what has come to light, I suspect Cemitrex's Washington lawyers are scrambling to block this inquiry from uncovering their dark and dirty secrets."

"Your Honor, I protest in the strongest possible terms." Yet even now there was an absence of real force, as if Jimmy Carstairs had become an actor already removed from the stage. "That is the most ridiculous thing I have ever heard."

"All right, enough." Judge Durnin's voice had grown placid. "Mr. Carstairs, your motion is denied. Mr. Barrett, you may recall your witness to the stand."

———

"We were speaking," Adrian began, "of control. And what this means to your patients."

Sonya appeared considerably calmer. She had made it to the witness stand on her own, and now she sat with her hands together in her lap, her gaze locked on Adrian. Alert. Ready. "As I said, when we offer the patient a risk-free method of alleviating their pain from at least half of the attacks, fear becomes less of a burden. It stops triggering *more* attacks."

Adrian stood behind his table, keeping the carpeted distance between himself and the three people at the front of the chamber—Judge Durnin, the court reporter, and Sonya. "What happens when the frequencies don't work?"

"They use the prescription drugs, of course. But these attacks happen less frequently, remember. Which means the risk of damaging side effects—"

Carstairs lumbered to his feet. "Your Honor, we have gone over and over this."

"Not in this form, Your Honor." Adrian studied the other attorney, as if confused by his opponent's lack of heat. "Not with the facts I am about to uncover."

"Overruled. Proceed."

Adrian returned his attention to Sonya. "The alleviation of chronic pain was not your only direction of research. Was it?"

Sonya's nervousness returned. "Of course it was."

Adrian went not just silent but utterly still. Ethan had the brief sensation that his brother had become poised at the edge of a cliff, gathering himself, readying for the dive.

"But there was a second direction you took," Adrian said.

"Briefly. It was a mistake. A terrible one." Each word added to Sonya's tension. "Why on earth do you want to talk about my failures?"

Judge Durnin's voice had gone as soft as Adrian's. "Witness will restrict herself to answering counsel's questions."

Adrian said, "What else did your lab seek to develop?"

"*Develop* is the wrong word. We tried to apply our research to a second chronic condition. Briefly. We failed."

"When was this?"

"We finally gave up hope five and a half months ago."

"That timing is crucial, don't you agree?"

Carstairs did not rise. "Your Honor, please."

"If you wish to make an objection, Mr. Carstairs, you may do so."

"Leading the witness. Asking for her to infer a conclusion."

Durnin gave him another tight inspection but merely replied, "Sustained."

Adrian asked, "When did Cemitrex announce their intention to acquire your company?"

"Five and a half . . ." Sonya released a tight breath.

"Yes? When precisely did they inform you of their intentions?"

"Five and a half months ago." Her voice had gone very soft.

"We'll come back to the timing in just a moment. First I ask you to explain to the court what you were studying." When Sonya did not respond, Adrian picked up his notebook and slowly shifted to the podium, drawing silent emphasis to what came next. "Explain to the court about this second application."

"Failed application," she softly corrected. "We sought to apply frequency modulation of brain-wave activity to epileptic seizures."

"Can you give us a bit more detailed information?" Adrian gave an actor's smile. "In terms we might hopefully be able to follow."

"Epilepsy is a condition in which repeated bursts of electrical activity in the brain cause bodily seizures." Sonya did not return his smile. Her gaze was hollowed by memories. Her voice was a mere shadow of the determined researcher Ethan had known before. "Some of the main causes of epilepsy include low oxygen during birth, head injuries, brain tumors, certain genetic disorders such as tuberous sclerosis, and brain infections like meningitis or encephalitis."

"But you did not succeed, is that correct?"

"That is too mild a term. We failed spectacularly. In some cases, we actually made the seizures worse."

"And in others?"

"We stopped the subjects' hearts."

"You killed your subjects?"

"Stone dead."

"We're not talking about human patients, mind you."

"No. This was one reason why we chose to at least try to help epileptic sufferers. Seizures can readily be induced in laboratory conditions, either through electrodes or by creating a chemical imbalance in the brain."

Adrian wrote in his notebook. He turned the page and continued writing.

Finally the judge demanded, "Are you through with this witness, Mr. Barrett?"

"Not quite, Your Honor."

"Then stop wasting the court's time and get on with it."

"Thank you, Your Honor." Adrian lifted his notepad from the podium. "Permission to approach the witness."

"Granted."

He lifted his podium, crossed the carpeted expanse, and planted himself directly in front of the judge's dais. "Can you tell us why your experiments failed here, yet you were able to help sufferers of chronic pain?"

"We *think* we know." It was just the two of them again, resuming a conversation they must have had a hundred times before. One that caused Sonya very real distress. "Chronic pain and epileptic seizures have several factors in common. Most importantly, they both impact a number of different areas of the brain simultaneously. But with seizures in adults, the key area appears to be the mesial part of the temporal lobe. This lies directly adjacent to the midbrain, the pons, and the medulla oblongata."

"And this is important because . . ."

"Those three regions control all the body's unconscious functions. Namely respiration, digestion, and the heart."

"So when you identified the correct frequency for that particular lab subject and applied it to the patient's brain . . ."

"In seventy-six percent of the patients, we completely halted all core bodily functions. Heart and breathing stopped instantaneously."

"But that is not all that happened . . ." Adrian stopped as Carstairs rose to his feet.

"Yes, Mr. Carstairs?"

"Once again, Your Honor, I must respectfully request an adjournment."

"Asked and answered."

"Your Honor, the situation surrounding this case has now changed." Carstairs had an oily sheen to his features. His forehead had become a fractured mirror for the overhead lights. "My clients have instructed me that certain lines may not be crossed. I am required to inform the court that this case has now entered restricted territory."

Ethan noticed then that his brother was not watching Carstairs. Instead, Adrian rested his right hand on the railing that surrounded the witness box and focused fully on his wife. Sonya started to reach for him, her features creased with a deep pain and something more. A realization, a new level of understanding. They both looked so very sad. Resigned. As if their worst fears had just been realized. Sonya did not quite touch her husband's hand. But Ethan had the distinct impression that the bond was complete just the same.

The silent communication was not lost on the judge. Durnin's gaze shifted from Carstairs to Adrian to Sonya. "Restricted in what way?"

"May the record show that I have formally requested an adjournment, Your Honor." Carstairs wiped his face as he bent over his table and lifted what Ethan could see was a handwritten sheet. "You will be notified by a senior official in the Department of Justice that the case must be shifted to federal court."

"In case the facts have escaped you, Mr. Carstairs, no one in Washington has the power to redirect actions taken inside *my* courtroom . . ." Durnin stopped when Adrian turned so that his sad smile was directed at the judge. "Yes, Mr. Barrett? You have something that might illuminate this situation?"

"Perhaps, Your Honor. I respectfully request a meeting in chambers."

FORTY-THREE

Ethan knew what happened next because Adrian shared the events with them over dinner. At the time, it felt like a sudden vacuum had swept in and overtaken the courtroom. Sonya was ushered off the witness stand by the security guard. Everyone stood. Judge Durnin filed out, followed by the court reporter and Adrian. Carstairs hesitated a long moment, then signaled for his two staffers to remain where they were. The young attorneys drifted slowly back into their chairs. Ethan had no idea whether their confusion was due to what had just happened or by their boss not wanting them along for the ride.

As soon as they entered the judge's chambers, Carstairs started talking a mile a minute. "This notification from Washington is actually a positive development, Your Honor. It will take us quite a while to identify someone within the group's senior executives who carries the same level of authority and insider knowledge as the absent Ms. Aldain.

This shift to federal court saves Your Honor a considerable amount of otherwise wasted time."

The court reporter plunked herself down in a hard-backed chair by the door and hastened to keep up with Carstairs's speech. Judge Durnin took his time rounding the desk and settling into his chair. All the while, he held his dark gaze on Adrian, who had taken up station by the side window. Adrian stared at the sky and the gathering afternoon clouds, nodding in time to Carstairs's words, as if everything he heard confirmed his reason for this meeting.

When Carstairs paused for breath, the judge said, "There are two incorrect elements to your statement, Mr. Carstairs. First, there is nothing positive about your informing me that a Washington bureaucrat, no matter how high up the food chain, might presume to remove a case from my courtroom."

"Your Honor—"

"I'm not finished. And secondly, you were the one who kept telling the court that this acquisition is a matter of utmost urgency." He glanced at Adrian as if expecting him to pounce on this opportunity. But Adrian merely continued to inspect the world beyond the courtroom. "If time is of such crucial importance to your clients, they will be able to produce someone who can illuminate this situation without delay."

"I can but ask, Your Honor."

"You do that." Durnin's chair squeaked loudly as he leaned back. "All right, Mr. Barrett. You've got us here. Let's hear why."

Thunder rumbled deep and slow as Adrian faced the judge. "Your Honor, I respectfully request this matter be discussed off the record."

For an attorney to make such a request in the middle of a hotly contested case was rare but not unheard of. Normally the judge would require the attorney to show some form of justifiable cause before agreeing. But today Judge Durnin merely asked, "How long do you need, Adrian?"

"Three or four minutes should do, Your Honor."

Durnin nodded to the court reporter. When the door shut behind her, the judge said, "Now both of you take your seats." When the attorneys were stationed opposite him, he said, "All right, Adrian, let's hear it."

Adrian turned and addressed Carstairs directly. "When I first showed up here in Jacksonville, your father went out of his way to help me get settled. Me, a greenhorn attorney working for another firm. Until that point, I'd never spent more than a day or so in your region. I felt completely out of my depth. And scared. But your father treated me like I was someone who deserved the finest this city had to offer."

Carstairs shifted in his seat like he couldn't find a comfortable position. He kept on with the tight little coughs. Small sounds, little more than a catch in his throat. "Is this going somewhere?"

"I respect you both," Adrian continued. "Always have. You are a fine attorney, and your firm deserves its good name. That's one reason why this case has been so difficult for me. Middle of the night, I keep waking up and wondering why you'd attack us like you have."

"Come on, Adrian. You know perfectly well that how we approach this case has nothing—"

"Let him finish," the judge said in a deep burr.

"Watching you in there today, it finally hit me," Adrian

said. "You're being duped, the same as us. Maybe even more so. They're your clients, and they're not telling you the truth."

Carstairs huffed. "Your Honor, this is getting us nowhere but farther and farther from a resolution."

Adrian went on, "They're using you, Jimmy. This has never been about a hedge fund wanting to buy a pain reliever that won't go to market for years, maybe never. You're a smart man. You're bound to have been facing the very same mystery. No matter what they've told you, down deep you're worried it's a lie. A total fabrication. And what they haven't said has begun to terrify you."

Carstairs heaved himself up on one side and pulled a handkerchief from his rear pocket. "This is ridiculous."

"Sooner or later the truth is going to come out," Adrian said. "You and your firm will realize this group is nothing but a shadow. And behind the shadow is something that is just awful, Jimmy. I realized this over lunch, when Ethan shared with me news about your missing DARPA agent. I know what their secret is, Jimmy. It's bad. And when it comes out, you and your firm had best be miles away."

Carstairs squinted at Adrian, his mouth open a fraction, far enough to emit the occasional cough. Nothing more.

Adrian pointed at the door. "We're going back in the courtroom, and I'm going to reveal the secret your clients are desperate to keep from having come out. And you're going to be faced with a choice."

"You don't know that."

"Here's what I do know. The man who tried to kill me on the courthouse steps has vanished. What's more, your firm represented his release from Raiford. In front of a federal judge no one can find."

Durnin demanded, "What are you saying?"

Adrian did not turn, did not even blink. He gripped Carstairs with an iron-hard gaze. "What happens when the press links this missing shooter and the evidence that's about to come out to your firm? Your family's good name is going to be dragged through years of slime, Jimmy. There's every chance you'll never recover." He stopped, giving the man time to apply the handkerchief to his face. "You're too good a man to be used in this way."

Carstairs gripped the handkerchief so hard his knuckles turned white as the cloth.

"Recuse yourself and your firm, Jimmy. Drop this case and walk away. Show the world you won't stand to be used like this." Adrian reached over and gripped the man's arm. "This is your one chance to break away clean. Take it."

When the lawyer remained silent, Durnin said, "Mr. Carstairs, we will resume testimony in five minutes. In the meantime, Adrian and I will step from my office. Feel free to use my phone."

The judge led Adrian from his chambers. When they entered the outer office, Durnin asked his aide to give them a moment. After the door closed, he demanded, "Why are you doing this? He's put you and your wife through the flames. Why not just let him burn?"

Adrian nodded. "It's a valid question, Your Honor."

"And your answer?"

"Ethan."

The judge narrowed his gaze. "Your brother."

"The man who saved my life. The man who . . ."

"Yes? Go on."

"Ethan has been teaching me what it means to see the

difference between the logical path and the right one." Adrian almost managed a smile. "That's as good an answer as I can give you today, Judge. Maybe in time I'll find a way to say it better."

Durnin studied him a moment longer, then said, "You know full well that Jimmy Carstairs would never voluntarily step away from a client in the middle of a trial."

"I know."

"So why insist on speaking with him here? Why not somewhere private?"

"Two reasons." Adrian pointed back to the judge's office. "After this conversation, the legal community will sooner or later come to know Jimmy's decision. And from this, if he was duped or if he served as a willing participant."

Durnin did not smile. Not really. He merely tightened the edges of his mouth. "Which was why you asked for this to be off the court record. So that you or I might speak of it."

"If necessary, Judge. Only if necessary."

"And the second reason?" When Adrian hesitated, he said, "It's just the two of us, Adrian. Off the record."

"It was never about Jimmy walking away," Adrian replied. "What happened in your chambers was my way of asking Jimmy not to block what happens next."

FORTY-FOUR

After Judge Durnin led the two attorneys from the court-room, Ethan was about to retake his seat when Gina whispered, "We need to talk." Without waiting for his response, she stepped to the center aisle and walked toward the exit.

Ethan had assumed there would be such a moment, when Gina made her demands or issued her ultimatum or offered a final farewell. But not here, in the brief interlude between courtroom dramas. As he followed her down the aisle, he assumed it meant something bad, as in, she was leaving and never coming back. He opened the rear doors for her and felt pierced by a keening sorrow.

Yet when he entered the courthouse corridor, Ethan was struck by the change. It seemed to him that he suddenly faced a second set of doors. Only this portal was the final exit. It was just beyond his vision, but it was there all right. And very close indeed. The sensation was so sudden and so potent, he stopped midstride. Whatever Gina was about to tell him became colored by a different lens. It was no longer about what made him happy or what might have suited them best, if only. The one issue he had to focus upon, while he still had time, was doing right by this lady and whatever she had decided. It was her choice. Her life. His responsibility began and ended with his response.

Gina wore the outfit from her first day, the pale grey pant-suit and navy blouse. The only change was a lovely gold brooch in a design Ethan did not recognize. The lapel pin was about as long as his little finger and swept in a half-moon shape that ended with a cuneiform that glowed in the corridor's overhead lights.

The hall was long and almost empty. Down by the elevators, two men and a woman were involved in an intense discussion. Gina walked to a long wooden bench running down the opposite wall. She seated herself and patted the place beside her. Once Ethan joined her, however, she showed no interest in coming to the point. She sat and stared at the opposite wall, as if she could read a message scripted upon the painted concrete.

He said the first thing that came to mind. "I don't recall seeing that brooch before."

"Sonya loaned it to me." Gina touched it with two fingers. "Adrian gave it to her for their first anniversary. She had miscarried. Things were hard between them."

"It's lovely."

"Sonya says it's the oldest known symbol from ancient Hebrew. It's the symbol for love. Human love, divine love, or both." Her fingers stroked the gold. "When he gave it to her, Adrian said such a symbol would not have lasted through the ages because it was easy. It was hard to love five thousand years ago. It is hard to love now. Sonya wears it in the hard times to remind her what is most important in this world. And the next. She had it on when they came back yesterday."

"From seeing her mother."

"From putting her mother in a home for dementia patients," she corrected. "And knowing it was only a matter of time."

Ethan found himself filled with a remarkable sensation. Perhaps it was the fact that his departure was as close as his next breath. Or maybe, just maybe, it arrived with the realization that he was wrong. Gina had not brought him out here because she intended to deliver her version of an ending. Instead, she was so filled with emotions she could hardly speak. She could not look his way. She could not hold back any longer. The ashes of a love Ethan thought lost and gone forever were burning anew. The embers were alive. He breathed the dusty air and shivered.

"Whatever you want, Ethan, I will do it." Gina turned to him. "Tell me what you think is best. I need you to do this for me. Because I really don't know. I don't have any answers. Every choice feels like one part maybe right and ten parts probably wrong."

"I've been there," he said.

"But you're not there now, are you?"

He shook his head. He had never felt further from that point in his life.

"I feel like such a mess." She turned to him. "Tell me, Ethan. Talk to me."

The answer was right there in front of him. "Yesterday I went looking for answers from a new friend. I've known about him for years. But I've only gotten to know him since the . . ."

"Transition."

It was good to hear her say the word as she did. Calmly, without the previous struggle and disbelief.

"What I really wanted most from him was a sense of clarity. How I should look at everything that was happening to me. And everything coming my way."

"Clarity. That sounds so nice. Like a favorite tune I've almost forgotten. Clarity."

"My friend said the difference between making the right moves now and making more wrong moves like before was that I had to seek out the eternal perspective."

"Did you make so many wrong moves, Ethan?"

"So many. So wrong." He pushed out a breath, expelling the bitter taste of regret as best he could. As he did so, he was struck by something he had not thought of in years. He started to speak, but the words became clogged in his throat.

Gina gripped his wrist. "Tell me."

"Sometimes when we fought, it felt like you didn't see me at all. You had this image inside you of who you wanted me to be. And what made you angriest of all was when I didn't live up to that set of expectations."

She released his arm, leaned back, and opened her mouth, but no words came.

"I think the reason you left me was that you finally gave up on that image. You became resigned. You realized I was determined never to change." Ethan saw in her lovely gaze a reflection of all that once had been. Of all he had never allowed to become. "I think at some level I knew all along that you only wanted the best for me. You saw what I could have become, if only I could have found a way to let go of all the barriers. All the stubborn resistance to change and growth and . . ."

She said it for him. "Love."

He nodded. "That most of all."

She reached forward and took another hold on his forearm. Gentle now, warm as her words. "And now?"

"You need to see beyond the now, Gina. I don't know how to say it any other way. I'm leaving, and you need to fashion a world and a future without me."

"It's so hard."

"You have friends and family who will help. And who need you." Ethan felt as though the fire in her heart and eyes was so strong, he could actually manage to catch a faint glimmer of what could perhaps be the way forward. "You asked me to tell you what to do. This is my answer: Stay here for the rest of this year. Talk to the university. Get them to set you up with a professor who will act as your thesis advisor. Go for a BA and MBA combined. Help Sonya form a new business model."

"Ethan . . ."

"No, no, hear me out. Sonya's team has no business manager in place. All of that was handled by the group that has become their enemy. If my investments are enough, they'll buy back the outstanding shares. And then what? They have to find another investor. They need to set up a business model. They need . . . well, they need you. Someone they trust completely."

She reached out her other hand and fit it into his. "I want to walk the riverbank and find a place we can claim as ours. Lie in a field of wildflowers with you and find faces in the clouds." She released one hand long enough to clear her cheeks. "No one has ever shown me how to see the world as I do with you. Like my heart was made to be open. Like it was made to love only you."

For once, the words did not make him sad. Instead, they felt to Ethan like a boon. He had said what she needed to hear, and this was his reward.

He leaned forward and kissed her cheek. "We need to get back inside."

FORTY-FIVE

Ethan entered the courtroom alone.

He had just seated himself when the guard ordered them to rise. Adrian accompanied the judge into the courtroom and returned to his table without meeting either Sonya's or his brother's eyes. Jimmy Carstairs followed a few seconds later, studying his shoes as he walked. Ethan had the impression that something that had happened inside the judge's office left the opposing counsel disconnected from events. When Carstairs took his chair, the two younger attorneys crowded in, whispering. Ethan doubted Carstairs was even aware of their presence.

Gina slipped into the seat next to him just as Judge Durnin demanded, "Mr. Barrett, are you ready to resume?"

"Yes, Your Honor. I recall Dr. Sonya Barrett to the stand." When she was seated, Adrian launched straight in. "We were talking about a sidebar research that you halted some six months ago."

"A bit less."

"At the time, you closed down this direction of study because you were negatively impacting your test subjects."

"You might as well say it, Adrian. We killed them."

Adrian half turned, waiting for Carstairs to object. But neither he nor the judge seemed to find anything worth voicing. He swung back to Sonya. "Before closing your research down, you made one final discovery, however."

"Yes."

"Will you tell the court what that was?"

"We tried to extract the specific frequencies that were impacting our subjects so negatively. Remove them entirely from the process."

"Were you successful?"

"No. We failed in a very dreadful way. We experienced the complete opposite effect of what we were hoping."

"Instead, what happened?"

"We increased our failure rate to almost a hundred percent." It sounded to Ethan as though Sonya dragged out each word, hauled it out by sheer strength of will. "We could not continue. We just couldn't."

Adrian rose from his chair and walked to the podium. His movement held the same sense of struggle as Sonya's speech. "Let us now return to the issue of timing. You completed this work—"

"I didn't *complete* anything. I gave up because we *failed*."

Adrian seemed utterly unaffected by Sonya's rising tension. "You ended this research. You set it aside, and then what?"

Sonya's only response was to take a fierce grip on the railing around the witness stand.

"You did not write it up, did you?"

She whispered, "I couldn't."

"It was too distressing. It meant reliving all the failed hopes and all those disastrous results. So you set aside making your report, didn't you? Until when?"

Sonya did not respond.

"When was it you finally decided you had to include this failure?"

She tracked her husband with her gaze and did not speak.

"You wrote it as a very brief sidebar," Adrian continued. "And you did so in the run-up to the semiannual visit of the investors' outside scientist. Is that not correct?"

She nodded. Once.

Durnin spoke in a remarkably gentle voice. "Witness must speak her response for the record."

"Yes," Sonya whispered. "Yes."

"Three paragraphs are all you wrote, isn't that what you told me?"

"Less."

"And yet writing that very brief summary caused you nightmares."

"Terrible," Sonya whispered. "Wrenching."

"Then the microbiologist arrived and asked you to go over that ground for the entire first day you spent together."

"It was horrible."

"At the time you blamed yourself. You thought it was due to the fact that you had done such a poor job of writing up the weeks you and your team spent on this futile direction."

"Five and a half months," she murmured, her gaze haunted.

Adrian stood by the central podium, rocking back and forth, heel to toe. Finally he said, "Your Honor, I need to ask the scientist a theoretical question. I suggest that it is within the parameters of her stated expertise."

Durnin glanced over. "Mr. Carstairs, do you have any objection?"

Carstairs seemed to experience the same unsteady struggle to speak as Sonya. "I . . . No, Your Honor."

"Very well, Mr. Barrett. You may proceed."

"Theoretically speaking," Adrian began, "would it be possible to use your discovery—"

"It wasn't a *discovery*. It was a terrible, disastrous *mistake*."

"But under certain circumstances, to a particular type of group or individual, it could conceivably be seen as a discovery, could it not?"

Sonya remained silent.

"Would it be possible to use your discovery," Adrian softly pressed, "and create a frequency that had the *intent* to halt all life functions?"

Carstairs punctuated the question with a loud huffing sound, just like he had taken a punch to the heart. Which, Ethan decided later, he most definitely had.

If Adrian or his wife noticed Carstairs's reaction, they gave no sign. Nor did either give any notice to how Judge Durnin shifted in his seat, moving from rapt attention to full alert. They were too involved as Sonya replied, "Not a single frequency, no. A specific combination of frequencies, which have been calibrated to the species in question."

"Including humans."

"Humans are a biological species." Sonya's words came more slowly now. It seemed to Ethan that she no longer saw the courtroom at all. Instead, her gaze was fastened upon the lab. "So yes. It stands to reason that frequencies could be identified and a specific process of application designed that would have this effect."

Adrian tapped the podium with his pen very softly in time to his words. A drumbeat that Ethan could feel in his bones. "Could this application be designed without the use of electrodes?"

This time it was the judge who punctuated the question with an indrawn breath.

Sonya's hands gripped the railing with bone-white intensity as she rocked in cadence with her husband.

"Answer the question, please."

"Theoretically." Sonya kept her gaze fastened tightly upon the unseen. "The required technology does not presently exist. But given a sufficiently powerful frequency array, and assuming it proved possible to precisely target the frequencies at the . . ."

"Victim," Adrian supplied. "Enemy combatant."

"Then yes. It is most certainly feasible that what we saw as a terrible mistake could be transformed into a . . ."

"Death ray," Adrian said. "Silent killer. A military game changer of exponential force."

Each of Adrian's words struck Sonya with such force she winced. "Yes."

Adrian stood there a long moment, watching his brilliant and mercurial wife restore her composure. Finally he asked, "All right?"

"Yes." She used her forefingers to compress the edges of her eyes. "Thank you."

Adrian turned to Carstairs. "Your witness."

Carstairs remained planted in his chair.

Durnin finally prodded him with, "Mr. Carstairs?"

Carstairs did not so much rise as lumber upward. The act was a genuine struggle against whatever internal forces had robbed his features of color. "Your Honor, I withhold the right to recall this witness at a future time."

"You have no desire to cross-examine?"

"Not at present, Your Honor. I have not been able to contact . . ."

"Yes? Go on."

"Nothing, Your Honor. No questions at this time."

"Very well." He turned back to Adrian. "Counsel, you may proceed."

FORTY-SIX

"Your Honor, I respectfully suggest that this case has never been about an investor making a lawful acquisition of my client's company and its products," Adrian began. "We have shown beyond reasonable doubt that there is no product. Instead, by sheer accident my client has discovered a terrible side effect that does the opposite of what she intended. This accidental discovery is utterly at odds with what she was contracted to do. Instead of healing and relieving pain, she has uncovered a process with potential military applications."

"Objection." Carstairs remained seated, not bored as much as disconnected. "Conjecture."

"Sustained."

"But we must accept, Your Honor, that this has become a very real possibility. I therefore request that the case be widened to include an official review of who precisely we are facing here." Adrian looked down at Carstairs and his minions. "I doubt very much my colleague has any idea who he truly represents."

"Objection."

"Sustained."

"I ask the court to force their hand, Your Honor. Make them reveal themselves. Either that or force them to unwind the deal with my client."

Adrian stopped and waited. The judge watched him intently and did not speak. It was as if they both were locked in silent agreement, insisting that Carstairs respond for the record.

When the opposing counsel finally spoke, he droned his words to his hands. "Objection, Your Honor."

Durnin leaned back and studied the ceiling. The silence lasted quite a while before he resumed his position and said, "Here is what we are going to do. We are going to treat this as final arguments. Whatever happens from this point, we can certainly assume that the ground has shifted under our feet. As a result, we need a clear sense of where we stand. So, Mr. Carstairs, you are hereby instructed to allow Mr. Barrett space to speak his piece uninterrupted. If he crosses a line into illegality, of course you may object. But until or unless this happens, you will listen in silence, and then I shall grant you the same right to offer rebuttal."

Ethan found it very interesting how Carstairs did not look up once during the judge's instructions. Even his minions looked confused by his silence.

Judge Durnin, however, appeared satisfied by his response. "Mr. Barrett, you may proceed."

"Thank you, Judge. First of all, I respectfully ask this court to order Cemitrex to show us Beryl Aldain's letter of resignation. If there is any hint of irregularity, I ask the court to declare this document a sham and serve an order on her personally. I suggest Beryl Aldain resigned merely to avoid appearing in this court. I suggest that she in fact has not unwound her connections with Cemitrex and thus should be held in contempt. I ask that you issue a writ of bodily attachment. If she fails to appear, she must be arrested by federal marshals and forced to testify. In chains, if need be."

Both Durnin and Adrian seemed to find nothing odd about Carstairs's utter lack of response. His two minions, however, were clearly stressed to the breaking point. The young woman leaned over and whispered something with such intensity, the muscles of her neck stood out like whipcords. Carstairs gave no sign he heard her at all.

Adrian stepped to the side, moved past his podium, and halted where nothing stood between him and the judge's bench except empty carpet. "Your Honor, failing the appearance of Ms. Aldain, I ask the court to order Cemitrex to supply a witness who can testify from personal knowledge. Hearsay testimony will not be permitted. This new witness must be capable of supplying the court with complete answers. Who are their ultimate owners? Are they involved with any branch of the military, here or overseas? And what is their true purpose behind seeking to acquire my client's company?"

Adrian took another step away from Carstairs and his own table and the safety of the known. "Finally, Your Honor, I ask that my client be permitted to file a sealed patent, to be held in absolute confidentiality, covering every aspect of the research in question. Clearly this potential weapon has nothing whatsoever to do with her contracted research or the intended product. Separating this accidental development from what Cemitrex is allowed to purchase will, in my opinion, be the only true way to safeguard her life's work."

As Adrian returned to his seat, the young woman's protest rose further in intensity. Carstairs waved at it like he would a circling wasp.

Finally Judge Durnin said, "Mr. Carstairs, you are free to offer rebuttal."

Carstairs shook his head slowly. Whether to the young woman's words or his own internal dialogue, Ethan could not tell. Finally he said, "Your Honor, at this point I feel I must speak with my clients before offering an official response."

The young woman leaned away from him, her mouth agape. Not just silenced. Poleaxed.

Judge Durnin, however, offered a tight nod, almost as if he approved. "Very well. At this time the court finds in favor of Mr. Barrett and his client. I deem there is ample evidence that Cemitrex and its ultimate owners have willfully sought to slip between the statutory cracks and, in so doing, have subverted the course of justice. As a result, a subpoena is hereby issued for the appearance of this absent executive, Beryl Aldain. If she fails to appear, this will be replaced by a formal writ, to be served by federal marshals. I also order Cemitrex to supply us with a second executive of senior status who can and will offer corroborative testimony. And finally, Mr. Barrett, you are hereby instructed to prepare a preliminary request for a patent, which the court orders must be held in strictest confidentiality until or unless I personally approve its release. Which I will not."

He rapped the gavel. "This case is adjourned."

CHAPTER

FORTY-SEVEN

Gina drove Ethan's car and followed Adrian and Sonya to their home. Ethan rode with his window down, letting the warm humid air wash over him like gentle September hands.

Twice during the drive, lightning flashed so close that Gina recoiled. Both times, Ethan felt himself endure another moment of partial separation. The charged atmosphere drove a wedge further between his consciousness and the physical body that would soon be no longer his. Even so, he observed the shift from an unemotional distance. Two storms were coming. There was nothing he could do about either.

The thunder was an almost constant rumble by the time they arrived. A deep-voiced warning that great events were about to unfold.

News of Jimmy Carstairs's withdrawal was waiting for them. There were three messages on the answering machine, two from Adrian's firm and one from a young woman who introduced herself as a senior associate in the Carstairs firm. She reported that Jimmy Carstairs had been unable to obtain valid responses to his queries. As a result, his firm had no choice but to halt their legal representation of Cemitrex and its pursuit of Sonya's company.

There was a distinct lack of celebration to the news. After all, the Washington-based group still owned fifty-one percent of Sonya's company. But for the moment, they were freed from any threat of her company being acquired. A major battle had been won. For now, that was enough.

Adrian and Sonya were clearly exhausted by the weeks of strain and uncertainty. They moved about their kitchen on automatic pilot. Gradually a buffet of salads and cheese and sliced melon and fresh vine tomatoes and bread took shape. Adrian pulled a bottle of wine from the fridge and asked if anyone wanted a glass, and when no one responded, he put it back.

They ate seated on stools around the counter. Ethan broke the silence only once, to explain what he hoped would become Gina's new role in the business. Sonya welcomed the news. Adrian merely studied his brother with a grave expression.

When they were done and the remnants cleared away, Sonya suggested she and Gina have a word about what form this new relationship might take. Ethan and Adrian left the house by way of the rear screen door and walked the long pier down to where the Saint Johns flowed. The late afternoon sky was alight now.

Adrian traced his hand over the shivering cattails growing alongside the pier and said, "I've been thinking about Pop."

"He always did love a good storm," Ethan recalled.

"It used to scare Mom to death, him hopping around the shore when a hurricane was on approach."

"I don't remember that."

"You were what, five years old the last time a hurricane hit?"

"I had just turned four. I remember because you and Dad used to talk about me missing all the fun."

Adrian laughed for the first time that day. "Oh, man. That's right. I loved giving you a hard time about how great life was before you showed up."

"You went on and on about how you and Dad raced around the backyard, Mom yelling at you both to get out of the storm. The two of you laughed every time the lightning struck, singing some crazy song."

"'Raindrops Keep Falling on My Head.'" Adrian kept laughing. "Pop couldn't hit a proper note with an Uzi."

A canvas-topped boat hung under a covered hutch, winched free of the storm's waves. The river was alive now, the greenish-brown waters frothing with excitement. The sky directly overhead was a pristine blue, so clear and deep it appeared almost black. Further east, however, the clouds held the dark menace of an approaching army. A wall of shadows marched toward them on a million flickering legs. More lightning flashed and boomed in the cloud bank itself.

Ethan felt each flash inside his head, prying loose his consciousness from his body. Every passing instant became filled with an impossible beauty. The water, the sky, the storm . . .

"You're a great brother. And an even greater man." Ethan reached out a hand. "Help me lie down."

Adrian's voice rose to a frantic whine. "No, man, you can't . . ."

"Please. Don't. It won't help anything, and I want . . ."

Speech became impossible then. His ability to shape any

sound at all became something that belonged to a fading past. He would have collapsed had Adrian not caught him.

"No, no, no . . ."

Ethan looked at the glorious sky, the majestic storm, the beautiful day . . . his brother. And then, with a clarity that came from that instant of further separation, he saw himself.

He was the prodigal son, the scourge of his family, the man who threw away his heritage and only took from life what he wanted. And only when he could do so in utter selfish abandon.

He had been granted the opportunity to come home. Not because he deserved it. Far from it. Even so, he had returned to the only family left to him. A brother who had abandoned Ethan to the fate he had demanded for himself. And then welcomed him back with open heart and arms.

This impossible gift of second chances had carried the immense challenge of making peace with a woman who before had loathed him, and who now counted him as her brother. And who trusted him with her own life's aims.

And then there was Gina.

It felt so good, so very good indeed, that his last thought was of her.

Read on for an excerpt of
ANOTHER THRILLING STORY
from **DAVIS BUNN**!

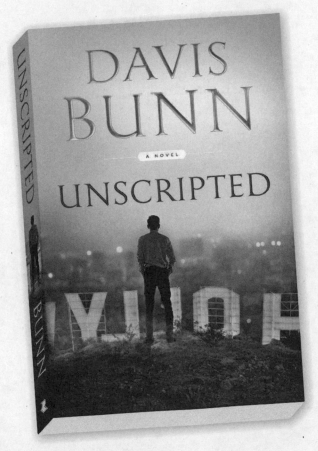

ONE

The entire Beverly Hills Jail was nonsmoking and air-conditioned. Four inmates to a cell. No overcrowding. Decent food for a prison. Three hours each day in the central pen rather than the customary one. Showers with hot water. And most importantly, the inmates were safe. All violent offenders were sent to Men's Central Jail, which was a totally different story. The threat of being reclassed and shipped out kept the Beverly Hills inmates meek as kittens.

Not that Daniel Byrd had much experience with prisons. Just one stint in juvie, convicted when he was twelve and released three days before his fourteenth birthday. For robbing a bank.

This time was different. For one thing, he was innocent. Totally.

Of course, he was guilty of a whole host of other offenses. The difference was, the things he had gotten so terribly wrong were not actually against the law.

Trusting the wrong partner. That was a lifetime felony, for

sure. This being the same person Danny had called his best friend since childhood. But that was before John Rexford had cleared out their accounts and skipped town with a would-be actress. Leaving Danny to take the fall.

———

It was probably just as well that Danny had no idea where the louse was, since the vengeance he spent so many imprisoned hours imagining was definitely on the wrong side of legal.

Which was exactly how Danny was spending the morning when his world shifted on its axis.

The first notice he had of pending change was when his cell door opened and the guard said, "Let's go, Byrd. Gather your belongings. You're being moved."

Danny protested, "I'm not due in court for another three weeks."

The guard was a pro at ignoring anything a prisoner might cast his way. "Don't keep me waiting, Byrd."

His three cellmates were an Israeli smuggler arrested with half a pound of conflict diamonds, a Rodeo Drive salesclerk who tried to play hide-the-turnip with an emerald pendant, and a professional cat burglar from Freeport, Bahamas, dark as the nights he loved. The smuggler shifted on his bunk, turning his back to the world. The salesclerk offered Danny a grimace. The thief said, "You just remember what I told you."

"Take a chill pill," Danny replied. "Keep my eyes on the next step. See nothing, say less."

The thief offered Danny a palm. "You stay cool now."

The guard pointed to the invisible line in the corridor.

Danny's month and a half in jail had taught him to keep his mouth shut and wait. The officer locked the door and started down the long hall. Danny fell into step behind him. His gut was one solid block of dirty grey ice.

Beyond three more steel doors loomed the shadow world of California's general prison population. Gangs. Drugs. Brutality. Danny knew with every shred of his being that he would probably not survive.

The guard's name was Escobar. Danny suspected he was the only prisoner who knew that. Most inmates in the Beverly Hills Jail were just passing through, held here for a few months or less. Once their convictions were set, they were processed into the California penal system. There was no need to bother with such trivialities as learning guards' names. But Danny had been memorizing people's names for so long the habit was ingrained. He knew the identity of every guard in their wing.

Escobar led him through four of the five steel doors separating Danny from daylight. They entered the octagonal booking chamber, and Escobar pointed him onto a side bench. "Sit."

Danny took one look at the others occupying his perch and felt his last shred of hope drain away.

When he didn't move fast enough, Escobar gripped his right shoulder and guided him over. "I said sit." He examined Danny's face. "You gonna be sick?"

"No."

"You better not get my floor dirty, you hear?"

Danny swallowed hard. "I'm good."

Escobar nodded, clearly satisfied his words had the desired effect, and turned away.

There were fourteen others lined up along the bench. They were cuffed and linked together by waist chains. Their ankles were bound by a flexible link just long enough for them to take little half-steps. They all wore orange prison-transfer jumpsuits with the dreaded MCJ lettering across the back.

Men's Central Jail was a bunker-like structure between Chinatown and the Los Angeles River. It looked like a windowless, high-security warehouse with an electrified fence and guard towers. MCJ held five thousand inmates in a space built to house half that. The place was overcrowded and highly dangerous.

Three weeks, Danny silently repeated. *I can survive three weeks.*

Three men down from Danny, a kid with pale golden skin started crying softly.

Forty-five minutes later, Danny was still waiting. Wasting time was just one of the daily punishments embedded into prison life.

Two guards Danny had never seen before appeared through the steel sally port. One of them carried the shotgun required for all prisoner transfers. "Stand up and face the right-hand door."

When Danny rose with the others, the guard behind the booking counter said, "Not you, Byrd. Plant yourself back on the bench."

The other prisoners looked his way. For the first time.

The chains clinked and rattled as the fourteen were led through the door, out to the transfer bus rumbling in the secure garage. When the last inmate had shuffled away, the sally port clanged shut and the remaining guards went back to pretending Danny Byrd was invisible.

Not that he minded. Not a bit.

———

An hour and a half later, Escobar returned, accompanied by an older inmate with the blue trustee stripe. "On your feet, Byrd." He gestured to the trustee. "Give him your gear. Let's go."

Danny followed the guard through two more doors, past the central visitation chamber, down the windowless corridor, to the room where he met with his rotten lawyer.

Escobar unlocked the door, pushed it open, and asked whoever was inside, "You need me to stay?"

A woman's voice replied, "That won't be necessary."

"Knock when you're done." Escobar waited for Danny to enter, then shut and locked the door.

Danny faced a woman seemingly his own age. Anywhere but Hollywood, she would have been considered a beauty. She compressed her attractiveness into a tightly severe package. Her raven hair was pulled back and clenched inside a golden clasp, her makeup designed to make strong features even more stern. Her white silk blouse was sealed at the neck by a high collar, her curves masked by a boxy, dark suit.

"Sit down, Danny. That's what you prefer to be called, correct?"

Danny stayed where he was. "Who are you?"

"Megan Pierce. I'm second chair on your legal team."

"In case you hadn't heard, I've been forced to declare bankruptcy. My company is in chapter eleven. I don't have a cent to pay you."

"Our costs have been covered. Sit down, please. We don't have much time." She gestured to the chair on the table's opposite side. "Unless you'd prefer to stay with your public defender."

"Not a chance."

When Danny was seated, Megan opened a file, slid a document across the table, and offered him a pen. "This appoints us as your legal representatives. Sign on the bottom of the second page and initial all the places that are highlighted."

Danny signed. "Who's paying for this?"

"I have no idea." She indicated a suit draped over a chair by the side wall. "We found these clothes in your former office. Am I correct in assuming they belong to you?"

"My court date isn't for another three weeks."

"Answer the question, please. I have to leave in . . ." She glanced at her watch. Her wrists were strong, her fingers long and tanned. "I'm already late."

"Yes, they're mine."

"Your lead counsel has requested a meeting with the judge assigned to your case. He needs this document to proceed." She rose from the table, crossed the room, and knocked on the door. "Be dressed and ready tomorrow morning."

"Ready for what?" Danny asked.

But the woman was already gone.

———

Escobar led Danny back down the hopeless corridor into the main block. Only this time . . .

Escobar waved to the camera, then started forward. When he realized Danny had become frozen to the cement floor, he demanded, "You keeping me waiting again, Byrd?"

"No sir." Danny forced his legs to move. "Not me."

Escobar climbed the stairs and led Danny down another corridor, waved to another camera, and was buzzed through the door.

They entered the Pay to Stay wing. The place of fables and disbelief.

When the city built their jail for prisoners awaiting trial in the Beverly Hills courts, they did what only a city with extra cash on hand could even consider. They built a second structure they didn't actually need.

The Pay to Stay wing was designed by city councillors who knew all too well how easily they could step over the invisible line and enter the realm of illegality. So they established a code whereby nonviolent offenders could make an official request of the Beverly Hills courts from anywhere in California's vast and deadly penal system. Only the rich need apply.

The criminal offense had to be white-collar. As in no drugs or violence. The offender paid the daily rate of 145 dollars. In exchange he was given a Beverly Hills version of life behind bars.

Danny could do nothing about his dumbfounded expression as Escobar led him through the commons room and over to . . .

A single cell.

Danny kept waiting for somebody to come rushing up and say there had been a mistake and he didn't belong. But Escobar stopped in the doorway and pointed Danny inside. "This is your lucky day, Byrd."

The cell was just as the burglar had described. He had been booked in here for his first few nights when the regular wing was overfull. The cell was a prefabricated steel pod. The bunk and table and stool and sink were all one piece. If Danny had stretched out his arms he could have touched both side walls. The ceiling was only a few inches higher than Danny's six-three frame. The bulletproof window was eleven inches square and overlooked the jail's interior courtyard.

A *window*.

"Look here, Byrd." Escobar waited for Danny to turn around. "The first time you make any trouble, the guards shut the door. You get fed through the slot here. You stay locked in for weeks, maybe months. The second time, you get shipped out. You read me?"

"Loud and clear, sir," Danny replied. "No trouble." He watched the guard turn and walk away. *Leaving his cell door open*.

———

At 7:15 the next morning, Danny was showered, shaved, dressed in his suit, and seated in the central hold. Waiting.

The court transfer bus left every morning at 7:30. Danny assumed there would be no more notice here than in the jail's other wing. If his new legal team had actually managed to shift the court system into a faster gear, Danny wanted to be ready.

Nine minutes later, his name was called over the loudspeaker. He rose and crossed to the guard by the exit. Danny and two other Pay to Stay prisoners were led back to the booking chamber. He was cuffed but not waist-chained. The steel access portal rose, and the prisoners were led forward. Danny entered the bus, and his cuffs were fastened to the steel panel linked to the seat in front of him. No one spoke.

The normal cursing and threats and harsh commands were absent here. The reality of what awaited them if they got out of line was too close.

———

The Beverly Hills Jail was located down an unmarked alley just off Glendale. The entire facility was rimmed by a pale stone wall that blended into the warehouses and small businesses to either side. There was no guard tower, no barbed wire, not even a sign. The only public access was a glass-fronted office on Rexford that led to the visitors' center, its windows stamped with the city seal. The bus trundled through the outer gates and down the narrow lane and . . .

Back into the real world.

Danny may have been watching the blooming trees and the fancy cars and the lovely ladies and the sunlight through wire-reinforced glass. He may have been chained to his seat. He may have been facing three to five. But today, for the first time since his arrest, he watched the world sweep past and tasted the faint flavor of hope.

The Beverly Hills courts were connected to the city's main administrative buildings, a stucco palace rimmed by palms and emerald lawns on Santa Monica Boulevard. Danny was led down the rear corridor into the holding pen where all prisoners on remand awaited their hour before the judge.

Fifteen minutes later a heavyset man with an intensely impatient air followed a deputy through the courtroom door. He crossed the concrete foyer and halted in front of the pen. "Daniel Byrd?"

"Here." Danny rose from the bench and approached the

bars. He had done this twice before, then entered the court-room and faced the judge with his rotten public defender. Each time he had felt his freedom slip one step further away.

Not today.

The man's first words were enough to assure Danny that this time was different. "My name is Sol Feinnes. As of yesterday, I serve as your principal attorney."

"How is this happening?"

"We don't have time for that. My associate has used her firm's considerable clout to shift your court date, and what I need—"

Another deputy pushed through the swinging doors leading to the courts and said, "Feinnes, you're up."

"Coming." To Danny he said, "Follow my lead, Byrd. Your future depends on it."

Davis Bunn (www.davisbunn.com) is the award-winning author of numerous national bestsellers with sales totaling more than eight million copies worldwide. His work has been published in twenty languages, and his critical acclaim includes four Christy Awards for excellence in fiction. Bunn is a writer-in-residence at Regent's Park College, Oxford University. He and his wife, Isabella, live in England.

Sign up for
DAVIS'S NEWSLETTER!

Keep up-to-date with Davis's news, book releases, and events by signing up at

davisbunn.com

f davisbunnauthor 🐦 davisbunn

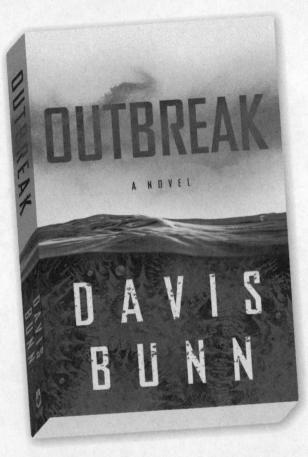

An Ancient Island Holds an
ANCIENT SECRET . . .

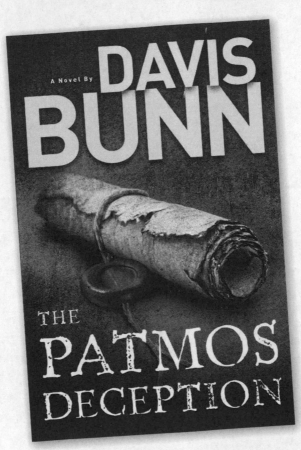

A Novel By **DAVIS BUNN**

THE
**PATMOS
DECEPTION**

While investigating the theft of Grecian antiquities,
journalist Nick Hennessy and archaeologist Carey
Mathers meet a local man who could be a suspect
or an ally. Will they learn the truth in time to save
Patmos's greatest treasure?

Be the First to Hear about New Books from Revell!

Sign up for announcements about new and upcoming titles at

RevellBooks.com/SignUp

@RevellBooks

Don't miss out on our great reads!

LET'S TALK ABOUT BOOKS

- Share or mention the book on your social media platforms. Use the hashtag **#BurdenofProof**,

- Write a book review on your blog or on a retailer site.

- Pick up a copy for friends, family, or anyone who you think would enjoy and be challenged by its message!

- Share this message on Facebook, Twitter, or Instagram: **I loved #BurdenofProof by @DavisBunn** or **@DavisBunnAuthor // @RevellBooks**

- Recommend this book for your church, workplace, book club, or small group.

- Follow Revell on social media and tell us what you like.

 RevellBooks

 RevellBooks

RevellBooks

pinterest.com/RevellBooks